THE WARLOCK'S KISS

TIFFANY ROBERTS

The Sundering toppled civilization, killed millions, and filled the world with walking corpses and supernatural monsters. It took nearly everything from Adalynn—her dreams, her home, her parents, and her chance of beating her terminal cancer—but it didn't take her little brother, Danny. She's come to terms with her inescapable fate, and she'll do everything she can to ensure her brother has a chance of survival in this new, unforgiving world.

When Danny and Adalynn discover a rundown mansion in the middle of nowhere, it seems like the perfect place for him to stay, but the mansion's owner—a tall, mysterious, intense man who exudes a strangely thrilling energy—complicates matters. Though Adalynn doesn't want to leave another person devastated when she's gone, Merrick has other plans for her—and he makes it clear he will keep her, no matter what price he must pay to make it so.

To you—you know who you are, and I love you. <3

Chapter One

Six Months after the Sundering

ADALYNN RELEASED a shaky breath and pressed her lips together. The revenant in the road ahead spun toward her car, its limbs swinging limply with the sudden movement. The creature's glowing white eyes met Adalynn's gaze, and the revenant stiffened, opening its mouth wide to release an inhuman cry. Even though Adalynn couldn't hear the sound with the windows rolled up, she'd heard its like so many times over the last several months that she could feel it in her bones.

She tightened her grip on the steering wheel. "We're safe."

"I know, Addy," said her brother, Danny, from the passenger seat. "It's just one, anyway."

But even a lone revenant was dangerous.

The revenant charged toward the car with no regard for its own wellbeing, moving in an unnatural, jerky gait that looked like it should've dislocated the creature's joints. The bits of flesh visible through its tattered, stained, and weather-faded clothing looked like it had been charred by weeks of exposure to the sun.

Even after six months of dealing with these things, Adalynn still sometimes had trouble *not* seeing them as human. When they were as damaged as this one, it was a little easier, but she'd been there in the beginning, when they'd first started getting up. She'd seen some of the worst of it.

Every one of these revenants had been a person once. But when the Sundering had split the moon in half, and the Earth had trembled like it was going to break apart, something had changed. Something had torn apart the laws of life and death as surely as the moon had been shattered. Distinguishing what was real and what wasn't had become significantly more difficult in the time since.

The old rules didn't seem to apply anymore.

She glanced down at the fuel gauge and clenched her jaw. The indicator was sitting on empty, and the little gas pump symbol was lit up red beneath it. They were running on fumes. They'd stopped at four gas stations—*four!*—and every one had been dry. She'd siphoned what she could out of some of the abandoned vehicles they'd passed, but the drops of gasoline her efforts had produced weren't worth the danger she'd placed herself and Danny in to obtain them. Either everyone else had driven until their tanks were empty or someone had already beat her to scavenging the fuel.

Adalynn had known this was inevitable the moment they'd lucked out and found this car—she'd known they would inevitably be forced to return to traveling on foot. Until then, she would use the vehicle to get them as far from danger as possible.

Looking back up at the revenant, Adalynn slammed her foot down on the accelerator. The car hesitated a moment before lurching forward, its engine roaring like a wild beast answering the call of the challenger charging toward it.

In her peripheral vision, she saw Danny throw his hand up and clutch the handle at the top of the door frame.

"Addy, what are you *doing?*"

Her entire body tensed. She tightened her grip on the steering wheel until her knuckles ached. "We can't let it follow us. You know those things will chase a car for miles if nothing else distracts them."

Adalynn stared into the undead creature's supernatural eyes just before impact. The revenant didn't deviate from its head-on charge. The car struck it with a loud *thunk*, and the creature vanished beneath it. The whole vehicle jolted and bounced as it plowed over the body.

Keeping the accelerator depressed, Adalynn glanced in the rearview mirror. The revenant was laid out on the pavement, but it was still moving—it rolled onto its stomach and turned toward the car, using its one remaining arm to crawl after the vehicle, its legs dragging uselessly behind it. The eerie light in its eyes had not diminished—and remained fixated on Adalynn.

How long before that's me? How long before I'm chasing Danny like that?

She didn't ease off the gas pedal until the creature was well out of sight and far, far behind them.

"That...was messed up," Danny said. "It's not like in video games at *all*."

Adalynn opened her mouth to tell him this *wasn't* a game, but she snapped it shut again before speaking. He'd known that already; the comment was just his way of coping with yet another horror in a world that had become hell for the living. He should never have had to face this reality. No one should've had to face it.

"Not like the games at all," she said instead.

Her racing heart only gradually eased, but her pulse remained as a dull, throbbing ache in her head. She drew in slow, deep breaths, trying to force herself to calm, trying to delay the impending episode.

Please just let us get a little farther. Let us find somewhere safe.

According to the dim clock on the dashboard, it had only

been seven minutes since the collision with the revenant when the car started sputtering. Adalynn glanced down at the fuel gauge again. She hadn't thought it possible, but it indicated the car was *less* than empty.

She lifted her gaze to scan the dense woods on either side of the road. They'd been traveling these country backroads for days, mostly at a snail's pace, trying to find a place to serve as their sanctuary—a place as far away from the revenant-clogged cities as possible.

Even small cities were too dangerous after the Sundering; more people meant more walking corpses, meant more *every-thing*—the kinds of monsters that were only supposed to exist in movies and books. The revenants seemed the most mundane of what Adalynn and Danny had seen so far. Were-wolves, ghostly entities, and creatures she could only describe as gargoyles had been amongst the dreadful beings she'd seen with her own eyes, and that wasn't even counting the surreally beautiful man who'd given off his own golden light and seemed to have some sort of *magic* at his command. They'd heard rumors of much more than that the few times they'd spoken with other survivors after breaking away from their original group.

All those things were very, very real now, and all of it was terrifying, but the most frightening part was that Danny would eventually have to deal with all of it *alone*.

Not going to think about that right now. Focus, Adalynn.

Though the surrounding woods were beautiful, they made it difficult to spot connecting roads and turn-offs until you were already driving past them. Adalynn would've preferred to park the car back on some logging road or backwoods trail —out of sight of the main road—but that wasn't feasible when the engine finally cut out. It wasn't worth the time and energy to try to push the car off the road.

There are abandoned cars all over. What's one more? If someone else finds it, they'll check for supplies and gas and move on when they don't find anything.

She guided the drifting car onto the narrow dirt shoulder. Rocks and gravel crunched beneath the tires. She winced; it was one thing to make some noise while they were driving and could outrun most threats, but it was quite another when they were about to go on foot.

Once the car was stopped and in park, Adalynn pulled the keys from the ignition and instinctively moved to slip them into her pocket. She stopped herself and glanced down at the keys in her hand. She didn't need them anymore. Even if they found more gas—which was unlikely at this point—it would be more practical to find a new vehicle rather than backtrack to this one.

She released a heavy breath and dropped the keys into the cup holder. "Well, we knew it'd come to this eventually."

Danny unbuckled his seatbelt and twisted around to reach into the back seat with both arms.

"We'll be fine," he said with that know-it-all-nothing-can-hurt-me attitude that was characteristic of many young teenagers who thought themselves wiser than the adults in their lives. He wrestled their bugout bags to the front.

Adalynn couldn't help but smile as Danny passed over her bag, which was heavy with food, water, and essential supplies. He could nail that snotty teenager tone when he wanted to, but she knew that wasn't her brother. He flopped back down on his seat, settling his bag over his lap.

"Thanks," she said, shifting her head to scan the woods outside the passenger-side window.

The forest was dense enough to provide some cover as they walked. So long as they kept the main road in sight, they wouldn't get lost—and they would eventually end up finding a building they could shelter in while Adalynn figured out their next step.

Unfortunately, she didn't have much time for planning. She didn't have much time for *anything*.

They needed to find someplace safe today, someplace secure—preferably before dark—and, sometime in the next week or two, a place for Danny to thrive.

Adalynn checked the mirrors to make sure there was nothing following on the road. She turned her attention to Danny just as he unsheathed one of the biggest knives Adalynn had ever seen.

Her eyes widened. "Danny! Where the hell did you get that?"

He grinned and turned his wrist back and forth, inspecting the blade. "Pretty cool, huh? I found it in one of the trucks at our last gas stop."

Adalynn held out her hand. "Give it to me."

"What?" he asked, eyebrows falling low as he yanked back the knife. "No way."

"Daniel Adam Jefferies, you hand that knife over to me right now. You're way too young to be handling that."

"Addy, are you serious? Look around us! I need it to help protect you."

"*I* should be the one protecting you."

Daniel rolled his eyes. "I'm not a little kid anymore, Addy. What if we *hadn't* seen that revenant back there? What if he'd snuck up on us? What would we have used to fight him off, your pocketknife? We should've gotten a gun by now!" He frowned and looked away. "We both know you're sick. Real sick. And I...I need to learn to take care of us, in case, you know...something happens."

Tears stung Adalynn's eyes. Twelve years separated her and her brother, and even though he was thirteen now, she'd always see him as that chubby little baby who'd smiled up at her as though she'd hung the moon, as the toddler who'd clutched her hand when he was scared, as the little boy who'd followed her into the deep end of the pool because he wanted to be as brave as his big sister. But he was growing up right before her eyes, and she couldn't ignore that.

He was right. She was treating him like a little kid, and it would only hurt him in the long run. She'd known for months what kind of world they were living in, even if she couldn't understand why it was like this. It was a world that chewed up the weak and spat them out as walking corpses. A world where everyone, even children, needed to know how to protect themselves. He needed to learn those skills, but how could she teach him things she didn't know?

The deeper truth of the situation enhanced the sting of her thoughts—even if she'd possessed those skills, she didn't have the time to pass them on to Danny.

Adalynn lowered her hand and sighed. "Okay, you can keep it. But just be careful! If you get cut—"

"I know, I know," he interrupted, shoulders sagging. He'd heard it a thousand times already, but he continued with surprising patience. "If I get a cut it can get infected, and our supply of antibiotics is limited."

A soft smile touched her lips. "Good. At least we know you're capable of retaining information other than the names and teams of soccer players or how to emote over someone you just killed in a video game."

"Uh, it's called tea bagging, and it's an art."

Adalynn laughed and shook her head. "You're so gross."

"You're just a prude."

Her jaw dropped. "A prude? I am *not* a prude. And where the hell did you learn that word?"

A slow grin stretched across his lips. "From one of your *romance* books." He puckered his lips and made kissing noises. "Oh, he's so handsome, so strong, so virile. And his co—"

"Okay, that's enough! New rule: you're not allowed to read. At all. Ever again."

"I learned about women in that book too, like—"

"We are not having this discussion. Didn't Mom and Dad talk to you about sex?"

Danny snorted. "Mom was even more prudish than you and told Dad to do it. I let him stammer on about it for a while and pretended that I hadn't already learned it all from the internet and other kids at school."

Adalynn twisted in her seat to look through the back window. "Where's that revenant? I think I changed my mind. I want it to catch me."

"But the sex in your romance book was pretty hot. Just sayin'."

"If you don't get your much-too-young-to-talk-about-this-stuff ass out of the car right now, I'm taking that knife from you and I will not be held responsible for what I do with it."

"Okay, okay." Danny laughed and opened the door. He stepped out of the car, pack in hand, and muttered, "Prude."

Adalynn couldn't hold back a chuckle as she exited the vehicle. "I am not! I'm the one that had the book to begin with. I just don't need to hear my *little brother* talking about it."

"I could talk about killing revenants instead," he said, thrusting the knife forward as though fighting an invisible opponent.

"*Daniel*," she warned, glaring at him as she quietly closed the car door.

He froze, staring at her with eyes wide, and lowered the knife. "You sound just like Mom when you say my name like that."

There wasn't any humor in his voice now; they'd healed enough to laugh and joke, to remember their parents with happiness and humor, but losing them still hurt. Adalynn knew that as much as it pained her, it was worse for Danny—and he put a lot of effort into hiding that pain.

She sighed softly. Slipping her arms through her bag's straps, she rounded the car and stopped beside Danny to give him a hug. "Let's go. We still have time before dark, but I'd rather not get stuck out here." She pulled away. "We'll walk in the woods to hide but stay close to the road so we don't get lost."

"'Kay." He sheathed the knife and clipped it to his belt before swinging on his pack. He shuffled away from the road and up the small embankment into the forest.

Adalynn checked the road one last time before following him past the tree line.

They kept close to one another as they walked, striking a balance between speed and quiet that Adalynn was satisfied with. Too slow and they risked being stuck out here at night, when the scariest things in this new world seemed to be most active. Too quick and they risked making enough noise to alert others—both the living and the dead—of their presence.

Out here, in the middle of nowhere, the chances of encountering anyone were slim—which was why Adalynn had been leading them away from most towns and cities. Of course, the lone revenant on the road was proof that low population wasn't synonymous with *no* population, but it was still better than a ravenous pack of dozens.

She saw it as a trade of risks—a smaller chance of being set upon by revenants in exchange for more potential difficulty finding food. Most of what they'd eaten over the last half-year had been scavenged from abandoned stores and homes. There were fewer of those places out here to search, but if they found the right place while there was still time, she could teach Danny to grow his own food.

Danny was quiet and alert, and Adalynn was grateful for it. She loved her conversations with him, but he was still a kid despite the growing up he'd been forced to do. The longer he talked, the more excited he became, and he tended to speak louder and faster as he went on. Addy had trouble keeping up with him sometimes even in the best circumstances, and right now, when their hike was combined with the weather—overcast but oppressively hot and humid—she knew she wouldn't

have been able to breathe if she had to walk and talk simultaneously. She was already sweating after only a few minutes,
and each step seemed to make her head pound a little harder.

Please let us find somewhere soon.

Though these headaches often started slow, they could be
debilitating when they ramped up, especially when they led to
nausea, dizziness, and seizures. Sometimes, she'd recover from
those seizures within an hour or so. Lately, they'd been
draining her more and more, and she often lapsed into unconsciousness for hours afterward. If it reached that point before
she and Danny had shelter…

It wouldn't be the first time Danny was forced to hide
them under a blanket in the middle of the woods overnight,
but she didn't want him to have to go through that again. It
was terrifying enough being out here together; she couldn't
imagine how much worse it was for Danny while she was
seizing or unconscious. He was helpless during her episodes
and had no way of knowing if she'd make it through an attack
—no way of knowing if it'd be her last.

She *hated* that she put him through that so often.

Before long, the back of her shirt was soaked, sticking to
her skin and pressed in place by her backpack, and sweat was
trickling down her face. Before she'd fallen ill, a hike like this
would've been enjoyable and refreshing, even in this weather.

Now it was a trek through hell.

Though she kept the road visible to her left, she didn't see
any mile markers as they walked; it was impossible to gauge
how far they traveled as they marched on.

"Hey, look," Danny said, turning to face her and jabbing
his thumb toward something up ahead.

Adalynn lifted her gaze to follow his gesture. A narrow
road, overgrown and unkept, cut through the forest a few
hundred feet away. Though it wasn't easy to tell from here, it
looked like little more than a pair of deep ruts with grass and
weeds growing in a strip between them.

"It might lead to a cabin or a campground or something," Danny said.

Pausing, Adalynn placed a hand on the trunk of a nearby tree and caught her breath. She lifted the collar of her shirt and used it to wipe the sweat from her face. After a few moments, she swung her pack down onto the ground and pulled out her road atlas, flipping through its worn pages until she found the area they were in. She nibbled on her lip absently as she traced the lines with a fingertip.

"I think we're somewhere around here, which means we're"—she counted off the distance using her fingers and the map scale—"at least twenty-five miles from the nearest town."

"So this might be our best bet," Danny said, peering at the map from beside her. He left unspoken what they both knew —Adalynn wasn't going to make it two more miles, much less twenty-five.

She closed the atlas and returned it to her pack. "We'll follow it and see where it leads."

When she bent to pick her bag up, Danny hurried to grab it first, and helped her get it on. She closed her eyes against a sudden wave of dizziness—and the fleeting sting of threatening tears that accompanied it.

Danny was thirteen years old; he was her baby brother. *He* wasn't supposed to be taking care of *her*.

"Drink this," he said, pressing something to her mouth.

Adalynn took the water bottle and drank slowly. Though it helped ease her, it couldn't cure what ailed her. Once the dizziness had passed, she opened her eyes and held the bottle out to Danny. "You too."

He drank faster and deeper than she had but didn't drain the bottle. He knew to limit himself until they found a reliable source to refill their containers.

They continued forward until they reached the edge of the dirt road. Here, the road was level with the rest of the forest floor, but as it continued into the forest to Adalynn's right, the ground to either side of it rose to leave the path in its own little valley for as far as she could see. To the left, it ran toward the main road, but overgrown weeds and brush cut it off from the shoulder.

Reluctantly, she sent Danny to the main road to check for any signs. Her heart thumped as she watched him creep toward the blacktop. He checked both ways and disappeared down the roadside embankment. Twenty seconds later—damn right she was counting—he reappeared and hurried back to her. The relief she felt in that moment seemed both overblown and wholly justified.

"No signs," he reported.

"Probably a private road, then…but it looks like it hasn't been used in a long time." Adalynn looked to the right again, drew in a slow, steadying breath, and nodded. "Well, let's see if it leads to anything."

Once again, they kept off the road they were following. Adalynn found something inherently unsettling about the thought of walking with the ground rising overhead on either side, about being surrounded by bare dirt and exposed roots.

Maybe on some primal level that seemed too much like walking in a grave.

After a little while, the road led up a small incline. When they reached the crest, Adalynn paused; there was something blocking the road up ahead—some kind of gate. She and Danny exchanged a glance and continued forward with a bit of extra caution.

The gate grew clearer as they neared it—it was tall, made of rusted wrought iron, its high spikes and arched structure reminiscent of a bygone, gothic era. It was connected to a stone wall that ran to either side and vanished amidst the trees. The wall looked as old as the gate—parts of it were cracked and crumbling, leaving her to wonder how *any* of it was standing.

A length of chain was wrapped through the bars at the

center of the gate, secured by a rusting padlock. Danny took hold of the padlock and tugged on it. "It's locked, but"—he crouched slightly and forced the creaking gates apart, opening a space barely more than a foot wide—"I think we can fit through."

Adalynn frowned. Though the gate and wall looked like they'd stood here, neglected, for decades, the lock and chain were in somewhat better condition, covered more in dirt than rust. This gate might've been sealed for a century for all she knew, but the chain and padlock were newer. She just couldn't be sure if they'd been here for years or for months.

It was likely that this place had been abandoned long before the Sundering, but they couldn't afford to assume that. They'd seen and heard signs of other people—living people— even out in these rural areas, and there was always a chance that Adalynn and Danny weren't the first to stumble across this place. And if the wall was in this condition, could they expect there to be any safe buildings beyond it?

But it was also likely that they wouldn't find another chance at shelter like this before Adalynn had to stop.

Adalynn stepped up to the gate, took hold of the bars, and leaned forward to peer through. The road continued beyond the wall, curving first to the left and then back to the right. Whatever lay beyond that second bend was blocked from view by a thick, dark copse of pine trees.

She sighed and nibbled absently on her lower lip for a moment. "We can check it out, but you need to stay close, okay?"

"Got it."

They slipped off their bugout bags, and Danny held the gate open while she squeezed through beneath the chain. The metal groaned and creaked, the chain rattled, and flecks of rust brushed off onto her clothing, but there was just enough of a gap for her to fit.

One of the few benefits of having too little food, I guess.

After he passed her the bags, she held the gate open for him.

Once Danny was through, Adalynn eased the gate closed again. Her muscles ached; even that bit of exertion was almost too much for her right now.

They continued along the dirt road, Adalynn scanning their surroundings ceaselessly despite the intensifying pounding in her skull. They'd had it relatively easy today, but they couldn't afford any mistakes, couldn't afford to be complacent.

As they rounded the curve and walked past the pine trees, Adalynn stopped in the middle of the road. Danny continued a few more steps before he, too, halted.

The area before them was wide open for at least sixty or seventy yards but for a few tall oaks and maples, bordered by thick forest along its edges. Scrubby, unkept grass, blanketed in places by fallen leaves, covered the ground. But Adalynn paid little mind to those details—it was the nearby building that demanded her attention.

It was a sprawling, ancient-looking mansion with wrap-around porches ringing both the top and bottom floors. Dozens of columns supported the roof and second-story porch, and a set of wide steps led up to the front door. The place had so many windows that Adalynn would've had trouble counting them even if she weren't suffering from a massive headache.

She couldn't guess when it had been built—it certainly appeared to be well over a hundred years old, but it could've been older for all she knew. The paint was faded and flaking, the exposed wood was weathered and worn, leaves and branches littered the porch, and all the windows were dark and clouded but unbroken. If anyone had lived here within the last decade, they certainly hadn't taken care of it.

And yet despite all that, it looked surprisingly sturdy. She would've expected to see a caved in roof, broken windows, or a sagging balcony, but everything stood tall and proud in defiance of the cosmetic wear it had suffered.

"Wow," Danny said.

"I…didn't expect this," she said.

"Let's check it out!"

"Danny!" Adalynn reached out and grabbed the back of her brother's pack. His forward momentum pulled her along behind him for several steps before he stopped and glanced over his shoulder.

"We can't just charge in there," she said. "We need to make sure there's no one here. It might *look* abandoned, but you never know. Caution, remember?"

"Come on, Addy, look at this place. Nobody's been here in forever."

"We don't know that. Please, Danny, just stay close, okay? Even if nobody's in there, it might be dangerous. The last thing we need is for a floor or ceiling to collapse on us."

Danny nodded—albeit with a frown—and fell into step beside her as they walked toward the manor. Her gaze rose to study the place as they neared. That it was standing at all was a testament to the craftsmanship and care that had gone into its construction; it must've looked beautiful when it was new. It seemed silly to feel bad about this house going uncared for after all the destruction, disaster, and death of the last half year, but she couldn't shake that sadness.

The front door was closed, and the narrow windows flanking it were dark. She leaned forward to peer through one; the room beyond was dimly lit, a mess of grays and blacks that offered little detail but suggested years of dust and neglect. She didn't allow herself any hesitation—she reached for the latch.

It was locked.

As quietly and carefully as possible, she and Danny walked around the porch to check the other doors—of which there were several—and the larger windows. Everything was locked, and the few windows they could see through offered glimpses of dusty, rundown rooms that seemed as dilapidated as the exterior. Adalynn couldn't help noticing, however, that the porch was incredibly solid despite its apparent age and wear.

"So...do I get to break a window?" Danny whispered when they arrived back at the front door.

"What?" Addy asked, brow furrowed. "No. It's locked up, so someone might be inside."

"Maybe they locked up when they left."

"*Or* maybe they didn't leave."

Danny gestured to the sky; the clouds were darkening as the evening deepened. "It's going to be dark soon, Addy, and we're both tired. Everything's falling apart, there are no cars, and the road is full of weeds. There's no one here. This is our best bet for tonight."

Adalynn frowned. Danny was right—this really was their best bet, especially because the structure seemed so solid despite its appearance. It'd be a perfect place for them tonight.

"Let's hope it's empty." *With no revenants inside.* She walked down the steps to the driveway and bent down to pick up a large rock nestled in the weeds.

Pain stabbed through her skull. Hissing through her teeth, she clutched her head in both hands.

"Addy?" Danny's voice was full of concern. The porch creaked as he stepped toward her.

She took in a few deep breaths, willing the pain away. "I'm okay."

Once the worst of the pain eased, she grabbed the rock, straightened, and returned to the front door. She could feel Danny's eyes on her throughout, but she refused to engage with his concern right now. They needed to get inside— because at this rate, she'd be out of commission within the hour.

She shouldered off her pack, swinging it around to her front, and settled it on the porch, placing the rock down beside it. She unzipped the bag and rummaged through its contents until she found one of her spare shirts, made of a thicker material—she'd been saving it for the colder days that would be coming over the next month or two. After wrapping her hand and arm in the fabric, she picked up the rock again.

Angling the rock so the pointiest tip was facing outward, she jabbed it into the narrow window beside the door. The glass shattered. She used the rock to break away the lingering glass shards around the window frame before setting it on the porch in front of her. For several seconds, Adalynn stood still, listening; no sounds emerged from within the building.

She carefully pulled her hand free of the shirt's protection and reached through the broken window, bending her arm to the side and feeling for the lock.

The deadbolt's thumb-latch required enough force to make her fingers ache, but it clicked open. Danny and Adalynn met each other's gazes for a moment.

Stepping back, Adalynn removed the shirt from her arm, shook out a few of the tiny bits of glass clinging to it, and wadded the garment up to shove it back into her pack. She zipped the bag closed, swung it back onto her shoulders, and reached into her pocket to draw her pocketknife. She pulled up its main blade.

"If anyone's home, they know we're here now," she whispered.

Danny's suddenly grave expression would've been comical before the Sundering. Kids his age usually didn't take things very seriously outside of whatever form of entertainment they preferred, and Danny had always been laidback and fun-loving.

He reached down and drew that massive bowie knife.

Adalynn stared at Danny's knife—it seemed just a step or two down from a sword. She hated the thought that he'd ever be put in a situation to have to use it, but if it could protect him…

"If anyone comes at you, Danny, you use that. You understand?"

Danny swallowed and nodded.

She turned toward the door and clenched her teeth against another bout of dizziness before grasping the handle. She didn't know what awaited beyond, and that scared the hell out of her, but they needed this place—*Danny* needed this place.

Depressing the latch, she pushed the door open and stepped inside.

For a few moments, a wave of disorientation swept over Adalynn, but she couldn't attribute it to her illness. Crossing that threshold had been like traveling back in time—that was the only way to explain the stark contrast between the exterior and interior of this home.

They were standing in a foyer that would've been the epitome of wealth and décor a century before—the floor was dark, polished wood, arranged in a pattern of circles-inside-squares, and the paneled wainscoting on the walls was made of even darker wood. The high ceiling was pure white with intricate, symmetrical patterns across it, culminating in a huge medallion at the center from which hung a crystal chandelier. A spiral staircase led up to the second floor, which had a railed loft overlooking the foyer. There was a large doorway on either side before the stairs and another set after, and straight ahead —beneath the loft—an arched, open entry led to a large sitting room. Despite the dim light, the elegant carved wood and patterned upholstery of the furniture was apparent.

And all of it was immaculate.

"Is this for real?" Danny asked.

It was amazing, Adalynn couldn't deny that—it was nothing like the dusty rooms she swore she'd seen when she looked in from outside. But it convinced her even more that someone was living here. There was no way this place could be in this pristine condition without someone taking care of it.

For a place this size? It probably takes a team *of people to keep it looking like this.*

Movement at the upper edge of Adalynn's vision called her gaze up to the loft, but there was nothing to be seen save the same gloom and shadows clinging to everything else in the place.

Dread coalesced deep in her stomach.

They needed to leave. It would be better to spend the night in the woods and avoid any potential trouble here. She didn't want to be in a situation in which they'd be forced to use their knives—there was too high a chance of one of them winding up hurt or dead.

Something unexpected came on the heels of those thoughts. The longer she stared at the darkness above them, the clearer that something grew—it was *music*, music unlike any she'd ever heard.

*I'm not hearing it, though. I'm…*feeling *it.*

Adalynn furrowed her brow, focusing on the muted, ethe-real song. She couldn't make out the individual notes, couldn't quite make out the melody, but there was something comforting about it. Something soothing. Something *right*.

She shook her head sharply, producing another jolt of agony. The song was in her head, and this was not the time or place to focus on it. The part of her life during which she'd composed her own music was long gone now, gone forever; all that mattered was getting out of this place before something bad happened.

As she turned toward her brother, she whispered, "Danny, we should—"

But Danny was already walking deeper into the house.

Damnit.

"Danny!"

Chapter Two

With a growl, Merrick slammed the book closed, flattened his palms on his desk, and shoved himself to his feet.

He'd been annoyed when the tingling sensation in the back of his skull—warning him that two people had crossed the ward at the front gate—had interrupted his concentration a few minutes earlier. That initial irritation had only intensified when he'd heard footsteps on the porch as the trespassers slowly circled the house; the relative quiet of the manor and his heightened senses had made the soft thumps audible from inside his study.

But irritation had flared into anger when he heard glass break down in the foyer. Apparently, merely *willing* someone to leave could not make it so despite the immensity of the power at his command.

Visitors—whether invited or not—had always been rare here. That had been one of the reasons he'd chosen this location. That it was situated along an ancient ley line was a bonus; he'd been more interested in its remoteness. Before the moon had shattered, most of his uninvited callers had taken one look at the manor and left, understanding the message

Merrick had intended the exterior to convey—*this is not a place for you; leave.*

Apparently, that message was lost on modern humans. Between these two and the group of teenaged vandals who'd wandered onto his property in a drunken stupor a few years ago, he'd well surpassed his tolerance for trespassers.

He strode toward the door leading out of the study, keeping his steps silent despite his anger. He'd never thought highly of humans, and this was more evidence justifying that opinion.

Whatever the situation was in the wider world—the plight of humanity was not Merrick's—it did not afford these people the right to come onto his land and break into his home. Avoiding interaction with humans had been impossible during his long life; though he rarely needed to eat, he still required food and supplies, and he had little interest in living in a shack in the middle of the woods without a single modern convenience. But he only dealt with humans on his own terms.

Electric tendrils of magic flowed over his skin as he opened the door and walked across the loft. The power thrumming through him was enough to annihilate any mortal he chose to turn it upon—that would be the quickest, easiest way to resolve this matter. If these humans had come with good intentions, they would've knocked on his door. They would've implored him for aid.

He still wouldn't have trusted them, but at least his irritation wouldn't have escalated into fury.

The energy gathering in his hands was raw and bristling— two scintillating spheres of chaos wrenched from the magical energies underpinning the universe—and it felt *good* to have that magic flowing through him in such a pure state. When the moon had broken—an event the humans had aptly dubbed *the Sundering* on the few radio broadcasts still operational in the days afterward—Merrick's power had been vastly amplified, but there'd been no reason to use it like this before now.

Merrick halted when the intruders, who were standing just inside the doorway below, came into view. Neither of them was looking toward the loft; their attention was directed else-where, their eyes wide and jaws slack.

One was a child, a boy too young to even sport hair on his face, and the other was a female. They both held knives, the boy's comically large in his hand.

The woman turned her face toward Merrick.

Reacting purely on instinct, Merrick curled his fingers into fists, snuffing out the gathering magic, and willed the nearby shadows to envelop his body like a burial shroud. The woman's gaze lingered on Merrick's position, but he could tell by the way her eyes moved that she couldn't see him amidst the gloom.

Human eyes struggled in the dark.

He studied her over the course of a few heartbeats. Her large, brown eyes gleamed with fear and uncertainty, and yet they were utterly beautiful—they were the most expressive eyes he'd ever seen. Her full lips were tantalizingly pink. She wore her brown hair pulled back in a ponytail, with a few curled strands hanging loose at the sides of her face.

Her features had an alluring, feminine softness to them, but they also bore evidence of the hard world from which she'd come—her cheekbones were accentuated by a hint of gauntness in her cheeks, and there were dark circles beneath her eyes.

Though she was clearly an adult woman, there was a certain innocence to her face—but it was an innocence that had somehow been sharpened and hardened by her expe-riences.

A strange but powerful urge rose inside him, fluttering in his chest. It took him a moment to realize that it was a magical resonance, a mana song, singing soft and sweet—a gentle melody existing beneath his own, existing within it.

Suddenly, he wanted to go downstairs, wanted to go to *her*. Not to kill her or frighten her, not to reprimand or confront her, but to be near her, to find out *why* she looked like she carried the world on her shoulders, to find out why she was so sad, so worn, and yet so *pure*.

The boy moved out of Merrick's view, proceeding toward the parlor.

"Danny, we should—" the woman whispered before hurrying along behind the boy. "Danny!"

Merrick's brows fell low. He stepped forward and grasped the railing, leaning over it to glance down, but the two had already moved beneath the overhang.

He tightened his grip and clenched his jaw. Why had he hesitated? Why hadn't he, at the very least, demanded an explanation from them? Instead of confronting the intruders, he'd hidden himself and stared at the woman like a smitten fool.

They broke into my home, he reminded himself, *and they are human. That makes them as dangerous as any monster that's awoken since the Sundering.*

Merrick shoved away from the railing and walked downstairs. The footsteps and voices of the humans drifted to him from the parlor; they spoke in hushed but excited tones—the boy's excitement fueled by wonder and the woman's by fear.

Ignoring them for a moment—he told himself it wasn't because he was concerned with how he'd be affected by taking another look at the female—Merrick turned his attention to the front door. They'd broken a pane of the left window, close to the latch. The damage, along with the fact that they'd left the front door open, was enough to rekindle his annoyance.

It would be overly merciful to toss them out unharmed.

He closed the door quietly and lifted a hand, drawing on the magical currents flowing through him. Everything in the universe, whether living or inanimate, whether organic or otherwise, was touched by magic and possessed its own magical resonance, each like a unique song wrought from mana.

He'd worked with glass before. He knew its energy, knew the way it felt, the way it resonated.

The glass shards rose from the floor, glowing faintly blue, as he cocooned them in magic, drifting to the empty window frame. After a few seconds of manipulation, the pieces were lined up and in place. With a final flare of energy, Merrick sealed the fissures between the shards. No indication of damage remained when the light faded.

It was a minor expenditure of magic. The Sundering had left him with immense stores of energy, which had been increased by the proximity of the ley line. Fixing the window-pane was like removing a cupful of water from the ocean. But he let the unnecessary usage fuel his irritation, nonetheless. Were it not for the humans, he'd still be upstairs in his study, reading peacefully rather than repairing a window that had been intact for over a century.

He turned away from the front door to see the humans exit the parlor and walk down the north hall. Releasing a heavy breath, Merrick pulled more shadows from his surroundings, thickening his shroud and venting a bit of the magic racing along his arms and crackling up his spine. He kept his gaze on the boy this time; it was concerning that Merrick's eyes seemed inclined to shift toward the female of their own accord.

"Danny, really," the woman whispered, "we should get out of here."

Yes, you should.

"It's okay, Addy. If someone was here, they would've already shown up, right?"

Merrick squeezed his fists; they trembled in his anger. That attitude—just another version of *because I can*—that *human* attitude, had tainted his life from his youngest days. But humans had squandered their time on top. They'd failed to cement their dominance before the world had shifted. Now was the time for beings like Merrick.

Now *Merrick* was the one with power, and humans would learn how helpless they truly were.

Silent as a stalking cat, he followed the humans along the hallway, keeping several paces behind them.

Addy hurried to keep up with Danny, falling behind more than once as she scanned her surroundings and peered into dark rooms, her concern apparent in her expression. She was the older of the two; why hadn't she asserted control? Why hadn't she reined in this child *before* they'd done wrong?

Danny stopped suddenly and turned his head to the right. "Look, Addy! I bet there's food in there."

Like a rat sniffing out grain.

Why was Merrick following them? He should've acted by now, should've confronted them. Did he simply want to see how far they would go to fuel his own anger?

The boy stepped into the kitchen. Addy hesitated, twisting to look toward Merrick. Her brows were knitted with worry, and her lips parted with a soft exhalation. She looked through him; he knew it was an effect of his magic, but it was oddly disappointing.

What would she look like with her features relaxed, with her luscious lips upturned in a smile? What would she look like when joy sparkled in her gaze rather than fear? What would she look like with those big, expressive eyes half-lidded in desire?

When he breathed in, the air was scented with a hint of lavender—*her* scent. A deep ache stirred in his groin, and prickles of heat skittered briefly across his skin.

When was the last time I bedded a woman? When was the last time I felt any sort of lust? Perhaps I've simply denied those urges for far too long...

But that didn't ring true to Merrick. He couldn't remember the last time he'd had such an urge. That could easily be explained by his tendency to avoid contact with people as much as possible, but for desire to stir so strongly within him after a single glance at an attractive woman...

The resonance he'd sensed when he first saw her reasserted itself; he'd let it fall to the back of his mind, but he couldn't ignore it now. It lured him closer to Addy, coaxed him with its gentleness, its sweetness, to approach her. Was it coming *from* her? He didn't understand how it could be—it seemed familiar somehow, and he'd never seen this woman before today.

He shifted his focus away from the mana song again; he needed to direct his attention toward the situation at hand.

This is more than attraction...and that I cannot explain it is infuriating.

Addy pursed her lips and headed into the kitchen to join Danny. Merrick trailed behind her, stopping in the doorway to observe.

Danny had already returned his knife to the sheath on his belt and was currently in the process of rummaging through Merrick's cupboards.

"What are you *doing*, Danny?" Addy hurried toward him.

"This is weird," he replied, stepping aside to show her the contents of one of the cupboards. "Look at these."

"It's just containers of flour and spices." Addy reached up to close the cupboard, but Danny stopped her.

"Not containers, though, Addy. Jars. Like...*ancient* jars. Look at the wire things on their lids. *And* most of the lids are wood."

Somehow, the crease between Addy's brows deepened. She glanced around as though she expected to see someone watching her—Merrick might have found that amusing under different circumstances—before taking out one of the jars and examining it.

"It's not weird, it's just old," she said. "It really kind of fits everything here, doesn't it?" She replaced the jar, and Danny didn't resist when she closed the cupboard this time. "Now let's *go*, okay? We have some light left. We'll"—she swayed slightly and blinked several times in rapid succession, as though to clear her vision—"we'll just…just have to find a decent spot in the woods."

"There's stuff we can eat here, I know it. And it's warm and dry, Addy."

A myriad of emotions flitted across Addy's features as she stared at Danny. She looked like she was at war inside her head, like her conscience was battling her desire to agree with the boy.

Who was the boy to her? Merrick studied them both; Danny's hair was straight and a few shades lighter than Addy's, but they shared similar noses, and their eyes—though different colors—were close in shape. Was Danny her son? She seemed far too young to have a child that old, at least by modern human standards.

For an instant, Merrick's mind flashed back over the long, bitter years to his own youth. He recognized the relationship Addy and Danny seemed to have, though it had been a great while since he'd experienced it himself.

They were siblings, separated by enough years that Addy had taken on a maternal role to the boy.

Addy sighed. "We really should go. The owner could be back at any moment."

"Come on, Addy. We need to eat. *You* need to eat." Danny narrowed his eyes. "Don't think I haven't noticed you've been giving me most of your share of our meals."

Her hand tightened around the cupboard handle, but her shoulders sagged. "Just a little."

Danny frowned, but he didn't say any more; instead, he turned to tug open more cupboards and rummage through their contents.

Addy released the cupboard handle and moved toward the sink, absently turning one of the knobs. She jumped in startlement when water poured from the faucet. "Danny! Water!"

"Oh shit!"

She turned her head and jabbed a finger at him. "Don't cuss."

"Oh, come on," he whined. "Who cares anymore?"

"*I* care."

Merrick—apparently having forgotten he was meant to be angry at them—felt his lips curl up in a wry smile. He wasn't sure if his amusement resulted from the confidence with which she'd admonished the boy or the absurdity of her policing his language while they were in a house they'd broken into and were planning to steal from.

Danny groaned and resumed his search.

Addy placed her knife beside the sink and slid off her bag, setting it atop the counter. She opened it and removed three bottles. Screwing off the lids, she filled the containers with water one at a time.

Once the bottles were filled and recapped, she cupped her hands beneath the running water, leaned forward, and drank several handfuls. After she was done drinking, she splashed water on her face and scrubbed some of the grime from her skin.

Merrick's eyes drifted to the curve of her ass, which was outlined through her pants. Between the faint hollowness of her cheeks and the slight bagginess of her clothes, it was clear she'd lost weight recently—likely due to scarcity of food—but she still had some tantalizing, feminine curves.

Heat coalesced in his veins and gathered low in his belly, intensifying the ache her scent had awoken.

"Peanut butter!" Danny pulled out a large plastic jar with a red lid. "Oh, man, I haven't had a peanut butter and jelly sandwich in *forever*."

Merrick's smile vanished as quickly as it had come. He

knew he had several more jars of peanut butter in the pantry, but that was something he could not make himself—and he happened to be extremely fond of it.

For most of his life, Merrick hadn't needed to eat as often as humans did—and his need had only diminished further since the Sundering—but when he did eat, peanut butter was high on his list of satisfying foods. He'd tried to ignore that these humans had trespassed on his property, had restrained himself despite them having broken a window and entered his home uninvited, and might even have been willing—at least up until a few moments ago—to give them some food and send them on their way, but *this* was too much.

He would not tolerate the theft of his Jif.

Energy crackled up and down his arms. Keeping his fists balled tight, he dismissed the shadows cloaking him. "Put that back."

Danny and Addy jumped. The boy stumbled backward, dropping the jar as he turned his wide eyes toward Merrick. Addy spun to face Merrick with more control and determination, snatching up her knife and holding it at the ready. Her hand trembled faintly, but her gaze held Merrick's without wavering.

"Danny, come here," she said.

The boy didn't hesitate; he drew his oversized knife and positioned himself in *front* of her. "Get back!"

"I do not take kindly to being threatened, especially in my own home," Merrick said, brows falling low.

"Danny, get *back* here," Addy whispered, reaching out with her free hand to pull the boy toward her. She didn't look away from Merrick for even a moment. "We're sorry. You…scared us. We didn't know anyone was here."

Looking into her eyes had a strange effect on Merrick—it produced a powerful, unfamiliar sensation within him that made his chest tighten and his stomach flutter. He couldn't pry his attention away from her.

But he couldn't forgive their transgressions because of some indefinable feeling, could he?

"Oh? Does that make it all right to break into someone's home?" he asked. "I must've been interpreting the law incorrectly for all these years."

"We're…we're…" She squeezed her eyes shut and pressed the heel of her hand to her head. "We're sorry."

"Sorry for breaking my window, sorry for entering my home uninvited, or sorry for intending to steal food from me?"

"A-All of it. We'll just…leave." She opened her eyes; they were unfocused for a moment before they rolled back to display their whites. The woman tilted to the side, teetered briefly, and collapsed. Her knife clattered on the floor as her body seized, limbs tense and jerking.

The boy wheeled around and dropped to his knees. "Addy!" He released his knife and grasped her arm to turn her onto her side. Tears brimmed in his eyes. "It's okay, Addy. It's okay. I'm here."

Merrick frowned. The tightness in his chest strengthened, but it was hot and acidic now, decidedly unpleasant. He stepped toward the humans.

The boy twisted to look at Merrick and frantically grabbed his knife off the floor, brandishing it in one hand while holding the woman's shoulder up with the other. Worry and anger warred on his face. "Stay back!"

"Put the knife away, boy," Merrick said.

Danny swung the blade. Merrick halted, and the clipped tip of the knife sliced through the air less than an inch from his leg. He couldn't deny the boy's bravery—nor his stupidity.

Merrick scowled. The long years had *not* granted him the patience to deal with this. "I said put your knife away. She's in poor enough condition as it is; would *you* like to be in worse?"

The boy hesitated, but finally lowered his weapon. "Don't hurt her."

Moving forward another step, Merrick knelt on the floor

beside Addy. Her convulsions continued, and foamy spittle trickled from her mouth. He didn't understand his concern for her. He didn't understand why he was about to try helping her when he should've cast them out—or killed them—the moment they'd broken the window.

"Who is she to you?" Merrick asked.

"Her name is Adalynn, and she's my sister. She's sick."

Merrick frowned, glancing at the woman again. "What did you bring into my home?"

"She's not contagious," the boy replied, a sharp edge in his voice, "and she's got it way worse than you right now. Sorry I touched your fucking peanut butter, dude, just...*help* her, please."

The boy's words shouldn't have held any sway over Merrick. How many humans had died during his lifetime? Billions? The number had been unfathomable when Merrick was born, and it made little difference to him now. And yet something about *this* human female called to him. Something about her urged him to do *anything* he could to help her.

And her brother's plea, however rude, *had* moved Merrick.

He knew this was another waste of his energy, another waste of his time, and he wasn't even sure it would work. His magic could do a great many things, but healing mortals was not amongst its strengths. And yet he was compelled to *try*.

Danny tensed when Merrick reached toward Adalynn, but the boy simply pressed his lips together and said nothing.

Merrick settled his hand over her forehead. He could feel the faint tremors coursing through her body, could feel the tension brimming in her. He closed his eyes and focused, careful to keep his magic from manifesting visibly.

Humans had their own magical resonance; it was a melody common to their entire species, but each individual had their own spin to it, had a unique harmony laid over it. Such mana songs were complex and difficult to learn. Hers was no less complex than any other he'd encountered, but it was *stronger*—and its familiarity extended beyond him having sensed it when he first saw her.

He altered his magic to suit her resonance, and a thrumming path—bridged by magic—opened between them.

There was immense beauty within her, he could *feel* it, but there was a thick, oppressive darkness clouding her mana— her impending *death*. Merrick nearly reeled back when he brushed against it; it was malicious, aggressive, *hungry*, not unlike the dead who now walked the Earth. But this was no magic-fueled monster. It was a mutation, a defect. A human imperfection that he knew he could not cure despite the power at his disposal.

He clenched his jaw and drew upon the energies swirling deep inside him, channeling them through his arm and into her—still careful to keep the magic from appearing on his skin and alerting the boy to Merrick's nature. He amassed that power in the shared space between their minds and souls, wishing that he were connected to her like this for a *good* reason, for the *right* reason, wishing he could enjoy the brightness of her beauty at his leisure.

And once the magic had swelled into a pulsating mass, he thrust it at her illness, turning his mana song—now mingled with Adalynn's familiar, exquisite resonance—against the discordant notes of the disease eating away at her.

The darkness in her receded. As it did, overwhelming pressure built inside Merrick's head—a throbbing, stabbing ache like he'd never felt. The heat of his magic intensified; it was not meant for this. So many texts warned against it, but all the texts concerning what he was and the magic he wielded were vague on such matters—the chroniclers who'd documented such things had, in accordance with their eras, often written in metaphors that welcomed a thousand conflicting interpretations.

Adalynn's body eased, and her head lolled. Merrick severed his connection with her and withdrew his hand like it was on fire, lowering it to his side to hide its trembling from Danny.

Her skin was sickly pale but for the purplish bags beneath her eyes, and spittle trickled from her mouth, but her features were no longer strained with tension, and she was unmoving save for the rise and fall of her chest with her slow breaths.

The pain in Merrick's head remained, each pulse of it filling his vision with star-like bursts. For the first time in a long while, he felt...*spent*.

Whatever illness had taken root inside of Adalynn, his efforts were meaningless. It was her end. Her doom. And that knowledge instilled in him a consuming sense of helplessness and despair he'd not felt in more years than he could count—if he'd ever felt their like at all.

Danny's voice was small and awed when he asked, "What did you do to her?"

Frustration flared within Merrick again; he didn't *know* what he'd done to her, only that he'd never attempted anything like it. She was relaxed now, was at rest, but he knew he hadn't defeated the malevolent presence within her.

He reached up with his other hand—which was also shaking—and snatched a dish towel from the counter to gently wipe the foam from Adalynn's mouth. He let it fall aside once he was done and shifted his position to slip his arms beneath her.

Danny tensed. His knuckles were white from his grip on the knife, but he didn't raise the weapon again. "What are you doing?"

"Moving her."

"To where?"

"To the dungeon," Merrick replied dryly.

Danny's brow furrowed, and his lips parted as though to speak, but it was a few seconds before he got any words out. "I don't know if you're serious or not. But...if you hurt her, I'll kill you."

The boy backed away warily as Merrick lifted Adalynn off the floor and stood. For an instant, the room spun around Merrick, but he locked his knees and settled his hip against the counter to keep himself steady. As soon as the dizziness had passed, he walked toward the door.

"Gather your belongings," Merrick said.

There was a flurry of movement behind him—boots on the floor, rustling cloth, the sloshing of bottled water, and the click of a knife being folded closed.

Merrick stopped at the doorway and glanced over his shoulder as Danny zipped up one of the backpacks. "And put my damned peanut butter back before I change my mind about helping."

Danny stilled, staring at Merrick with eyes as large and round as dinner plates. Slowly, he reached into the small opening of his bag and withdrew a red-lidded peanut butter jar. He set it on the counter without breaking eye contact.

"Good boy. You might survive the night after all." Merrick stepped into the hallway and carried Adalynn toward the parlor. Danny's boots thumped down the hall behind him.

The woman seemed so slight and frail, so delicate, so precious. Even her resonance was diminished now. Merrick struggled against the urge to hold her tighter; he feared anything more would break her. How had she survived so long in a hostile world?

It was a foolish question. He'd seen her spirit. He knew its light, its strength. That was all that had kept her going to this point, he was sure. Her spirit...and her protective little brother.

The deepening evening left the parlor gloomy. The shadows were nothing to Merrick, but he doubted Danny could see very well. Those doubts were confirmed when there was a loud bump, and the coffee table rattled. The boy muttered a curse.

"Mind your step," Merrick said. He stopped at one of the

couches—the one facing the fireplace—and carefully laid Adalynn atop it. Her resonance called to him through the discomfort in his head, and, despite everything, he was sorely tempted to make that connection with her again.

He thrust the urge aside and stepped to the fireplace. Danny set their bags down on the floor near the couch and knelt in front of his sister.

"She gonna be okay?" Danny asked, brushing a strand of hair away from Adalynn's face.

Merrick's fingers twitched; he wanted to brush her hair aside like that, wanted his fingertips to trail lightly over her pale, soft skin. Instead he turned his back to Danny and Adalynn and leaned down to light the fire. "How should I know?"

Once the fire was burning, Merrick stood up, bracing himself with a hand on the mantle as a rush of lightheadedness threatened to topple him. Using his magic had never affected him like this before, and it shouldn't have now regardless of the amount of energy he'd expended—he was still far from his limit. What was this? What had he done?

He looked back over his shoulder. Danny was crouched near his sister's feet, digging through one of their bags. The couch was cast in the soft orange firelight, which was reflected in the beads of perspiration on her skin and sparked coppery highlights in her brown hair.

Who was she?

Merrick drew in a deep breath and pushed away from the fireplace, allowing himself not even a moment's hesitation before stepping to the couch, reaching forward, and plucking a hair from Adalynn's head. Electric jolts coursed up his fingers and along his arm when his fingertips briefly brushed her skin, but she made no reaction.

Was the sensation the result of his magic, or something more? Perhaps Adalynn wasn't as human as she seemed at a glance.

Danny rose with a thin, worn blanket in his hands, meeting Merrick's gaze. The boy's earlier bravado had vanished, leaving only concern and a lingering hint of fear.

I'm not going to sympathize with a boy who broke into my home to steal from me, who threatened me, regardless of their circumstances.

It doesn't matter that they aren't a real threat...

"Tend to your sister," Merrick said, "and *stay here.*" He turned and walked toward the hall, keeping himself steady only through sheer willpower—and by squeezing that single hair between his fingers, clutching it like a lifeline.

Danny said nothing, but Merrick felt the boy's gaze on him until he'd turned the corner.

Merrick didn't know whether that should reassure him or reignite his suspicions.

He hurried up the spiral staircase, taking the steps by twos, and crossed the loft to return to his study, shutting the door behind him. Now that he was alone again, his annoyance resurged—this time directed as much at himself as the two intruders.

Humans were trouble. That had always been true and would always *be* true, no matter how the world changed. All they could possibly do was bring him headaches—and they had *literally* done so within the first few minutes of their arrival!

By the time he reached his desk, his vision was blurred from the pounding in his head. He dropped into the chair, propped an elbow atop the desk, and clamped his finger and thumb over his temples to massage them. Somehow, he'd taken a bit of whatever ailed Adalynn into himself. A touch of her darkness. He wasn't concerned for the long term—human ailments meant nothing to him either way—but it was frustrating to feel so...weak.

He'd only experienced sensations like this after receiving horrible wounds—wounds that would have killed a mortal—and those had been fortunately few given the length of his life.

While he soothed his temples with one hand, he absently twirled Adalynn's hair between the fingers of the other. How did she endure this pain? How had she survived like this?

The hair resonated with her mana song; he found himself focusing on it, letting it wash over him, and it brought unexpected comfort in its sweetness and familiarity.

Merrick knew there were human bloodlines carrying magic, and he had to assume those bloodlines had awoken fully with the Sundering, much like his own magic had come into its fullness. Was she the same? He'd read accounts of inherent arcane powers consuming mortals from within because they didn't know how to vent the building power—their physical bodies could not handle the excess energies. Was that what ailed her?

Was that why he was so drawn to her? Power calling to power was a simple explanation, a neat explanation, a convenient explanation, but it wasn't the *right* one. He'd felt no substantial power brimming within her apart from the impressive strength of her spirit.

He squeezed his eyes shut and increased his focus, separating his mind from his discomfort, from his other concerns, from the physical world, until only magic remained. Only magic—and Adalynn.

Her mana song reverberated through him from her hair, and as he attuned himself to it again, he suddenly understood why it was so familiar, why it was so soothing—he *had* sensed it before her arrival. It was there, deep within him, underscoring his own song. He'd felt it since his magic had first woken during his adolescence.

Adalynn's resonance had been playing in Merrick's heart, ever-present but barely noticeable, for more than a thousand years. The sound of his own heartbeat filled his ears, providing the rhythm for their mingling songs.

He dropped the hair atop his desk and severed his connection with it, with *her*, but he felt it still at the back of his conscious mind. Felt the call like a siren's song, luring him down to her. Why should a human have such sway over him? Why should he be compelled to go to her side, to help her, after actively seeking solitude for so long? Why did he have so deep-seated a connection to a mortal?

A sick mortal.

A *dying* mortal.

Chapter Three

Adalynn returned to consciousness slowly, as though drawn out of a dream she didn't want to wake from—a dream in which an ethereal presence had wrapped her in its comforting embrace, freeing her from pain, fear, and guilt. She wanted to stay in that embrace. Why return to a world where everything was falling apart, and only suffering awaited her?

But that wasn't quite true—Danny was in the real world. He was waiting for her. *He* needed her.

She opened her eyes. Her blurry vision cleared slowly, finally focusing on the ceiling. The flickering light of a nearby fire was just strong enough for her to make out the intricate patterns on the plaster overhead—sweeping, symmetrical flourishes radiating outward in circles and squares from a central light fixture, cast in stark relief by the contrast between shadow and light.

Her brows creased.

Where am I? What happened?

That man confronted us and…and I had a seizure.

Where's Danny?

Alarm flooded Adalynn; her only concern was for Danny.

Was he okay? Was he here? She turned her head and shifted to rise. "Danny?"

"Addy?" Suddenly, Danny was beside her, his face filling her vision as his wide, worried eyes scanned her face. "How do you feel? You okay? You scared the shit out of me."

"Don't. Cuss."

Danny laughed. "You *are* okay." His laughter faded as quickly as it had come. "Really though, you okay?"

Adalynn opened her mouth to tell him she was fine purely out of habit—she was never without some sort of pain or discomfort these days—but it occurred to her that she really *did* feel fine. Her seizures were usually followed by disorienta-tion, anxiety, and physical exhaustion, but she felt none of that now—only an odd but undeniable sense of *rightness*. Her mind was clear, and she felt like she'd just had a solid ten or twelve hours of restful sleep.

"I…feel good. *Really* good, actually." She sat up slowly, not wanting to push her luck, and Danny shifted back to give her space.

She looked around, her gaze moving from the crackling fire in the grand fireplace to the old-fashioned wallpaper, from the antique, upholstered chairs and sofas to the expertly carved coffee table, finally landing on the patterned rug. With a little light, the place was even more immaculate than it had seemed earlier.

"You sure?" Danny pressed a hand to her forehead. "You don't feel…strange? Weak? Anything?"

She offered him a smile and reached up to guide his hand away. "No. I feel fine, Danny. Don't worry." She glanced around the room again, brows furrowing. "Where's that man?"

"Upstairs, I think? I'm not sure."

"Did he say who he was? If he's…going to hurt us?"

"No. He just carried you in here and left." He leaned

closer and narrowed his eyes at her. "Are you *sure* you feel okay?"

Adalynn laughed and nodded. "Yes, Danny, I'm fine. Why don't you believe me?"

Danny shrugged and sat back on his heels. "I don't know. It was just weird is all."

"What was weird?"

"I mean, you've had seizures before, some pretty bad ones —and this one looked real bad—but when he touched you, you just…stopped."

"Stopped?"

"Yeah. You kinda just went limp. You looked like you were just sleeping, almost like it never happened."

Adalynn frowned. She hated the worry in her brother's eyes and voice—it tore her heart to pieces knowing she was the cause of it. A kid his age shouldn't have had to worry about much more than schoolwork and getting his chores done. Instead, Danny had been forced to deal with the sudden loss of both parents, the inevitable loss of his sister, and surviving in a harsh, unforgiving world.

She leaned forward and wrapped her arms around Danny. He embraced her without hesitation.

"It was probably just a coincidence," she said. "You know the seizures vary in length. Maybe this one was just shorter and happened to end when he touched me. But I'm okay, really." She pulled back. "I'm assuming since we're both still here and he made the effort to carry me to a couch that he doesn't intend to kill us?"

Danny snorted. "So long as we don't touch his peanut butter."

Adalynn chuckled. "Then I guess we better not touch it."

"I grabbed our water though." He dragged his pack closer, unzipped it, and pulled out one of the bottles, handing it to her. "You should drink some."

"Thanks." She unscrewed the top, lifted it to her mouth, and drank the whole thing in a matter of seconds. There was no need to conserve right now; this place had running water! They'd just refill everything before they left; so long as they showed respect to their *host*, she didn't think he'd deny them that.

After she handed the empty container to Danny, she studied the room again, frowning. It was dark, aside from the gentle light coming from the fireplace. Rising from the sofa, she walked to the nearest window, drew back the curtain, and looked outside.

Night had fallen. The sky had an eerie gray glow, a result of the halves of the shattered moon backlighting the clouds, and everything below it was varying shades of black and gray. The cleared ground behind the manor led to the impenetrable darkness of the surrounding forest—though there was something different straight ahead. It looked like an overgrown wall of hedges, but it was difficult to tell for sure in the gloom.

"How long was I out?" she asked.

"A while. At least a few hours."

Adalynn released the curtain and returned to her brother's side as he stood up and stretched. "And he hasn't come back?"

"Nope."

That had to mean he wasn't going to hurt them—or she hoped it did, anyway. If he'd planned to do them harm—and he had reason to, considering what they'd done—he could've done so several times over. She'd been helpless for hours, but he'd left her and Danny alone.

Adalynn sat on the sofa, grabbed her bugout bag by the strap, and dragged it closer. She opened it and rummaged through its contents until she found a couple protein bars.

"Here," she said, offering one to Danny. "Eat."

Danny groaned, his posture sagging. "Those things taste like cardboard and sand, Addy. I know he's got real food in the kitchen." He held his empty hand up, palm toward the ceiling and fingers slightly curled. "I had peanut butter right here, in my hand."

She smiled. "But this is *our* food, and that's *his* food—food he didn't offer us. Do you really think it's a good idea to press our luck?"

With a comically exaggerated sigh, Danny accepted the protein bar, tore the wrapper, and slowly—so slowly it almost seemed to pain him—peeled it down. He lifted the bar to his mouth and nibbled the corner, shuddering as he chewed.

Adalynn opened her protein bar and took a bite. It really did taste like cardboard and sand. She chewed anyway, forcing herself to swallow—it was better than nothing. Supplies were scarce, and their stores were limited; they couldn't afford to be picky. Food was food. Survival trumped taste.

She'd only eaten half of the bar before she curled the wrapper around it and stuck it back in her pack. Danny finished his despite his complaints and followed it up with a big gulp of water.

He wiped his mouth with his arm and grinned. "We should check this place out."

Adalynn shook her head. "We should stay here and wait for that man to come back."

"Addy, it's been hours. He might not come back at all until morning. Why not explore the place?"

"Even if he doesn't check on us until morning, this is his house, Danny. He's being gracious enough to let us stay for now, despite everything." She looked her brother over and frowned; his clothes were tattered and filthy, there was dirt smudged on his cheeks, and his hair was a tangled mess. She probably didn't look any better, but at least she'd had a few hours of rest. "You need to get some sleep, anyway."

"I can't sleep. I'm bored, and restless, and I just need to move."

Adalynn, strangely, felt that same restlessness—as though she were brimming with energy. But that didn't mean they should sneak around a house that didn't belong to them, no matter how curious they were.

"Danny, we—"

"Please?" he begged, lacing his fingers together and staring up at her, pleading with his big, baby blue eyes. That look always swayed her. "I won't touch anything. Promise."

Adalynn flopped against the backrest, tilting her head back to stare up at the ceiling. "Ugh, why do I always give in to you?"

He smiled. "Because you love me."

She sat forward and jabbed a finger at him. "Don't touch a *single thing*. Nothing. Got it? If he catches us, we'll just say we're looking for the bathroom."

"I mean, I really do have to pee, so it's not exactly a lie, right?" Danny's smile shifted into a mischievous grin.

Adalynn chuckled. "Me too, so no, not really."

There was running water here, so there had to be a working toilet, right? God, to be able to use a *toilet* again! It was one of many conveniences she'd taken for granted before the Sundering. Her parents had taken her camping once a year when she was younger, but even then, digging a hole in the ground and squatting had never been her idea of a fun time.

Adalynn closed her bag and, as she stood up, swung it into place on her back. Danny followed suit. They'd learned early on that they could be forced to run at a moment's notice in this new world; it was always best to keep their belongings with them no matter the situation.

They exited the sitting room together, pausing just beyond the entry; it was *dark*. Every curtain in every room must've been closed.

This is silly, Adalynn thought as she reached back and pulled her little flashlight from the small pouch on the side of her bag. Batteries were a rare commodity, and using some of that juice just to explore this place seemed wasteful, but she couldn't shake her curiosity. How many places like this still existed?

She clicked on the flashlight and swept its beam around the foyer, taking a few moments to admire the craftsmanship, before steering Danny into the left hall—*away* from the kitchen. She knew he'd try to talk her into checking for food again if they passed that room, despite what they'd already been through, and that was an issue best avoided.

The hardwood-floored hallway had a patterned rug running its length. There were paintings on the walls—all of them depicting landscapes and inanimate objects, totally devoid of people—and sculptures in a few of the alcoves. The sculptures were primarily of animals, all of which were in that classical, realistic style.

All the rooms they peeked into were elegantly furnished—even the bathroom, which they both hurriedly used—and Adalynn couldn't guess at what some of their purposes were. A living room? A family room? A den? How many rooms did a person need for sitting?

But it was the room at the end of the hall that called to her the most. It was a large, open space with a polished wooden floor—a dancefloor—and a high ceiling with intricate patterns in its wood. The windows were at least ten feet tall, running along the walls to either side, and three large, tiered chandeliers hung in a row down the center of the ceiling.

When her flashlight's beam fell on the far end of the room, Addy's eyes widened, and she froze. The low stage situated there was empty save for a grand piano with a leather-upholstered bench. Its black exterior gleamed in the light.

"Wow," Danny said.

"Yeah, wow," Adalynn echoed, entering the room.

As she crossed the distance to the stage, the little hairs on the back of her neck stood up; she had the sudden, disorienting sense that there was something here, that she was being watched. She paused a few feet away from the piano and looked behind her, swinging the flashlight around to scan the room. No one was there but Danny, who'd walked to one of the tall windows and was peering through a tiny gap in the curtains.

"This place is huge," Danny said. "And he has it all to himself."

Adalynn smiled and brushed the strange sensation aside—it was likely just an aftereffect of her seizure catching up with her. "We don't know that, just like we didn't know he'd be here. There could be others."

"True."

She stepped up onto the stage and approached the piano. The instrument was so much more beautiful up close. She ran her fingers over the top of the fallboard; there wasn't a single speck of dust. How could a place this large possibly be kept so clean, especially if the owner really was here alone?

That question was swept away on a rising wave of excitement as she lifted the fallboard to reveal the keys beneath. It had been so long since she'd last played. Unable to resist, she settled her fingers on the keys and tapped a few notes. The sounds echoed across the room. She cringed at how loud the piano was, at how out of tune it was, but those notes were still the most wonderful things she'd heard since the Sundering had birthed a world lacking in music.

"Addy! You said no touching!"

Grinning guiltily, Adalynn turned toward her brother. She gasped, nearly dropping the flashlight, when she caught a flash of glowing blue eyes—there and gone in an instant—in the shadows near the door.

"And I told *you* to stay in the parlor, boy," the man said, his deep voice amplified by the room's acoustics.

As that voice swept over Adalynn, it raised goosebumps on her skin—just as it had the first time she'd heard it. But her head was clear now, no longer clouded by pain and dizziness, and her goosebumps were accompanied by a thrill that raced straight to her core.

No one's voice had ever affected her so strongly.

"Uh…we were looking for the bathroom?" Danny glanced at Adalynn. "Right, Addy?"

Adalynn jerked her hand from the piano and took a step away from it. "Right. The bathroom."

"Oh?" The man entered the ballroom, his steps silent. His features grew more distinct as he neared the glow of Adalynn's flashlight. "I suppose you missed the bathroom two doors down the hall on your way here, then?"

Cheeks warming, she shifted her weight from one leg to the other and cleared her throat. "Um, actually, no, we didn't. We were exploring. We didn't touch anything though! Well, except…" She waved toward the piano. "Sorry. It's just that your home is so big and beautiful and…"

Her breath caught as the man closed the remaining distance between them, granting Adalynn her first clear look at him. Long, dark hair hung past his shoulders and framed a strikingly handsome face that was only enhanced by his hard expression. His features were sharp, with a short, neatly trimmed beard and mustache framing his sculpted lips. He had a straight, narrow, aristocratic nose, and thick, slashing, arched brows which rested above bright citrine eyes. A scar began an inch or two over his left eyebrow, slicing it in half, and continued just beneath his eye to end midway down his cheek.

It didn't mar his appearance in the slightest. If anything, it only made him *more* attractive.

The man was straight-out-of-a-romance-novel hot.

With him this close, she smelled a hint of leather and cedar in the air. The scents were strangely calming…and enticing.

She stared up at him—he was at least a foot taller than her —and Adalynn could've sworn there was music playing from somewhere near him. It was a faint melody she *felt* rather than heard, tickling the edges of her consciousness but too intangible to define. "…and…oh, wow."

He arched one of those devilish brows—the one with the scar—and held her gaze. His shoulders were broad, and she could tell he had an athletic figure despite the old-fashioned black suit he wore.

Was it possible to orgasm just from looking at someone?

"Oh, wow?" he repeated in a dry tone. "Why are you here, Adalynn? Of all the places you could've attempted to burgle, why mine?"

"Burgle? Who says that?" Danny asked.

The man glanced briefly at Danny. "People who speak English."

"Sick burn, man," Danny replied in a bored voice.

Their exchange pulled Adalynn out of her trance, but she couldn't take her eyes off the man. "Danny, hush. Our car ran out of gas down the road and we were looking for shelter."

He was silent for a time. Adalynn had heard people say things like *he looked right through me*, but this was different, this was more—she felt like he was looking straight *into* her. And there was something familiar about him, something that made her want to take a few steps closer to eliminate the remaining distance between them. Something that made her want to reach out and touch him.

The muscles of his jaw ticked. "You may stay until morning, but you will leave with the sun whether by choice or by force."

His words were enough to wipe away whatever ridiculous, girlish, romantic fantasies she might have entertained. This was real life. Things didn't work like in her books. Her shoulders sagged, and she looked away from him, nodding. His offer was more than she could've hoped for; at least he wasn't kicking them out into the night.

But that still left her to worry about Danny. For a few

moments, this had seemed like a perfect place for him to have stayed after she was gone. What were they going to do now?

"Thank you," she said.

The man's brow furrowed as though he were uncertain of how to take her response, but his mild confusion vanished faster than it had appeared. He turned and walked toward the door, saying over his shoulder, "Keep to the parlor."

"Got any food we can have?" Danny asked. "We're starving."

"*Danny*," Adalynn warned.

The man paused mid-stride, his posture stiffening. "Yes, you must be. I imagine breaking and entering is hunger-inducing work."

Adalynn frowned, her body tensing. "We said we're sorry. We thought this place was abandoned."

"And I said you may spend the night. If that's not enough for you—which it clearly isn't—then by all means, come to my pantry. I'll feed you little beggars, too, so your bellies are full before I kick you out."

Little beggars.

She pressed her lips together as anger roared through her. She had no right to be angry, not now—the world had fallen apart, leaving everyone to fend for themselves, and she was the one who'd broken into *his* home—but she couldn't put it aside. That he was being more helpful than necessary didn't mean he wasn't being an asshole—or that she and Danny had to stay here and endure that treatment.

Danny scowled and opened his mouth, but Adalynn moved to stand beside the boy and grabbed his hand tightly, silencing him.

"No, thank you," she said. "We wouldn't want to bother you any more than we already have. We'll find somewhere else to sleep and spare you the inconvenience of having to be a decent person for one night."

The man turned to face her, his brows low and eyes narrowed. "You come into—"

"I don't need to be reminded of the circumstances," Adalynn snapped, stepping toward him. Her heart was racing; this was foolish, *dangerous*, but she couldn't stop herself now. "I was there, remember? All we're looking for is a safe place to live and a little food to eat. We made a mistake in breaking in. You don't owe us anything after that. But we don't have to stand here while you insult and belittle us." She looked at Danny, who was staring at her with wide eyes, and gave his hand a tug. "Come on, Danny. We're leaving."

She led her brother past the man, keeping her gaze fixed ahead.

THIS WAS what Merrick had wanted—the humans gone, along with all the potential problems and complications they would've caused. His house would be spared further damage, his stores would be spared unnecessary depletion, and his mind would be spared the constant irritation of having mortals nearby. It should've been a moment of petty triumph —which was sometimes the most satisfying sort. It should've been a moment of quiet celebration.

Adalynn and Danny leaving on their own was the ideal outcome for all concerned parties.

Why, then, did her walking away—without giving Merrick a second glance—sting tenfold more than the angry words she'd hurled at him?

He was angry, yes, but he was also…disappointed. Sorrow-ful. Confused. *Panicked.* These were not emotions befitting an immortal being with unfathomable arcane power at his command. Catering to the needs of a pair of humans was beneath him. Humankind was beneath him—over his long years, they'd certainly demonstrated that they saw beings like

Merrick as little more than monsters and abominations. Why should he show *any* compassion toward their species?

But the thought of Adalynn spending the night out there —though she must've spent so many nights out there already —sparked unexpected concern in him.

How could he be so concerned and yet so frustrated all at once?

He spun on his heel to face the humans just as they reached the ballroom entryway.

"You will join me in the kitchen presently, Adalynn. Even if your pride is too large to exist in this home alongside my own, that is no reason to deny your brother security and food tonight."

She stilled. A moment later, she released her brother's hand, turned, and marched back toward Merrick, her expression hard.

She raised a hand and jabbed a finger at him. There was fire in her dark eyes. "Don't you *dare* use my brother to guilt me."

There was something...exciting about her anger. It charged the air with energy he'd scarcely encountered, a fleeting, mortal energy made more intriguing by its ephemeral nature. The crackling power coalescing deep in his belly seemed to be in direct response to her. It was a gathering of magic, but it was something more, something impossible to define because it was entirely new.

"I'm simply concerned about his wellbeing. Someone has to be," he said.

She stared at him incredulously.

"Dude," Danny muttered, "it's like you *want* her to stab you."

Merrick glared at Danny only long enough to say, "The adults are speaking, boy."

"No, he's right," Adalynn said, glaring at Merrick.

"Food and shelter for tonight," Merrick continued, though

part of him didn't know why he was so adamant she stay; he'd certainly not made it an appealing choice. "Tomorrow you can swear at me as much as you like—despite my generosity— on your way out."

Adalynn clenched her jaw, and her brows fell even lower. Her nostrils flared with a heavy inhalation. "Do you even know how to offer someone help without being a condescending prick about it?"

Merrick felt an echo of the headache that had developed after he'd fought back her sickness—a dull, distant pulsing between his temples and behind his eyes. He squeezed his eyes shut and caught his lower lip between his teeth to prevent himself from snarling.

"I am not what you would consider a…*people person*," he said in as measured a voice as he could manage.

"Obviously," Danny said.

"Danny," Adalynn growled.

Danny threw his hands up. "Okay, okay! *I'm* not the bad guy here, remember?"

Keeping her eyes locked with Merrick's, Adalynn crossed her arms over her chest. "Do you want us to stay or not?"

More than I would've thought possible mere minutes ago. More than I even realize.

"It would be my pleasure to have you," he grated through his teeth.

The corners of her mouth twitched, and her lush lips slowly stretched into a grin. Mirth sparkled in her eyes. "You need to practice sounding sincere, but was that so hard? It would be an *honor* to accept your invitation."

Part of him wanted to be annoyed at her, annoyed that she could so quickly shift her mood, annoyed because he should've viewed her change in attitude as smugness, as arrogance, as her exerting power over him she did not possess. But he *wasn't* annoyed.

Maybe she *did* have some inexplicable power over him.

Seeing her grin like that was nothing short of arousing. That hint of mischief, of wickedness, on her otherwise innocent face urged his imagination toward something much more titillating; he knew he could not allow himself to dwell on such lustful thoughts.

He raised a hand and waved toward the hallway. "After you, then. I trust you remember the way."

Adalynn and Danny preceded Merrick into the hallway, and he followed them toward the kitchen on the other side of the manor. Danny, who remained in the lead, turned and walked backward, his gaze flicking between Adalynn and Merrick. His attention finally settled on Merrick.

"So, uh…what's your name?" Danny asked.

"Merrick."

"Cool. Mine's Daniel, but most people call me Danny."

"I didn't ask."

Adalynn released a dismissive huff.

Merrick sighed and shook his head as they crossed the foyer and entered the north hallway. "Your whispers carried well down the hallway while you were *sneaking* around my home. I overheard your names several times."

Danny grinned, but his expression swiftly turned into startlement when he tripped, stumbling back a few steps with his arms wheeling.

"Danny, watch where you're going," Adalynn said.

"It was the rug," Danny said. "Jumped up out of nowhere."

"If you think I'm unpleasant already, wait until you break something else," Merrick grumbled.

"We haven't broken anything!" Danny said.

"So the window broke itself mere moments before you came inside?"

"*I* didn't break that. Your window's on her."

"Wow, thanks, Danny," Adalynn said.

Merrick couldn't stop the corner of his mouth from tilting up. "Quite the dashing young gentleman you are."

"I know, right?" The boy managed to match Merrick's sarcasm, if not his dryness.

Danny turned into the kitchen. Adalynn and Merrick followed close behind.

Merrick walked toward the pantry. "Go sit down."

The humans moved to the table positioned near the back corner of the kitchen. Adalynn set the flashlight atop it, pointed upwards to create a wide circle of light on the ceiling. Slipping their packs off their shoulders, they dropped them onto the floor, pulled out their chairs, and sat next to one another.

"Do you always wander around this place in the dark, Merrick?" Danny asked, drumming his fingers on the table's surface.

Merrick paused in front of the pantry door and glanced back to see Adalynn reach out and place her hand over Danny's to still his fingers. However poorly Merrick thought of humans, they were perceptive, and it was in his best interest to mask his true nature from them—to hide, just as he'd done for so many centuries.

"There are candles in most rooms, but I've lived here for many years. I'm quite familiar with the layout of my home. I find it wasteful to use candles when I don't require additional light for navigation." Merrick opened the pantry door. "And I don't often make a habit of wandering the halls in the dead of night, young Daniel. Circumstances tonight have dictated otherwise."

"Does anyone else live here?" Adalynn asked.

"No." Merrick entered the pantry; he assumed it would've been black as pitch to their human eyes, but he could see the stores he'd built up over the last several years quite clearly. Whatever his qualms about interacting with humans, he couldn't deny the convenience of the food preservation methods they'd innovated over the last century or so.

"So, you're alone here?"

"Yes."

Just as he preferred.

Merrick selected a few tomatoes and cucumbers from the baskets on the shelves—he preferred to hold onto his jars of preserve and canned goods for when the fresh crops ran low during the long winter months—and a sleeve of buttery crackers.

He carried the food into the kitchen.

Danny stared at Merrick with huge, excited eyes. "I knew it! I *told* you there was food here, Addy."

Adalynn's eyes widened when they settled on the food in Merrick's arms. "You have *fresh* produce?"

Merrick leaned forward to place the food atop the table, letting the produce roll gently from his arms. "Yes. And you, apparently, have an endless supply of questions."

A flash of irritation crossed her face, and she pressed her lips together.

"A jest, Adalynn," Merrick hurried to say; he *wanted* her to stay, so why was he pushing her away? "Forgive the dryness of my tone."

I suppose the years have made me somewhat cantankerous, haven't they?

Her expression softened, and she nodded.

He tore open the package of crackers and placed it on the table between the two humans. "I've always kept a bountiful garden, even before the world changed."

Danny tore into the crackers the moment they touched the table, shoving two into his mouth and chewing noisily. He released a satisfied groan.

Adalynn looked at the vegetables. "It's a good idea, but a lot of people, especially in the cities, didn't have the space to grow anything. These days…it's more a matter of not being able to stay in one place long enough."

Merrick moved to the counter, taking two plates out of the cupboard and a knife from the block. "I imagine its more difficult now to maintain one than ever. Things are…bad out there?"

"*Real* bad," Danny said before stuffing another cracker into his already full mouth.

When Merrick returned to the table, he frowned; it was already covered with crumbs around Danny. Merrick slid one of the plates directly in front of the boy, catching a few of the falling crumbs. This was going to be harder to tolerate than he'd thought.

Merrick set the other plate in front of Adalynn and settled the knife atop it.

"Thanks." Adalynn picked up the knife, grabbed a tomato, and began cutting it.

"My only expeditions into this altered world were made soon after the moon split," said Merrick, "and I imagine the small towns in this region are not exemplary of the wider world. *Real bad* how?"

Danny swallowed audibly. "You haven't seen? The cities are pretty much just hunting grounds for *monsters*."

Merrick had been aware of monsters throughout his life—he was one of them, after all—but his encounters with other supernatural beings had been limited. His few treks into the nearby towns after the Sundering had been enough to confirm his suspicions—just as the moon breaking had amplified Merrick's magic beyond his imaginings, it had brought about a resurgence of inhuman beings. But his experience was with a tiny portion of the country; he found himself eager to hear more, to *know* more. His isolation hadn't been kind to his ravenous appetite for information.

"Monsters of what sort?" Merrick asked.

Adalynn paused in slicing a cucumber and looked at him

curiously, head tilted to one side. "You really haven't heard anything?"

Danny snatched a slice of cucumber off her plate and popped it in his mouth.

"I've been self-sufficient since well before all this happened, but there were a few supplies I deemed important enough to warrant a couple of trips. I saw many strange things during those journeys, but it was some months ago, and I deemed it best to remain here in security. Any other means I possessed of obtaining information from beyond my walls lasted only as long as the electricity. I'd like to know what *you* have seen."

"Lucky," Danny muttered.

Adalynn frowned, her gaze shifting from her brother to the sleeve of crackers. She took five of them before placing the remainder on his plate.

Merrick's mouth fell into a frown of his own. Though he had no intention of eating with the humans, he pulled out a chair opposite them and eased onto it. "That isn't necessary, Adalynn."

She turned her gaze to him. "What?"

"There is plenty of food for both of you. You do not need to split your portion for your brother tonight."

A blush colored her cheeks. "We've already taken from you, and you've made your stance on that pretty clear."

He leaned back in his seat and folded his arms across his chest. "After all the arguing that brought us to this point, you are going to eat a fair portion. Isn't she, young Daniel?"

Danny had stopped eating to look at Adalynn. He glanced at his plate and seemed only in that moment to realize how much he'd eaten—despite his sister having taken only five crackers, the sleeve was better than halfway depleted. His brows lowered, and he frowned. The guilt that flickered across his face was accompanied by a deep sadness.

"It's okay, Addy. You can eat more," Danny said, returning the sleeve of crackers to the table between them.

When Adalynn looked at Merrick questioningly, he dipped his chin toward the food. "Eat—and talk. Consider the information payment; a fair exchange for food and lodging."

"You talk funny," Danny said.

Adalynn elbowed her brother before slipping a wedge of tomato into her mouth.

Merrick arched a brow and returned his attention to the boy. "And you don't?"

"Nope," Danny said, popping his lips when he made the *P* sound.

Merrick took a slow, deep breath, and paused for a moment to assess his motivations. He wanted isolation, wanted to be alone. But he wanted Adalynn to stay, wanted her close, wanted to touch her and hear her voice and see her happy, wanted to feel her mana song. Getting her to eat was part of that. Obviously, those were conflicting desires...but his want of isolation had dropped to a distant third, now behind his craving for information in addition to his inexplicable craving for Adalynn.

And her eyes were on him, so big and dark, full of curiosity and wariness, so different from those fleeting moments in the ballroom when they'd brimmed with fire and lust.

"I'm not originally from the area," he finally said. He had little desire to delve into his origins; lying to humans had been necessary for survival, but he'd always felt degraded by having to do so.

"Huh," Danny said. "Cool." Apparently bored with the subject, he dove back into his food.

Merrick's relief at the boy's sudden disinterest was ridiculous in its strength—but it was short-lived.

"Where are you from?" Adalynn asked.

Damn it.

"Europe," Merrick replied dismissively, "but I emigrated a long time ago. You were speaking about monsters?"

She took a bite out of a cucumber slice. "It's basically a bunch of monsters you might've seen in horror movies or heard about in old legends. They kind of appeared after the moon broke, and there were rumors early on that some people actually…well, *turned into* them."

"I haven't watched many movies. Would you mind elaborating?" Merrick had seen walking corpses and a plethora of spirit-like entities when he'd left his estate; he needed to know what else was out there, needed to know how many of the ancient texts he'd spent so long studying were accurate in what they described.

"The werewolves are scary as shit," Danny said.

"Danny," Adalynn warned.

"What? They are! We saw one when we were trying to get out of the city. The only reason it didn't come after us was because someone else shot at it. The thing didn't even flinch!"

"We've heard them a few times after that," Adalynn said, frowning. "They sound like howling wolves, but much deeper. It's…I don't know, otherworldly. And it's terrifying, especially when you realize they're communicating with each other."

"And there are revenants everywhere," Danny said.

"Revenants?" Merrick asked.

"Walking corpses," Adalynn replied. "The wolves are scary because they're so monstrous, but the dead…a lot of them still look human, but they're not. They go after anything that's living, almost like they can sniff out life, and they're vicious. Like rabid animals. You can damage their bodies, slow them down, even incapacitate them with enough damage—or just the right kind of damage, I guess—but the only way to make sure you stop them is by burning them."

"What do you mean by *the right kind of damage*?"

Adalynn's brow furrowed, and she lowered her gaze. There was a mild strain on her features now, and Merrick's heart thumped restlessly in response; he didn't like causing her distress.

"Injuries affect them sort of like they would a living person. Not that they seem to feel pain, but...you hack into their leg, and their leg doesn't work right. You know what I mean?"

"Addy had to hit one with the car before we got here so it wouldn't follow us," Danny said.

"And it just dragged itself down the road behind us anyway," Adalyn added. "I was driving almost fifty miles an hour when I hit it. That would've killed a normal person instantly."

Merrick raised a hand and brushed his fingers over his short beard. Their testimony only served as more proof in support of what he'd suspected based on his research—the moon had served as a balance of some sort, as a mystical lock on the forces of magic, on the forces of life and death. Its destruction had disrupted what had previously been the natural laws of Earth.

Adalynn worried her lower lip for a moment. "After the moon broke, Mother Nature went *nuts*. There were earth-quakes, floods, tornadoes, crazy lightning storms...we even think the coasts got hit by tsunamis. Power went out right away in a lot of places, and it was out everywhere else within a few weeks. No internet, no cell service, no radio or TV. And as if all those disasters weren't enough, everyone who died just... got back up and tried to rip the survivors to pieces.

"Me and Danny saw that werewolf, but we've seen other things, too. There was an impossibly beautiful man who was glowing all golden, and he had *wings*, but his eyes were cold. Once we saw these demonic-looking things perched on a roof —I swear, they looked like gargoyles come to life. We've seen some...spirits at night, too. And other survivors have told us about all kinds of other things."

Irritation and alarm flared in Merrick's chest; he did his

best to suppress them, but the sudden worry was justified. "Other survivors? You don't have companions out there you've not told me about, do you?"

Eyes rounding, Adalynn shook her head. "No, we've been alone for months. When it all started, we got out of the city as fast as we could. A lot of people had the same idea. We kept in groups for a while, but as time went on, and resources got scarce, and more and more scary stuff crawled out of the darkness...people got desperate. They got mean.

"The last group we were with ended badly. A couple of the guys got into an argument over food, and it turned into a shootout. Three people died, and a lot of people were hurt. It only got worse when the dead people got back up. So, we grabbed whatever supplies we could and took off on our own. I kept us away from major cities, using as many country roads as I could find, and we've avoided people as much as possible."

Such was the nature of humanity—even when confronted with inhuman terrors and widescale disaster, they still couldn't avoid conflict with one another. Her story wasn't surprising, at least in that regard, and Merrick shouldn't have felt anything over it...but he did. He felt the immense weight Adalynn carried on her shoulders, felt the fear, the sorrow, the utter weariness in her heart, felt her pain.

And he felt her spirit, her willpower, her protectiveness. Despite her sickness, she'd kept herself and her brother alive through all that. Merrick had some understanding of what it meant to be mortal, of the struggles she must've faced, of the fear she must've felt, and he was impressed with her for having overcome them.

He was proud of her.

"How long have the two of you been on your own?" Merrick asked.

Lowering her gaze, Adalynn used her fingertip to push a

crumb around in a small circle atop the table. "One hundred and three days."

The ease with which she'd offered that number suggested she'd kept careful track.

Was that because she knew her time was limited?

Merrick wanted to reach for her, wanted to comfort her, but even if she wanted that—which was unlikely—he wasn't sure of what to say or do.

Danny's mouth opened wide, and he released a loud, prolonged yawn.

Adalynn glanced at her brother, then down to her own plate, which was nearly clear. She seemed surprised, as though she'd not realized how much she'd eaten as she talked.

Her eyes rose to meet Merrick's. "Thank you. For the food, and for letting us stay the night. We can find our way back to the...parlor? And I promise we won't break anything on the way."

If they were going to stay, that was the easiest arrangement; it kept them in a centralized location with little they could damage, and they'd be close to the front door when he kicked them out in the morning. But Adalynn still looked so worn, so tired, so weak. He couldn't make her sleep on the couch—the cushions were firm, the armrests were hard, and the pillows were overstuffed and lumpy. It was a fine room for sitting with company, if one were inclined to do so, but it wasn't adequate for comfortable sleep.

"I'll show the two of you up to a bedroom," Merrick found himself saying after a few moments.

Adalynn's eyes widened. "A room?"

"You mean, we get to sleep in an actual bed?" Danny asked.

Merrick flattened his hands atop the table and pushed himself to his feet. "Yes. A room. With a bed. That is implied by the term *bedroom*, is it not?"

Adalynn's confusion didn't ease. "But I thought—"

"I am attempting to be a good host," Merrick said. "For tonight, you are my guests, and the recipients of my good will." He stepped to the side of the table and extended a hand, palm up, for Adalynn to take. His skin hummed in anticipation of her touch. "Will you accept, or do I have to be a *condescending prick* before you take my offer into consideration?"

She blushed again, looking contrite, but lifted her hand and placed it in his. "Well, you kind of were being one."

A thrill arced up his arm, raising gooseflesh over his skin. He barely suppressed a shudder. The sensation continued down to a place low in his belly, where it sparked a flame. "Were?"

She smiled at him, one side of her mouth rising a little higher than the other. Her dark eyes, even in the dim light, were warm and filled with good humor. "I think your social skills are improving already."

"I suppose I'd better ensure I kick you out promptly at dawn, then," he replied, feeling his own lips curl into a small smile, "before your behavior influences me any further."

"Are you flirting with my sister?" Danny asked from beside Merrick.

Adalynn whipped her head toward her brother and quickly pulled her hand out of Merrick's. "Danny!"

Merrick curled his fingers into a loose fist—as though that could assuage his sudden sense of emptiness—and dropped his hand to his side. "Daniel, are you familiar with the saying *children should be seen, not heard?*"

"Nope. Are you familiar with the saying *dude, don't be a dick?*"

Adalynn pressed her lips into a tight line and covered her face with her hand. "Danny…"

"What? Isn't dick and prick the same thing? You called him a prick before!"

"So, young master Daniel will be sleeping in the front yard tonight?" Merrick asked.

"Oh, come on! Why is it okay for her to say that stuff but not me?" Danny demanded. "It is because you're flirting, isn't it?"

Struggling to suppress his irritation, Merrick cleared his throat. He didn't have to answer to anyone, especially an adolescent human—though it didn't help that, were he to be honest with himself, he had to admit the boy was correct. "Shall I show you to a room?"

"Please," Adalynn replied, "before he says something else and *I* make him sleep outside."

Chapter Four

Adalynn lay in bed staring at the dark ceiling, wide awake despite her fatigue. Sleep tugged at her consciousness, but there was a strange energy flowing through her that kept her from closing her eyes and succumbing to her weariness.

It was frustrating. She had a roof over her head, good food in her stomach, and she felt genuinely safe; not once since the Sundering had she had all three of those things simultaneously. And yet she couldn't rest.

Danny snored softly beside her. He'd conked out as soon as his head hit the pillow. She could admit she was jealous of that, but she was glad to know he was safe and resting soundly. She was glad Merrick was allowing them to stay, even if it was only for one night.

Merrick.

She couldn't stop thinking about the man, couldn't stop thinking about how it'd felt when they'd touched. Dealing with him had been like riding a roller coaster that was so rusted and worn it could collapse at any moment; she wasn't sure how to feel about him. The first impression he'd made—while justified—certainly hadn't helped anything. He was a mystery.

One moment he'd wanted them gone, and the next, he'd wanted them to stay. He'd thrown a fit about them eating his food only to offer them fresh produce a few minutes later. She had a feeling he would've given them *more* if they'd asked.

But even if her emotions concerning him were jumbled and confused, she couldn't deny that looking at him and touching him had roused something powerful in her.

Desire.

Adalynn lifted her hand off the bed and looked at her palm. They'd exchanged such a simple touch, yet it had evoked a sensation so thrilling that it still lingered on her skin. And her denial didn't change the fact—he *had* been flirting with her. There'd been heat in his eyes as he looked upon her, a teasing twist to his lips.

Maybe he's not as bad as he makes himself out to be.

Sighing, she closed her eyes, attempted to push those thoughts away, and willed sleep to come.

It didn't.

She turned onto her side, facing Danny.

Come on. Sleep!

She released a heavy, frustrated breath. When she inhaled, she caught a whiff of body odor—and she knew it wasn't just Danny's.

Thankfully, that helped turn her thoughts away from Merrick. She focused on how odd it was to be lying on a comfortable bed with clean, soft bedding, on how restrictive her clothing felt, on how filthy and stinky she was. All of that tumbled through her mind in an endless loop, each thought gaining strength every time it came around again.

She and Danny were likely staining Merrick's sheets with dirt and sweat.

When her next breath renewed her awareness of the smell, Adalynn tossed the covers off and quietly slipped out of the bed. She glanced back at her brother; he slept undisturbed.

Why had this not bothered her before?

Because it didn't matter. We were always on the road, in a car, on the run, too preoccupied or too terrified to notice or care about personal hygiene. Now, we're in a fancy home, lying in a fancy bed, with fancy, clean sheets, and it all belongs to a sexy—

No, Addy! Not supposed to be thinking about him right now!

But it was hard not to; the house itself reminded her of Merrick. It was old, out of its time—and even though he didn't look older than thirty-five or forty, she somehow had the same sense about him.

Everything here was so amazing, and in impossibly good condition. Hell, there was *running water* in this house. Nowhere else they'd stopped had had running water thanks to the lack of electricity. She and Danny had been taking water from rivers and streams over the last few weeks, filtering and boiling it as thoroughly as possible.

Running water.

She straightened. Merrick had shown them a bathroom down the hall and had said they were free to use it as necessary—so long as they cleaned up after themselves. And there'd been a tub in there, one of those old-fashioned, claw-footed tubs. Even if the water was cold, it would feel *good* to finally be clean. A dip and a quick scrub down in a stream wasn't the same.

Anticipation thrummed in her.

She looked at Danny. He'd been a magnet for dirt even before the Sundering, and probably needed a bath even more than she did, but she didn't have the heart to wake him. The bed was likely soiled by now, anyway. He'd just have to bathe before they left in the morning. She'd make sure of it.

Adalynn picked up her pack, made her way across the room, and slipped into the hallway, closing the door softly behind her. She paused; everything was silent except for the occasional creaking bough and gust of wind from outside— but this wasn't the sort of oppressive silence so common beyond these walls, wasn't the silence of a dead world. This was almost…comforting.

Without bothering to take out her flashlight—her eyes had adjusted adequately to the darkness—she walked to the bathroom. Once she was inside, she set her bag down and crouched beside it, unzipping a small pouch in front. Merrick had said there were candles in most rooms, so she assumed there was at least one in here.

She took out her lighter, stood up, and flicked it on. It didn't take long to find a candle; there were at least a dozen scattered around the room—at the sink, on a high shelf, in a small cut-out nook, and along the windowsill. It was like something out of a movie.

The perfect romantic bathroom.

Adalynn could just imagine the glow those candles would emit, could imagine sinking down into that clawfoot tub with it full of steaming, hot water and a mountain of bubbles.

But those luxuries were gone. Perhaps, one day, things would get back to that…though it wouldn't be in her lifetime.

She wasn't about to complain—even if she didn't have the hot water and bubbles, she had running water and candles. She didn't have to overindulge to appreciate what was available.

She lit two candles—one on the sink counter, the other on the windowsill near the tub. After putting her lighter away, she plugged the tub and turned the left knob all the way up. Water blasted from the faucet.

As the bathtub filled, Adalynn undressed, pausing once her shirt was off to give the garment a narrow-eyed, disgusted sneer. It was stained with dirt and sweat. She couldn't suppress a groan when she lifted it to her nose and sniffed; it stank. She couldn't begin to guess at the thoughts that must've run through Merrick's head when he'd first seen Adalynn and Danny—when he'd *smelled* them.

Maybe he was being polite. She doubted he would've have held his tongue otherwise.

She'd just have to wash her clothes after her bath and hang them up overnight. Danny's wouldn't have time to dry, but at least she could clean them in the morning.

She tossed her shirt onto the floor beside the tub. Unbuttoning her jeans, she hooked her thumbs beneath the waistband and shoved her pants and underwear down, tossing them atop her shirt. Her bra followed. Finally, she reached up, pulled the hair tie from her ponytail, and slipped it over her wrist. She shook her hair out; it felt dirty, greasy, and tangled.

It'll be so nice to feel clean again.

Dropping her arms to her sides, Adalynn stepped closer to the tub and braced herself for the shock of cold.

Best to just get in the water fast and get it over with. Just like we used to do a when we went swimming.

Taking a deep breath, she stepped in quickly and dropped down into the water—only to scream and leap back out, stumbling and slamming against the wall, knocking over a couple candles and toppling a low shelf in the process.

Panting, limbs shaking, she stared at the tub in shock as a stinging pain—made worse because it was so unexpected—swept over her flesh and radiated through her body.

The water was *hot*.

MERRICK CURLED his fingers in his hair, tugging on the thick strands. He sat leaning forward, elbows on the desk, staring down at the book lying open before him—a latter translation of ancient documents pertaining to beasts lurking within mankind. About *monsters* dormant in human blood, their essences diluted over millennia of interbreeding. If there was useful information in the text, it was currently lost on him.

He'd reread the last paragraph half a dozen times without retaining anything. His mind kept shifting toward Adalynn. At first those shifts had occurred between pages, then between paragraphs, then in the space between each sentence. Now it seemed that after each individual word, he thought of *her*.

He couldn't shake the knowledge that she was in a bedroom just down the hall from his study—that information was lodged in the back of his mind, producing a soft but ceaseless hum that served as a constant reminder. His palm still tingled with the residual energy of her touch, and flashes of her smile danced through his mind's eye unbidden.

"It will be for the best when she departs on the morrow," he muttered, but hearing those words aloud didn't lend him the resolve he'd hoped they would. Instead, they produced a sinking feeling in his gut.

Exactly *who* would benefit from her departure? Certainly not Adalynn or Daniel; they'd be returning to a horrifying new world that had been transformed by the resurgence of true magic, a world in which humanity—who'd for so long been the Earth's apex predator—had suddenly become prey.

Certainly, it would restore the quiet in Merrick's home, but had they *really* disturbed it that much to begin with? Despite Danny's tendency to chatter endlessly, there was something heartening about hearing warm, friendly voices in these halls.

He growled deep in his throat. No good could come from sheltering humans. What would they bring but more of their kind? Their numbers always multiplied eventually, more of them always came, and when they banded together, they tended to be at their worst. Regardless of the immense increase in magical power from which he'd benefitted since the Sundering, Merrick was under no illusion—he was far from invulnerable. Humans had killed powerful witches and warlocks throughout history, and they would do so again.

He did not intend to become the latest name on a long list of victims.

But from what Merrick had witnessed thus far, Adalynn and Danny weren't like that. They were just trying to survive. Just trying to get by. Merrick was undoubtedly drawn to Adalynn, but even Danny had admirable traits—even if those traits were wallowing in a mire of youthful disrespect and rambunctiousness.

The humans needed to leave.

Merrick *wanted* them to stay.

A scream—high and feminine—sounded from down the hall, followed by the sound of several objects clattering to the floor.

Adalynn.

Merrick shoved himself away from the desk, darted out of his study, and raced toward the source of the scream, heart pounding. He stopped outside the bathroom. Candlelight flickered from within, visible through the gap at the bottom of the door. Images of blood staining the tile floor and dripping down the sides of the tub flashed through his mind. Humans were such fragile creatures, especially when they were ill.

He grasped the doorknob, turned it, and entered the room. His eyes immediately fell upon Adalynn.

She stood with her back pressed against the wall and arms spread, her fingers splayed and curled like claws as though they could somehow dig into the wall and support her weight. Her chest heaved with her panting breaths, and her skin, completely exposed from head to toe, glistened with moisture in the candlelight. Her hair hung loose around her shoulders. Merrick's gaze dipped down her body, taking in her bare breasts, which were tipped with pink nipples, her flat stomach, and the small patch of dark hair between her legs.

His cock throbbed, hardening rapidly within the confines of his trousers. Her body was the same as her face—the faint lines of ribs at her sides and the slight pronouncement of her hip bones spoke of a woman who was underfed, though now he couldn't be sure if it was due to scarcity of food, her illness, or a combination of both. Still, she was stunning, and the near-overwhelming urge to close the distance between them and run his hands over her skin roared to life within Merrick.

Adalynn swung her gaze to his. Her eyes widened, and recognition lit within them before she screamed again, crossed her arms over her nakedness, and dove for the pile of clothes on the floor. She snatched up her pants first, tossed them aside, and grabbed her shirt instead, holding it up to shield her body.

"What are you *doing?*" she demanded.

"Making sure you were all right. You screamed like you were attacked by something." His eyes dipped, and the fire in his belly flowed into his veins as his gaze trailed down her supple thighs. The skin of both her legs was reddened, as though she'd spent too much time in the sun, but that didn't reduce their appeal.

She clutched the shirt tighter. "The water was hot."

"Hot water *is* what tends to come out when you turn the knob marked *H*," he replied distractedly; he was far too occupied with running his gaze lower still. His memory was impeccable, but the brief glimpse he'd had of her bare body was simply not enough. He needed *more*.

"The water isn't supposed to *be* hot."

Adalynn was hot. Did humans still say that? He had trouble keeping up with the way their languages changed, which had seemed faster and faster with every generation.

Merrick forced his eyes up to meet hers, but he did so slowly. Her cheeks were now flushed—with embarrassment, perhaps? Or something more?

"Why wouldn't it be?" he asked.

"There's…no electricity. Usually no running water at all, especially not *hot* water. But you have both."

"People have had means of heating and pumping water long before they learned to harness electricity."

Her brow furrowed. Merrick sensed that she wanted to argue, but she seemed hesitant to do so; perhaps she simply wasn't informed enough on the subject to feel she could argue with any confidence? Modern conveniences had made life easy for humans, but they had also enabled an immense loss of knowledge—the way their ancestors had been forced to live and survive had become unnecessary information.

Of course, he didn't *want* her to argue—he'd been pumping and heating his water with magic since the power went out, and she didn't need to know that. There were only two possible outcomes to him sharing that information with her—either she'd flee in terror, eventually rounding up more humans to destroy Merrick like the monster they'd see him as, or she'd seek to take advantage of his power to obtain her own comfort and security.

Be destroyed or be used. Neither option was appealing.

But *she* was appealing, and he wouldn't mind if she used him for something else…

Merrick took a step closer to her. That small movement was enough for him to feel the heat wafting off her body. He *knew* it wasn't all because of the bath. "*Are* you all right, Adalynn?"

"I-I'm fine. You can go now."

He extended an arm to brush Adalynn's hair away from her shoulder. His fingertips trailed over her soft skin, sending a thrill through his body that nearly made him groan. Her breath hitched, and her eyes flared infinitesimally. Despite the other scents clinging to her—sweat and dirt, primarily—he could still smell the fragrance that was undeniably, entirely *her*. It was reminiscent of lavender blooms beneath a warm summer sun.

Merrick released a soft but strained breath; he yearned to touch more, to tear away her shirt—and his own—and pull her against him. "You don't sound very certain."

Movement below caught his attention, and his eyes dropped to see her little toes curl inward against the floor. One candle lay to her right, and another to her left, undoubtedly knocked over when she'd leapt out of the water.

"I'm fine. Really," she said a little breathlessly. "It doesn't even burn anymore."

He lifted his gaze again, stopping it this time at her collarbone. It would be so easy—and so satisfying—to lean forward and trace it with his lips.

When he sank slowly into a crouch, leaving his face mere inches from her sex—with only the dangling fabric of her shirt serving as a barrier—Adalynn released a soft whimper and pressed herself even more firmly against the wall. Her scent was different here; he could detect the earthy, sweet notes of her arousal.

Merrick nearly groaned. His cock ached with want for release, with want for *her*, and his lips parted to let out a shaky breath. In an instant, he could have swept her shirt aside and devoured her. In an instant, he could have had her up against the wall, legs spread, crying out in pleasure as he worshipped her sex with his mouth and tongue.

Maintaining his deliberately slow pace, he reached aside with both hands and—leaning just a little closer to her, close enough that his breath moved the cloth of her shirt—plucked the fallen candles off the floor.

When he finally stood, delirious heat suffused his chest, and the desire-driven discomfort in his groin was almost too much to bear. He set the candles on the shelf over Adalynn's head and looked down at her. "Is there anything I can do for you, Adalynn?"

With head tilted back, lips parted, and pupils blown wide, she stared up at him. She caught her lip between her teeth for a second, and the action sent a jolt straight to his cock, making it twitch.

Smiling, Adalynn shook her head. "No. I mean…maybe a little more light? And some, um…privacy."

He couldn't help but smile himself, though her answer—even if he'd expected it—disappointed him. He stared at her lips for a few more seconds, letting himself wonder what they would feel like, what she would taste like, before he finally stepped away. Raising a hand, he snapped his fingers.

The unlit candles flared to life, bathing the room in their soft, flickering glow.

Adalynn gasped, looking around in wonder before her gaze returned to him. "Merrick?"

Oh, fuck. Merrick, you twice-cursed fool.

"Enjoy your bath, Adalynn," he said, dipping his head in a shallow bow. He spun and exited the room before she could say anything more, pulling the door shut behind him.

He lifted a hand and buried his fingers in his hair, tugging it back sharply as he muttered under his breath, "After all that, why be so *stupid*? What, did you think she wouldn't notice?"

But he hadn't been thinking *at all*; it had seemed so natural in that moment to use his magic to cater to her whims, to fulfill her wish as quickly and wholly as possible.

And now there'd be a conversation in the morning that he was neither prepared nor willing to have, because Adalynn was intelligent, observant, and protective of her brother. His only consolation was that he'd be sending them on their way with the sunrise…

But even *he* wasn't entirely certain of his conviction on that matter.

He returned to his study and sat at his desk, restless and fully aware that his research wasn't likely to progress much further tonight—his mind was even more preoccupied with Adalynn than it had been a few minutes earlier. Now he had that fleeting, exquisite glimpse of her naked body to fuel the flames of his desire, now he had her mouthwatering scent

lingering in his nose, and his skin still pulsed with her resonance, her mana song, which seemed to play just for him.

Merrick dropped a hand to his groin and squeezed his
hard, aching cock, but the gesture provided no relief.

Why, after all this time? Why am I suddenly craving a human?

Chapter Five

A peal of thunder rattled the window. Merrick's frown deepened, but he did not move away from the glass. He'd slowly woven magic into every piece of this manor over the years since he'd purchased it, infusing it with arcane energies to ensure it remained in the best possible condition; before the Sundering, repairs had meant calling human laborers, and he preferred to avoid that whenever possible. Those enchantments on his home had been bolstered by the invisible barrier he'd shaped around it to protect it from a world that seemed hellbent on destruction—lightning and fallen branches would never touch the manor, even if the rain could.

That protection hadn't meant anything when a little human woman had picked up a rock and smashed in his front window.

But he couldn't bring himself to feel sorry for that.

Though morning had come, there was no sunlight— everything was drab gray, and the heavy rains had already made the ground mucky. The dirt lane that led from the manor to the main road would've been impossible to traverse by this point.

He watched the fat raindrops fall, watched them turn the

surfaces of countless puddles into rippling bastions of chaos, and told himself this was the time to send the humans on their way. What did the weather matter to him? It was their problem, not Merrick's.

At least one of them was awake already. Merrick knew it was the boy—he sensed that Adalynn was down the hall, in the bedroom he'd let the humans use, though he wasn't sure how or why he was aware of her location.

Lightning streaked across the sky—at least seven strikes all in rapid succession, blasting over the trees to create a wall of blue-white electricity. It was there and gone in a flash, though its web-like afterimage lingered in his vision for several seconds.

The fleeting nature of those lightning strikes—which came and went in the blink of an eye but could have such profound impact on whatever they touched—reminded him of Adalynn.

Adalynn, who'd already so deeply affected him.

Adalynn, who'd kept Merrick awake all night, who'd sparked consuming arousal and unfulfilled lust in him.

Adalynn, who would be gone so soon whether he sent her away or not.

That ominous thought was punctuated by deep, booming thunder—thunder that seemed intent on shaking his manor apart despite its magical protections.

Those protections suddenly seemed inadequate.

He knew, in his heart, that if he sent Adalynn and Danny away, he'd spend the entire day standing at this window, watching the rain and thinking of her. *Feeling* her absence. Feeling…guilty. Even now, he wanted to go to her. He could imagine entering the bedroom to find her curled up on the bed asleep, could imagine himself climbing in to lie beside her, could imagine himself wrapping his arms around her and drawing her close.

After more than a thousand years, is it really going to be this little human to drive me mad?

And while I am here brooding, young Daniel has already gone downstairs and raided my pantry.

The thought of his precious supply of peanut butter being decimated was just the distraction Merrick needed in that moment. He stepped back from the window, tugged the curtains closed, and exited his study.

Despite a powerful urge to glance down the hall toward Adalynn's bedroom, he kept his attention directed forward—lest he find his body turning toward her—and strode to the staircase, descending swiftly.

When he reached the kitchen, he stopped in the doorway.

Danny was indeed at the table, an open sleeve of crackers set before him—with the jar of peanut butter beside them. Merrick's eyebrows fell, and his jaw muscles tightened, but he stopped himself from charging at the adolescent.

Lips pressed together as though in concentration—or perhaps anticipation—Danny opened the jar before raising a cracker in one hand and a butter knife in the other. He delicately dipped the knife into the jar. When he lifted it clear, a pea-sized bit of peanut butter was on its tip. The boy stared with wide eyes as he spread the peanut butter on the cracker; it didn't go far.

Danny licked his lips, inhaled deeply, and exhaled. He moved the cracker to his mouth and took a little bite from the edge. His body sagged as he tilted his head back and moaned in appreciation. "So, so good," he muttered.

He finished the cracker in several small bites, pausing to relish each one. After the cracker was gone, Danny shifted his gaze between the red lid and the open jar, worrying his lower lip as though he were contemplating having more. That he was hesitating at all was impressive to Merrick, but what the boy did next was surprising.

Danny nodded to himself, took another cracker out of the

sleeve, and scooped out a slightly larger glob of peanut butter. He smeared it over the cracker, scraping everything off the knife along the cracker's edge. Then, holding the cracker between forefinger and thumb, he carefully set it down on the table in front of the empty seat beside him. The seat his sister had occupied the night before.

Once the cracker was down, Danny picked up the lid and screwed it back onto the jar.

Something shifted inside Merrick, something deep, old, and powerful. Something that had shaped his life since he was even younger than this human.

Merrick hadn't been able to bring himself to hate this boy and his sister, even when they'd broken into his home, but he still should've been as indifferent toward them as he had been toward most every other human he'd ever encountered. Their lives should've been of no consequence to him. Whether they lived or died should've been unimportant so long as they were out of his home. Danny, in particular, represented much of what made humans dangerous—their easily roused passion, their volatility, their disrespectfulness.

But this simple act—even if it violated the boundaries Merrick had established—showed a different side of humanity. A side that had been so easy for Merrick to ignore in his isolation and bitterness. Because Danny and Adalynn both exemplified the human capacity for loyalty, for compassion, for sacrifice.

Merrick had gone hungry many times in his life, especially during his youth. Though it had been long ago, and his appetites for physical food had diminished since—even if his enjoyment of it had not—he'd never forgotten. He never would forget. The pleasure Danny had expressed in that taste of peanut butter reminded Merrick of himself as a child.

But in setting a cracker aside—with more than he'd taken for himself—Danny had proven his maturity, his appreciation, his thoughtfulness. And that spoke to Merrick more deeply than he would've thought possible.

Merrick stepped into the kitchen and approached the table.

Danny lifted his head, meeting Merrick's gaze, and his entire body went taut. Guilt and fear gleamed in the boy's eyes and paled his skin. He gulped and forced a wide grin. "Morning?"

"It certainly is," Merrick replied as he slowly pulled out the chair across from Danny.

The boy's grin crumbled. "Please don't kill me."

Merrick sat down and dipped his chin toward the cracker on the table. "Who is that for?"

Danny glanced at the cracker. His shoulders sagged. "Addy. But you can have it if you want it."

"I think she's earned it, don't you?"

The boy cocked his head, his brows furrowing. "You're not mad?"

Reaching forward, Merrick picked up the peanut butter jar. He kept his eyes on Danny as he unscrewed the lid and set it aside. This had been a fairly fresh jar—Merrick himself had only eaten a little after opening it—and Danny seemed to have used a negligible amount.

Merrick slid the jar in front of the boy. "I should be."

Danny stared at the jar for a moment before returning his gaze to Merrick. "But...you're not?"

"Eat some more."

The boy perked. "Really?" He reached for the jar and dragged it closer only to pause suddenly, his features falling in suspicion. "Wait...it's not poison, is it?"

Merrick's brows rose. "You *just* ate some, Daniel. Now that I offer it freely, you ask if it is poisoned? Should you not have considered that *before* you snuck a taste?"

"Did you forget how you were acting about it yesterday?"

"No, but you must have."

"Um, sorry, but if you're so protective over your peanut butter you *clearly* understand that this stuff is like the greatest thing ever invented. How was I supposed to resist it?"

Merrick couldn't hold back a smirk. "I should drag you out into the storm by your ear for violating my wishes, boy, but I find myself impressed by your restraint—and your thoughtfulness toward your sister. *That* is why you may have more."

Danny grinned. "I changed my mind. You're pretty cool."

"And all it took was some peanut butter?"

"You mean the nectar of the gods?"

"Nectar implies a liquid."

Danny shrugged and dipped the butter knife into the jar. "I could drink this stuff." He smeared a bit on a cracker and held it out to Merrick.

"No, thank you." Merrick was hungry—more so than ever since reaching immortality, perhaps—but there was no food that could sate his current appetite.

"So what'd you do? Before all this?" Danny took a bite of the cracker and released a satisfied hum.

Leaning back in his chair, Merrick rested a forearm on the edge of the table. "I was an eccentric millionaire. Little has changed for me."

"Huh. So, your family was rich?"

"No. I earned my fortune by my own toil."

"That's what every rich person *says*," Danny replied, "but it's usually bullshit, right?"

Merrick arched a brow. "Pardon me, young Daniel? Did you imply I'm being dishonest *and* use a word your sister would frown upon?" He reached toward the peanut butter jar. "Perhaps I misjudged your maturity…"

"Aw man, not you too!" Danny grabbed the jar and pulled it closer. "Sorry, okay? Don't tell Addy."

"I won't. This time. What did *you* do before all this?"

Danny smiled proudly. "I was a B student and played loads of soccer. Our team placed third in the state tournament.

Another year, and I think we would've taken first. We had a really good team put together, you know?" He popped the rest of the cracker into his mouth.

Despite the relative casualness in his tone, Danny's passion and love for the sport came through in the way he spoke. It *sounded* like nothing had changed for the boy, like he was going to meet with his friends when the summer was over and get back to practicing, even though *everything* was different.

Merrick had already glimpsed a deep-running strength in Adalynn; it seemed Danny possessed a similar quality.

Though he couldn't bring himself to mourn what humanity as a whole had lost, Merrick could sympathize with what these two humans—*his* humans?—had lost.

"And what of your sister?" Merrick asked. "What did she do?"

"Addy was a straight A student, graduated college with honors and all that. She's been playing the piano since she was little, and she's *really* good. She plays—well, *played*—in an orchestra and everything. She was always pushing her music, even when she had to work a day job to pay her bills. She always talked about playing a solo concert one day, and I know she would've made it, but she, uh…" Danny frowned, and pushed aside the crackers as though he'd suddenly lost his appetite. "She got sick. And then, you know, all *this* happened."

"Did she get sick immediately before everything fell apart?" Merrick asked, voice uncharacteristically soft.

Danny shook his head. "I guess she was having headaches and stuff for a few months before she was diagnosed. The first doctor she went to said it was just migraines and basically told her to deal with them and take the medicine they gave her. It was different doctors a couple months later who figured it out, after her first seizure. That was like two months before everything went bad. They said she had brain cancer."

Merrick frowned deeply. He possessed only passing knowledge of the many ailments that plagued humanity, but he knew of cancer—it was amongst the more serious illnesses. Even if he'd never heard of it, he would've known that it would kill her—he'd felt it firsthand, had brushed against it with his magic, had felt her impending doom. And that troubled him greatly.

Even if Adalynn had a chance of living to seventy or eighty years old—or however long it was humans lived these days—her life would have gone by in a blur for Merrick. As years built up behind him, the present seemed to move faster and faster. Humans were born, lived, and died while he simply persisted; the life of a single person being cut short was nothing new, was nothing unnatural.

But he *hated* it in this case.

"Were they working to heal her before the Sundering?" Merrick asked. Perhaps they'd been using some method he could replicate. Perhaps, with enough research, he could figure something out, could hone his magic into a refined, delicate blade to neatly slice the sickness out of her.

Have I already made the decision, then? Do I already intend to let them stay?

The boy shrugged a shoulder, turning his palm toward the ceiling. "I don't really know the details. Our parents either thought I was too young to understand or didn't know how to tell me, so they didn't really say much about any of it other than she was really sick. But Addy sat down with me one night and explained it. She said it was *terminal*. The only thing that had a chance to stop it was an experimental treatment, but there wasn't really any guarantee."

Tears welled in Danny's eyes. He lifted his hand and swiped at them angrily, bowing his head. "Didn't matter, because the first day she went in to start the treatment was the day of the Sundering."

"Where are your parents?" Merrick asked gently.

Danny fiddled with a corner of the cracker sleeve, crinkling the plastic. It was clear when he answered that he was struggling to control his voice, that he was battling against raw emotion, that he was *trying* to rise above the pain. "They died. They were driving to meet Addy at the hospital, and just as they got there, everything just…happened. And, um…well, an ambulance hit their car."

Merrick's heart ached; that made Adalynn *and* Danny who'd been able to produce that feeling in him, who'd touched his soul with sorrow like he'd not felt in a long while. He sensed there was more to Danny's story, but he dared not press the boy further; Merrick understood this sort of pain. He had been close to Danny's age when he lost his own parents— before he'd even come into his magic. And in the years following, he'd lost his siblings, as well, both of whom had been older and stronger than he.

The sense of loss, loneliness, and displacement—like he'd never belonged anywhere—lingered with Merrick to this day.

"My parents died when I was very young," Merrick said, "and it was also very sudden. I will not lie to you and say the pain goes away…it never does. But the *weight* of it lessens over time. The sting fades. And you will carry on."

"I was lucky to have Addy. Without her…" Danny lifted his head and looked at Merrick. "I'm sorry about your parents."

Merrick's brow furrowed, and for a moment, he was at a loss for words. No one—not in a thousand years—had ever offered him any consolation. Even if logic suggested it was because he'd always been so guarded, had always kept himself isolated, he couldn't help but feel a rush of warmth in his chest now. Merrick had lived for so long without any emotion apart from bitterness that he wasn't entirely certain how to react.

"And I am sorry about yours," he finally replied. "Perhaps I'll have one of those crackers, after all."

ADALYNN WOKE WITH A JOLT, her eyes snapping open as a deafening peal of thunder shook the room around her. She lay on her stomach, facing the window, through which dull gray light streamed around the edges of the closed curtain. Rain drummed against the windowpane and the roof above. The storm would make traveling on foot difficult.

That thought instilled her with sudden dread. They'd be moving on today. They'd be leaving behind a sturdy, safe, dry shelter, running water—*hot*, running water—warm, comfortable beds, and an abundance of supplies and fresh food. This place would have been perfect.

But it wasn't theirs. It belonged to Merrick.

Her mind shifted to last night, producing startlingly crisp memories of Merrick barging into the bathroom while she was naked and completely exposed to his captivating, citrine eyes. Despite everything, she hadn't been scared.

Well, perhaps she'd been a *little* frightened, but beneath that fear had been excitement, had been *desire*.

Adalynn knew that any sane woman would've demanded he leave, would've reached for a weapon when he advanced on her, would've *fought*. She was sure that, had she told him to leave, he would have. But she hadn't. She'd stood still as his hungry eyes ran over her body, as he closed the distance between them and touched her. That simple brush of his fingers on her shoulder had sent a shock of electricity through her, sparking her body to life, had made her sex pulse, flooding her with delicious heat.

And she'd wanted *more*.

It hadn't mattered that he was a stranger. All that mattered, in that moment, was that she had *wanted*. With every bit of herself, she'd wanted *him*.

She'd resisted. She wasn't sure if it had been out of habit or because he'd be sending them away with the morning, but her will had held longer than she would've expected. He was so damn sexy, and so intense—even if he had a talent for being abrasive when he wanted to be—and what would the harm have been? What was a little mutual pleasure between consenting adults?

Even after she'd asked for privacy—as close as she'd been able to come to asking him to get out—she might've stopped him, might've given in to her urges, were it not for the *candles*.

At first, she'd thought she was dreaming. The entire situation had been surreal—a secluded, rundown mansion that was in perfect condition inside; *hot*, running water; her standing naked in front of a mysterious man she desired without any concern for her own safety. The candles suddenly flaring to life must've been her imagination completing the fantasy in which she'd found herself.

But the heat of the flames had suggested that it was all *very* real.

There had to be an explanation for it. Maybe she'd lit more than two candles and had forgotten? It wouldn't have been the first time she'd spaced doing something, especially with her condition—memory loss was a common symptom, according to the doctors, and her experiences had supported that.

Maybe her interaction with Merrick had never happened, and she'd just had a particularly vivid dream after taking a cold bath, brushing her teeth, and getting back into bed.

But it had felt so *real*.

Another crack of thunder pulled her out of her thoughts.

It was time to go.

Her stomach cramped with hunger; she hoped Merrick would be kind enough to offer something more to eat before they headed out into the storm.

With a sigh, Adalynn pushed herself up and swung her legs around to get into a sitting position. "Danny, it's time to wake up. We don't want to overstay our welcome and anger our host."

There was no movement, no response. Not even a groan of protest.

Turning her head, Adalynn reached out to shake her brother awake. "Dan—" Her eyes widened.

He was gone.

"Danny?" she called, scanning the room. He was nowhere —he wasn't rummaging through the tall, dark armoire against the wall, wasn't standing by the door bouncing impatiently, wasn't standing in front of the window or sitting on the floor. But his bugout bag *was* sitting on the floor. A flare of frustration joined her alarm, but she quickly stamped them both down.

We're okay. Danny's *okay. This is our first taste of comfort and security in a long time, and he just…just got a little complacent. He's just a kid.*

But he still needed to remember. As much as she hated being hard on him, she wasn't going to be around forever, and he needed to be careful. He needed to stay alert regardless of how safe things seemed. Merrick was a stranger, and people hid their true nature all the time; why would he be any different? That didn't mean he *was* crazy, or a killer…but it didn't mean he *wasn't*, either.

Oh, so now *I take that into consideration, after I stood there and let him gawk at my naked body. Way to go, Adalynn.*

Sitting on the edge of the bed, Adalynn grabbed her boots and shoved her feet into them, tying them quickly. She stood, picked up their bugout bags—swinging one over each shoulder—and left the room to find her brother.

As she walked down the hall toward the spiral staircase, she glanced into the currently unoccupied bathroom, where her drying clothing dangled from the curtain rail over the tub; she'd have to collect her clothing after she collected Danny. But she lingered at the doorway, finding herself again fighting back the memories of what had transpired within.

Just a dream. It wasn't real—couldn't *have been real.*

She descended the steps, and when she reached the bottom, her eyes flicked to the front door, catching a glimpse of the rain through the windows flanking the entrance. She stopped abruptly as she was turning away and swung her gaze back to the left window—a fully intact window.

Brows falling low and eyes narrowing, Adalynn slowly approached it.

"I broke it," she whispered. That was how they'd entered —she'd broken the window, reached through, and unlocked the door.

Wasn't it?

She lifted a hand and lightly tapped on the glass, producing a soft clinking sound with her nail.

I'm not going crazy.

She looked down. There wasn't so much as a sliver of broken glass on the floor. Adalynn pressed the heels of her hands to her eyes until flecks of color danced behind her eyelids. When she pulled her hands away, she looked at the window again; it was still intact.

Not. Crazy.

Laughter carried into the foyer from down the hall, faint but undeniably Danny's. Adalynn followed the sound, and the voices that came on its heels, to the kitchen. She slowed when she reached the doorway and leaned forward to peer around the doorframe. Danny and Merrick were seated at the kitchen table, sharing crackers and peanut butter.

"You've really never heard of *Stranger Things*? It's like the best piece of entertainment ever created," Danny said before shoving another peanut butter-laden cracker into his mouth.

"Several thousand years of human civilization may disagree with that assessment, young Daniel," Merrick replied. He was leaning back in his chair casually, exuding effortless sensuality; Adalynn wouldn't have thought him capable of it were it not for their brief encounter in the bathroom.

"Whatever, man. Just 'cause it's, like, really old doesn't mean it's better. *Stranger Things* is pretty much set in old times, anyway."

"Given what I know of modern entertainment," Merrick replied, "I doubt I've missed anything."

Was this really the same man from the day before? The one who'd seemed ready to shed blood over the very peanut butter they were eating now while discussing TV shows?

Danny's eyes shifted past Merrick to meet Adalynn's, and his smile widened. "Morning, Addy!"

Now that she'd been spotted, she had no choice but to enter the kitchen. She tightened her grip on the shoulder strap of Danny's bag as she neared the table. "Morning."

Merrick turned his head to look at her and arched one of his dark brows. The corner of his mouth rose along with it. A subtle light flared in his eyes, reminiscent of the light they'd contained last night in the bathroom.

Oh no, it wasn't a dream at all. That was real.

"Good morning, Adalynn," he said. "How did you sleep?"

His voice, deep and sultry, washed over her, making her nipples tingle and her heart beat just a little faster.

"Good. Very good, actually. Thank you," she replied.

"Are you hungry?" Merrick's eyes suggested he was —for *her*.

Instantaneous heat suffused her. How had things changed so drastically, so quickly?

"Merrick's sharing his peanut butter," Danny said. "I have a cracker waiting here for you."

Her gaze shifted to her brother. "I am hungry, but… Danny, did you forget something this morning?"

He cocked his head, brow furrowed. "Huh?"

Adalynn swung his bugout bag off her shoulder and dangled it in front of him.

Danny ducked his head, cheeks coloring. "Ohhh. Well, I mean…it was with you, right? So it's…okay?"

"Not okay. What if something happened to me?"

Danny's shoulders sagged. "Sorry, Addy."

Adalynn placed both packs on the floor beside the table before slipping her arm around her brother in a quick hug. "Just don't forget next time." She pulled back and straightened. "There's hot water. You need to take a quick bath before we go. That is"—she turned her face toward Merrick—"if it's okay with you, Merrick? I don't want us to overstay our welcome."

Merrick's smile faltered, falling into a faint but troubled frown. "He may bathe, yes, and take some time to enjoy it if he is inclined. As for leaving…you do not yet have to go."

"It'd be best if we leave soon. We have a long way to go before we reach the next town, and we're losing daylight already."

His tongue slipped out for a fleeting instant to slide over his lips. "I said you would have to leave with the sun. It could be argued that the sun is not currently visible, and therefore you are under no obligation to go."

Adalynn studied Merrick for a few seconds before her lips slowly stretched into a smile. "Are you asking us to stay until the storm is over, Merrick?"

"I am simply pointing out a technicality by which you may convince me to allow your stay to be extended."

His features softened briefly; it was enough for Adalynn to know that, however he'd behaved when they first arrived, however rough a start they'd had, Merrick was a good man at heart.

She grinned. "Merrick, would you be so kind as to allow us to stay until the storm passes?"

Merrick waved a hand dismissively. "I suppose I'd feel guilty if I made you leave in this weather. You may stay."

"Yes!" Danny pumped his fist before he looked at Adalynn and wrinkled his nose. "Do I *really* need to take a bath?"

"Yes," Adalynn said. "You stink."

"I do not!" Raising his arm, he turned his head and sniffed his armpit. He jerked his head back immediately. "Okay, so I *do*."

"Then go," she said, "and don't forget your bag this time."

"Fiiiine." He pushed his chair back, picked up a cracker covered with peanut butter, and held it out to her. "This one is for you."

Adalynn stared down at the cracker. The peanut butter's scent was mouth-watering; she could almost taste it on her tongue. Her heart flipped in her chest at her brother's thoughtfulness. It was a small gesture, but those little things meant more than ever after the Sundering. Even while indulging himself, he'd set a bit aside for her.

"Thanks, Danny," she said, taking the cracker carefully between her thumb and middle finger.

Danny beamed at her. "Welcome. Guess I'll go take a bath." He swiped the remnants of his half-eaten cracker off the table, shoved it in his mouth, and grabbed his bag. As he walked out of the kitchen, he said through his mouthful of food, "See you later, Merrick."

Mindful of the cracker in her hand, Adalynn pulled out a chair and sat down across from Merrick. His eyes, intent but unreadable, were already upon her.

"Thank you," she said, "for letting us stay longer. And for what you did with Danny."

His lips curled upward; Adalynn couldn't tell if he was smiling or smirking. Either way, the scar across his left eye granted a rakish air to the expression.

"And what was it I did?"

"Distracted him, made him laugh. Let him have one of his favorite foods."

Adalynn took a bite of the cracker, and she barely stopped

her eyes from rolling back in bliss. Her tongue darted out to lick peanut butter off her upper lip.

Had she just moaned?

Merrick's eyes dipped to her tongue for the instant it was exposed. "He seems to amuse himself well enough. The boy never runs out of things to say."

"Only because you're someone new. He's already talked my ears off about the same subjects more than once." She slipped the rest of the cracker into her mouth.

"Perhaps." Merrick slid the jar of peanut butter—which had a knife already plunged into it—from the center of the table to stand directly in front of Adalynn. "Help yourself. I fear it will be all gone the next time your brother gets into it."

A pang of guilt struck her, and when she swallowed, the food went down thickly. Frowning, she glanced into the jar. How much had Danny eaten? She should have woken when Danny did, should've stopped him, should've—

"He *was* into it when I came down," Merrick said, as though reading her thoughts. "He had one cracker with barely any on it for himself, and then he set the one aside for you. After that, he put the lid on and was done."

Adalynn's brows rose as she returned her gaze to Merrick. "Really?"

He nodded.

Pride replaced most of her guilt but couldn't overpower it completely—despite some of the things she'd said last night, she couldn't quite let go of the circumstances that had brought them into his home. She smiled a bit sheepishly. "Well, um, thanks, I guess, for not throwing us out."

Merrick chuckled; it was a deep, rich sound, warmer than she would've expected. "Do not thank me too soon. I may yet throw you out. A bored, idle child is a dangerous thing."

"We wouldn't mind helping out with whatever you need."

"There's little that requires tending, at least while the rain persists. It is enough, for now, that you simply respect my home. I ask that neither of you enter my study, which is the room at the top of the steps, or my bedroom, which is at the end of the north hallway—just down the hall from your room. Keep the noise down, don't break anything, and clean up your messes. You may eat from my stores, but be responsible with your portions."

Adalynn nodded. "We will. Thank you."

Silence stretched between them as Adalynn ate. She used only a minimal amount of peanut butter on the crackers she took. Even if he'd offered it freely, she didn't feel right taking too much, especially considering things like peanut butter had become a rarity in the modern world.

"I must insist you take more than that, Adalynn," Merrick said, "lest you insult my hospitality."

Adalynn paused as she was spreading peanut butter on a cracker to look up at him. Heat flooded her cheeks. "I…I don't need very much."

"Which is no reason to take too little. I grant you permission—*indulge yourself.*" As he spoke those last two words, fire rekindled in his gaze.

Adalynn didn't think he was talking about the peanut butter anymore.

Her body reacted to those words, and she recalled how close he'd been to her in the bathroom, how warm his breath had been on her skin, recalled the feel of his touch, the powerful energy he'd exuded—and the *candles.*

But the candles weren't all—the window by the front door was intact this morning, as though it hadn't been broken last night.

She dropped her gaze to the butter knife in her hand, brows creased as she dipped it back into the jar and added more peanut butter to her cracker. Her guilt at what she saw as excess lingered, but he'd insisted, and she wasn't about to decline a second time—this was an opportunity she wasn't likely to get again. Besides, she needed the nutrition as much as Danny did, so she could help him on his journey for as long as possible.

Adalynn ate a few more crackers; in her mind, the candles flickered to life in unison on a ceaseless loop, and she could almost feel their heat on her skin.

"What troubles you, Adalynn?"

Adalynn started; she hadn't realized that she'd been sitting there fiddling with the cracker packaging and staring off blankly. "Nothing." She twisted the package closed, reached across the table, and grabbed the lid to the peanut butter jar. Setting the knife aside, she screwed the lid onto the jar.

"It's in your face. In your eyes." He sat forward, leaning his arms on the table. "A great many things trouble you at every waking moment, I imagine, but there's something bothering you more than the rest now. What is it?"

"The window," she blurted.

"The window?" he asked flatly.

"By the front door. It's not broken."

"Good. I don't need the wind blowing in rainwater to ruin my floor."

Adalynn frowned. "But it *was* broken. *I* broke it."

His brow creased infinitesimally. "I've not seen broken glass in the foyer. Perhaps you're mistaken?"

"What?" Adalynn drew back, confused. "But you mentioned it last night, right before you brought us back in here."

Merrick turned his gaze upward and drummed his fingers over his chin. "Ah, yes. I *do* recall. The repair was so simple it must've slipped my mind. No harm done."

"*Repair*," she repeated with undisguised disbelief. "I don't know much about repairing windows, but there is no way that you could have repaired that overnight. There wasn't even the faintest crack on the windowpane this morning. You would've had to at the very least have replaced that whole pane, and I doubt you just had one on hand."

He shrugged. "I've a fondness for puzzles and a healthy supply of fast-drying glue."

"That…that doesn't make sense."

"Think about everything going on beyond these walls," Merrick replied. "Does *anything* in this world make sense?"

He was right. She couldn't make sense of anything out there; none of it should've existed, none of it should've been *real*. But the window… She *had* broken it.

"What about the candles in the bathroom?" she asked, fresh warmth flooding her cheeks. There was no way to think about the candles without thinking about what had transpired between her and Merrick, and she guessed his mind was going to the same place. "How did they all light up at once?"

His expression faltered, but only long enough for her to wonder if it had happened at all.

"You were somewhat…*flustered* last night, Adalynn. You had the candles lit when I entered."

"But I hadn't. I only lit two of them."

"Perhaps you're just misremembering?"

"I told you what was happening out there, Merrick, and I wasn't lying or exaggerating about any of it. There's…I don't know, *magic* in the world. It *doesn't* make any sense, but it's there. If you're involved in that somehow, well…it doesn't matter. I just…I need to know that Danny is safe."

For the second time since she'd come downstairs, Merrick's features softened. He reached forward and settled his hand over hers. His palm seemed to thrum with unseen energy, which zipped up her arm in a pleasurable thrill that nearly stole her breath. That faint, barely perceptible song entered her awareness again, a bit clearer than before but no less mysterious.

"Danny is safe here, Adalynn. As are you." Just that quickly, Merrick withdrew his hand and stood up. "If you'll excuse me, my routine has been disrupted. I've research to resume. Help yourself to more food."

Before she could ask why his touch affected her like that—before she could respond at all—he strode out of the kitchen and vanished into the hallway, leaving her alone.

But she couldn't shake the feeling that he'd somehow taken a part of her along with him.

Chapter Six

Adalynn grasped the patterned, velvety cloth in both hands and drew the curtains apart, allowing grayish light into the ballroom. She lowered her arms and stared through the tall window.

The rain hadn't let up since it had begun yesterday. The puddles around the house were closer to ponds now; if the rain continued like this for much longer, it was possible the manor could be classified as a lakefront home. Thankfully, the building was on slightly higher ground, and the first story was raised about six feet from ground level.

The thunder and lightning had persisted, though their occurrences had become infrequent—and the lightning never seemed to strike near the house.

Adalynn found a certain beauty in the dreary weather; apart from the rumbling thunder, the storm was soothing. Despite that calming effect, she felt on edge—partly because she felt *good*. She couldn't recall a single day passing without some degree of a headache or at least a bit of discomfort over the last few months. She felt perfectly...*healthy*, which was bizarre.

The rest of her unease was because of Merrick.

She'd been unable to shake her suspicions regarding him. There was far more to the man than he let on. She knew that was true about everyone, but it felt truer regarding him. He had some kind of magic, but she didn't know enough about it to draw any concrete conclusions.

Neither she nor Danny had seen him since he left her in the kitchen yesterday morning. True to Adalynn's word, she and her brother had occupied themselves in their room and kept away from both his study and his bedroom. Though Merrick had told them to help themselves to his food, Adalynn had reined Danny in, ensuring he ate only what she deemed a reasonable amount.

Adalynn didn't care how crazy the rest of the world was right now, there were things *here* that didn't add up. The front door window—which she'd checked for cracks again and found only smooth, unbroken glass—was only one of those things. The way he'd lit the candles was another. In fact, *all* the candles here were suspect—she'd used a few last night, and this morning noticed that none of them seemed to have burned down at all.

But that wasn't all; his home was completely devoid of dust and dirt even though she hadn't seen him dust or clean *anything* since she'd arrived, and *everything* here was in like-new condition despite its apparent age. And she hadn't forgotten what she saw when she'd first looked in through the windows from outside—broken-down, dust-blanketed rooms, a far cry from the reality of the manor's interior.

All that couldn't be mere coincidence, couldn't be the result of Adalynn losing her mind. And when she'd given him a chance to come clean, to tell the truth, he'd taken the escape route she'd left open—he'd avoided the matter entirely by saying she and Danny were safe.

How could she *not* take that as some sort of admission that he had magic at his command?

How am I even standing here considering all this rationally? Six months ago, this would've seen me committed to a psych ward for a mental evaluation.

Why wouldn't she believe in magic after everything she'd seen?

And if Merrick was *other*...wouldn't it be best to grab Danny and run, to face the storm rather than let her guard down and trust this man?

Yet despite all she and Danny had been through, despite the supernatural *things* that now roamed the world, Adalynn *did* trust that Merrick wouldn't hurt them. She felt it down in her bones, in her very *soul*. If Adalynn had to leave Danny with anyone, it would be Merrick. This late in the game, what more could she possibly do?

Nothing.

Her chest tightened, and she raised a hand to gently rub between her breasts as though it could erase the pain.

The world was big, and without modern technology, it felt impossibly larger. She slowed Danny down every time she suffered an episode. How long before she became a liability? How long before she slowed him down so much that she'd be placing him in danger rather than protecting him from it?

I'm already doing that. Every time I have a seizure, it forces him to choose whether to stay and protect me or to run and save himself—and Danny's always going to stay.

This reprieve from the headaches, the dizziness, the seizures was just an unexpected lull in the storm—she was in the eye of the hurricane.

Sighing, Adalynn turned and stepped away from the window to look at the rest of the ballroom. Though the light provided by the open window wasn't the best, it was enough to grant her a clearer view of many of the details that had been lost to her in the dark that first night.

The ceiling was made of the same golden oak as the floor, with thick borders around the edges of the room and encircling the lowered portions of the ceiling from which the three crystal chandeliers hung. Intricate designs were carved into the borders and the ceiling itself, including radial patterns around the bases of the chandeliers stylized like rays of sunlight. The frame of each of the tall windows extended beyond the top pane in an arch; those spaces were adorned with painted images of blue skies, clouds, and delicate flowers, adding brightness to the room. The walls were off-white, intersected between each window by gorgeously carved wooden pillars that ran from the floor to the ceiling borders.

She could just imagine the chandeliers above shining in the evening, casting their glow upon the polished wooden floors and ceiling. Their light would reflect upon the windows running along the length of the room. Music would fill the air, drifting through the side doors and into the garden where dancers would sneak away for a moment's solace.

But those days were long gone.

Why did Merrick live in such a grandiose house? Why had he let the exterior fall into such disrepair?

She supposed none of that mattered.

The thumping of her boots echoed across the wide-open room as she walked to her pack. She crouched down, opened the zipper, and dug inside. She found what she was looking for closer to the bottom of the bag, carefully wrapped in one of her clean T-shirts—a cassette player. If not for *Stranger Things*, Danny wouldn't have had a clue what the device was when Adalynn had discovered it in an abandoned pawn shop.

She hadn't meant to take the cassette player. It was unnecessary; the batteries were better used in flashlights and other handheld tools that contributed to their survival.

They'd gone to the shop in search of supplies—camping equipment, knives, and guns, all of which had been picked clean—when she'd passed a small tower of cassette tapes with familiar names like Beethoven, Mozart, and Tchaikovsky printed on the sides. Without thinking, she'd slipped them into her bag, along with one of the cassette players sitting in the bin beneath them—one that had a built-in speaker—and a pair of headphones.

Returning the T-shirt to her bag, Adalynn opened the player to check which tape was inside. *Beethoven's Greatest Hits*. Snapping the player shut, she rewound the tape until she found the beginning of the song she wanted, stood, and walked to the piano. She set the player gently atop the closed fallboard and pressed play.

The hauntingly beautiful notes of *Moonlight Sonata* spilled from the speaker and drifted across the ballroom. Adalynn closed her eyes and raised her hands, her fingers moving in the air as though she were the one playing as she swayed to the music.

Her earliest memory, from when she was only four years old, was of her father—who was sitting at the piano in the spare room downstairs—helping her up onto the bench beside him. He'd placed his fingers on the keys, given her a smile, and played this song.

Adalynn had been in awe; that moment had sparked her love for piano. It had set her on the path she'd walked until half a year ago, when all that had been taken away forever. That life was gone. Her father, who'd been her very first piano teacher, so patient and nurturing, was gone. Her mother, who'd taken her to every practice, recital, and competition, whether it was for dance or piano or volleyball, who'd always cheered her on, was gone. Only Danny and Adalynn were left...and soon she'd be gone, too.

But this moment, this place...it was a chance to take a little of that back, wasn't it?

I've never danced in a ballroom. Why not knock something off the old bucket list while I feel good?

She smiled as she swayed in wider motions, ceasing her pantomimed piano playing. Toeing her shoes off, she let herself get swept away by the music.

MERRICK PACED BACK and forth across his study, hands clasped behind his back—he couldn't trust them not to expel rogue bursts of magic in his heightened agitation. Everything he'd learned over his life told him this whole situation was a problem, a *massive* problem. Close interaction with mortals never ended well. He could only suffer loss and pain as a result.

Adalynn had dominated his thoughts even though he'd kept himself isolated from her since yesterday morning. He'd locked himself in his study, meaning to continue searching the books lining the bookshelves for useful information regarding this new world, the awoken ley lines, and the nature of life, death, and magic.

Instead, he'd found himself seeking a way to turn his power toward healing. He'd perused tomes for hours and hours, flipping through countless pages—many of which would've crumbled to dust at his slightest breath were it not for his magic holding them together. All that searching had come up with nothing. Warlocks, it seemed, could not use their magic to heal mortals. Healing was the forte of witches —who were separate from Merrick's kind, despite the misconceptions of humans—and the fae-blooded.

Even after he'd finally pried himself away from that search —well after night had fallen, when only occasional flashes of lightning brought any illumination to the sky—he'd thought about Adalynn. About the way she looked, the way she sounded. About the little he knew of her life and circumstances. About the strength, courage, and character she'd displayed in her short time here.

About his overwhelming desire to be near her, to touch her, to *taste* her.

That undeniable attraction unsettled him. He'd been in control of himself for centuries, had honed his discipline and detachment to a fine edge—a blade to wield in self-defense against an unforgiving world. Magic was in his blood. Magic was in the very fiber of his being. It was his calling, his purpose, and humans had always stood against that.

But perhaps even more unsettling was that a deeper instinct—deeper than those that urged him to send the humans away—suggested *she* was his calling. They suggested *Adalynn* was Merrick's purpose. How could he accept, after *two days*, that he'd been wrong for over a thousand years?

It was lust. Dangerous lust, powerful lust, but nothing more than that.

He swept his gaze over the open books atop his desk as he turned to resume his pacing. This was all a distraction, a waste of time that would have no reward in the end.

Storm or not, he needed to cast the humans out. He couldn't risk *anyone* having control over him, not when his power had risen to such immensity. If he'd grown so obsessed after the brief time he'd spent with her so far, how bad would he be in a week? In a month? Would there be room for a single thought in his mind that didn't involve her?

And that wasn't even taking into consideration the question of his magic. For his own security, he needed to keep his abilities hidden from them. They seemed to think of him now as a grumpy-but-kind stranger, and once they'd all worked past their initial tensions, they got along well enough. How quickly would that change once they learned what he was? In Merrick's experience, humans tended to view what they didn't understand—magic being high on that list—as an intolerable evil.

He doubted the resurgence of magic and monsters in the wider world would make them any more accepting; it would *all* be terrifying to them, regardless of its source.

But their fear made no difference—if Adalynn and Danny had survived the harsh world she'd described, that made them dangerous. What would stop them from making an attempt on Merrick's life while he was vulnerable?

"I cannot risk it. They *must* go. They must go...tomorrow."

Yes, he would send them on tomorrow, rain or shine, and then he'd be free to carry on with his existence. Then he could turn toward the future and embrace the new world with a clear mind and an unburdened conscience, for the lives of these two mortals were of no consequence, and he was not responsible for them.

To send them away today, with half the day gone, would be unnecessarily cruel.

Being firm didn't require being unfair. They would appreciate the gesture, would be grateful for an additional night in a warm bed beneath a sound roof, would appreciate a few more decent meals before they'd need to find sustenance for themselves again.

Though...what would *two* more days matter, in the grand scheme? It would allow them more time to rest and prepare for whatever trials awaited them...

No. I need to tell her now. Tomorrow, they need to leave.

He allowed himself no further internal debate; he halted his pacing, turned on his heel, and stalked to the door, which he tugged open a bit too hard before exiting the study. Halfway across the loft, he paused. A soft, eerie sound was drifting up from downstairs, unidentifiable but somehow familiar.

Merrick descended the staircase. The sound grew more distinct as he entered the space between the foyer and the parlor. It was music—piano music—emanating from the southern hallway. There was something *diminished* about the notes, however, something flat and almost metallic; he couldn't understand why, but they lacked the fullness and subtle power piano music usually contained.

Merrick followed the music down the hall. By the time he

was a few paces away from the ballroom's entrance, he knew what the music was, knew why it was familiar. It had been a long time since he'd heard it, but he couldn't forget Beethoven's Piano Sonata Number Fourteen, *Sonata quasi una fantasia*. Whatever his opinions on humans, Merrick could not deny that they sometimes produced works of immense beauty.

His stride faltered when he reached the entryway—his eyes were called immediately to Adalynn, who was dancing to the melancholy music in an impromptu ballet. Her arms and legs moved with an expressiveness as haunting as the notes of the song, even if she seemed a bit uncertain and out of practice. The patter of rain and occasional peals of thunder seemed only to urge her on, and added another somber layer to the scene; she danced like it was the last time she would ever do so, danced like she was mourning the world, danced like she was *alive*.

Merrick's chest tightened, and for several seconds, it was difficult to draw breath. Her emotions were clear in her movement, in her features—she was feeling *everything*. Joy, sorrow, pain, fear, comfort; she carried it all with her, and it was both terribly *human* and more beautiful than anything he'd ever seen. He knew there were dancers with far more skill and grace—he'd seen some in his time—but he knew also there was no dancer in the history of the world who could've moved him as much as his Adalynn did right here, right now.

My Adalynn?

Yes, his soul replied. *Mine*.

His body responded, flooding with arousal, with desire, with *need*. Only the overwhelming beauty of her dance kept him in place, with eyes transfixed, until the song finally ended. To interrupt had seemed like the gravest crime he could possibly have committed. The little cassette player she'd placed on the piano went quiet, emitting only static for several seconds, which was largely swallowed by the steady sound of falling rain. Adalynn came to a halt, her chest heaving with her quick breaths.

She straightened and turned toward the piano, halting abruptly when her eyes fell on Merrick. She sucked in a startled breath, her eyes rounding, and raced toward the piano to press a button on the cassette player. The device fell silent with a click.

"I'm so sorry," she said. "I didn't realize it was that loud. I didn't mean to disturb you."

Merrick crossed the threshold and approached her. His mouth was dry, his blood heated. Each step closer to her was easier than the last, as though her pull on him only increased as the distance between them shrank. "It wasn't loud, you didn't disturb me, and there's no need for you to be embarrassed. That was *lovely*, Adalynn."

Her already flushed cheeks colored further. She ducked her head slightly and smiled. "Um, thank you. It's...been a while. It felt good to dance again."

"Your brother mentioned you being a talented piano player, but he did not mention you were also a dancer." Merrick stopped a few feet away from Adalynn and slipped his hands into the pockets of his jacket to prevent himself from reaching for her.

She grinned. "I think you're just being nice. I'm not that great a dancer. I stopped in my senior year of high school, so I'm especially rusty."

"As with any art, the true power lies in the emotion. And the emotion you expressed while you were dancing...it was *powerful*, Adalynn. Do not discount yourself."

"Thank you." Adalynn shifted her weight from one leg to the other and slid one of her palms along her forearm to grasp her elbow. She glanced away briefly, her soft smile curling into a smirk. "So, Danny was talking about me, huh?"

God, those lips...

Merrick wanted nothing more than to kiss her, to feel her

soft, pliable lips against his, to feel the heat of her body directly, to sample her taste.

"He was," he said. "He is incredibly fond of you, and remarkably protective."

"He is. That protectiveness is a trait that I both love and fear."

Merrick tilted his head slightly. "What about it do you fear?"

"That he won't leave me when he needs to. We already lost our parents, and I know I'm all he's got now, but…"

"He mentioned that, as well. To have lost them both so suddenly must've been difficult on the two of you. But you've both demonstrated immense inner strength."

Her features tightened. "He told you about our parents?"

The sudden pain in her voice wrapped around Merrick's heart and squeezed.

"That they were killed in a car accident while going to visit you in the hospital," he said.

Tears welled in her eyes, and after a moment, she looked toward the window. "Danny was in the car with them. They were coming to support me for the first round of my new treatment when the quake happened. I was standing at the edge of the parking lot waiting for them when I saw them driving up…and saw the ambulance plow into their car. My parents were in the front seat and took the brunt of it. They… they were dead by the time I got to the car. Danny was in the back, shaken up pretty badly, but he didn't seem hurt.

"I calmed him down as best I could and was helping him get out of the car when we heard a choking sound from the front seat. We thought maybe they were alive, maybe there was a chance to save them. We were at the hospital, so close to help. But the things in the front seat…those weren't our parents anymore. They were like wild beasts, with glowing eyes and gnashing teeth and…" She shook her head. "They were trying to grab at Danny, making these inhuman, gurgling growls. It was like they wanted to *eat* him. But they couldn't reach because they were pinned in their seats by all the mangled metal. I got him out of there as quickly as I could."

She turned her face back to Merrick. Her gathering tears fell, rolling down her cheeks. "They were our parents, and that was the last thing he'll remember about them."

Frowning deeply, Merrick closed the remaining distance between them and settled his hands on her shoulders. That pulse of energy—which he'd already come to crave—raced up his arms, but he ignored it this time. "He didn't mention any of that."

"No, he wouldn't have. I think he's tried to block it all out, has told himself it didn't happen. That he wasn't there."

"That's how he made it sound when he told me about it."

"He has nightmares sometimes. He never talks about them, but I'm pretty sure it's about that accident. Even with all the other things we've seen, that was the *worst*. The most traumatic. To see the people you love most killed, and then to see their faces contorted in rage and hunger, to see *nothing* left of who and what they were but their…their soulless husks…"

Merrick slid one hand up along her neck and over her jaw, settling it on her cheek. He brushed his thumb lightly across her cheekbone, wiping away her falling tears. Her skin was so smooth, so soft, reminding him again of how delicate and precious she was.

"And you fear it will happen again if he is still with you when you succumb to your sickness," he said in as gentle a voice as he could; the words hurt to speak aloud.

Adalynn nodded. "I don't want him to see me turn into one of those things. I don't want him to stay with me and get hurt."

Her voice held an unsettling degree of certainty that made Merrick's stomach churn. She had no question of what would happen to her—only of what would become of her brother afterward. Everything within Merrick railed against it, but his magic couldn't help now. She wasn't looking for a cure, and he didn't have one to offer, but he could provide some sympathy, perhaps, however inadequate it felt.

"I witnessed my parents' deaths when I was young," Merrick said. "Not much younger than your brother. I carry that pain, carry those scars on my heart, to this day. But it is possible to continue on."

Her eyes searched his as she gently tilted her head, pressing her cheek into his palm. After a few moments, she lifted her hand to cover his. "I'm so sorry, Merrick. It's hard to have lost people you love, no matter how long ago it happened."

This was the second time in two days that someone had offered Merrick sympathy and condolences for the loss he'd suffered so long ago. It was no less strange than the first time, but he found a certain sense of peace with Adalynn that he'd never experienced before.

Despite their short lives, perhaps mortals weren't so different from him as he'd told himself for all those years—or at least Adalynn and Danny weren't.

"Daniel is strong," he said, "just as *you* are strong. It is not fair that he must deal with this world, especially that he must deal with it alone, but he'll survive."

"I know he's strong, but I worry for him. This world…it's so dangerous, and he's so *young*. Nothing's guaranteed out there. Nothing but…but hardship and death and terror. He doesn't deserve that. *No one* deserves that. And if I can't even be there to protect him…"

Fresh tears spilled from her eyes, running hot over his hand.

Merrick shifted his hand to hook his finger beneath her chin, guiding her face up so he could look into her dark, glistening eyes. He'd come down here to tell Adalynn she would have to leave tomorrow. He'd come down here because he couldn't risk growing attached, because he couldn't risk the potential danger she posed.

But it was already too late. Even if he hadn't realized it then, he'd been attached to her from the first moment he saw her.

"So stay here, Adalynn."

She sucked in a sharp breath, her eyes flaring. "What?"

"Stay here—you and Danny—for as long as you'd like. I can offer you safety, security, comfort…all the things you don't have out there."

She grasped his wrist. "You mean that? You want us to stay? With you?"

The way she clutched his arm was oddly satisfying; he wanted her to need him, wanted her to depend on him, because in the back of his mind he knew, somehow, that *he* needed *her* regardless.

He nodded. "I do. This house…it's been so quiet, so *lifeless*, for so long. Of course," he hastened to add, "my offer cannot be without stipulations."

Her expression faltered as a hint of wariness entered her eyes. She stiffened and pulled away, and the distrust she must've harbored toward him from the beginning was suddenly palpable.

"I will not lie to you, Adalynn. I *want* you. But I will ask nothing untoward of you in exchange for what I'm offering." Merrick lowered his arms to his sides and clenched his fists to keep from reaching for her, to keep from pulling her back, from drawing her against him.

She frowned. "Sorry. It's just that…people have offered food or supplies before, but what some of them asked for in exchange…"

"I would never ask that of you," he said, swallowing a sudden surge of possessiveness and anger. "As I've stated, my study and bedroom will remain off limits. I expect the two of you to clean up after yourselves and be responsible with the food stores. And…I would ask that you and Daniel contribute. There is not much work to be done, but the harvest is approaching, and assistance in the garden would be welcome."

"And that's really all?"

"That's all."

Her tension faded, and she smiled. "Then yes. We'd love to stay here with you. You have no idea how much it eases my mind knowing Danny will be safe."

When I'm gone, were the words she'd left unspoken, but Merrick heard them all the same. The reminder of her impending death jolted him like an electric shock. If he couldn't find a means of saving her, she would be gone soon.

Even if he *did* save her from her current illness, her life would run its course so quickly, *too* quickly. She was mortal—her existence was ephemeral whether she lived to the limits of the human lifespan or not.

"It eases my mind knowing *you* will be safe." He raised a hand and tucked a dangling lock of Adalynn's curls behind her ear. "We do, however, have one more serious matter to address."

There was a shyness in her stance, in her smile, and a light blush stained her cheeks. She tilted her head and arched a brow. "What other serious matter?"

"I've not had a dance partner in many years. Would you do me the honor?" He stepped back and offered his hand. "I'm certainly more out of practice than you, but if it's all for fun, it shouldn't matter."

Her eyes lit up, and her smile widened. "Really? You want to dance with me?"

Warmth blossomed in Merrick's chest at the sight of that smile. "At the risk of embarrassing myself, yes. I do."

Adalynn placed one hand in his and reached back toward the cassette player with the other. "I don't have anything current. Just some classical."

He curled his fingers around her hand, marveling at the way his skin thrummed when in contact with hers. "Perfect. I wouldn't know anything current, anyway."

She pressed the play button and turned to face him fully, settling her free hand on his shoulder. He put his arm around her, settling his hand at the small of her back. She looked up, met his eyes, and smiled again.

The lightly crackling static from the tape player gave way to the lively opening notes of *Für Elise*—a song which itself had not emerged until some decades after its composer's death. But it was lively and upbeat, and Merrick led Adalynn into a spinning, waltz-like dance that sped and slowed in time with the music.

Her smile grew with each step, her eyes sparkled with excitement, and she laughed as the ballroom whirled around them. He couldn't help but laugh, too; her joy was infectious. She followed his steps expertly, as though anticipating his every move. Merrick's heart sped, and the heat in his veins intensified.

They stopped with the music, which ended only a few short minutes after it had begun. Though the next song began, they remained still, panting softly.

"I would swear you're from another time," Adalynn said.

"Though I don't appreciate you implying I'm an old man, it often feels that way," he replied.

She chuckled. "That's not what I was implying." She lifted her hand from his shoulder to touch his hair, brushing it aside from his forehead. "You don't look old at all."

Tingles pulsed across his skin, and he nearly shut his eyes against the bliss of that simple touch. It meant more than should've been possible; it meant she was growing comfortable with him.

"And you look...*beautiful*," he said. He lifted her hand to his lips and brushed a kiss over her knuckles.

Her breath hitched and her eyes dipped to his mouth. Desire flared in the depths of her eyes, and it sparked an answering desire in his core—sparked it in his *soul*. His magic swelled, bolstering the heat in his veins as it flowed along his arms to gather in his fingertips as though it were desperate for her, desperate for a connection beyond anything he'd ever known.

She eased toward him, her lips parting, and Merrick tightened his grip on her, pulling her pelvis against his.

It was, apparently, too much, too quickly.

She drew back, her wide eyes snapping to his. "I…I should check on Danny. Make sure he's behaving."

Her body tensed as she prepared to pull away from him, and it triggered something else atop his need—that same possessiveness he'd felt at the idea of other men lusting after her. This time, these moments, belonged to Merrick and Adalynn, and he wasn't willing to give them up. Not when they were finite. Not when they could end forever in an instant. It was an instinctual drive, still fresh, still new, and one that was proving difficult to ignore.

"Do you fear me?" he asked.

"I…" Her cheeks flushed and she shook her head. "No."

"Then why are you trying to flee?"

"I-I'm not. I just… I'm not scared of you, Merrick. I'm… scared of what you make me feel."

"If it's anything like what you make *me* feel, Adalynn, there is *nothing* to fear." He turned her hand over and kissed her palm, trailing his mouth first to the tips of her fingers and then to her inner wrist.

She shivered, her breath quickening. Her pulse raced beneath his lips.

Never in a thousand years had he wanted a woman as much as he wanted Adalynn. Never had he burned so hot, never had his thoughts been so clouded by desire. There shouldn't have been *any* connection between them, especially considering how little time she had left. It could only lead to complications, to unwanted, unwarranted pain.

Even if she only had a few weeks of life remaining, Merrick had eternity to carry the pain of her loss. Why torture himself like that? Why allow this to go any further?

Because I want her. She has consumed my mind during every minute since her arrival. So, I will take from her all I can while she is here—and give to her as much as I am able.

"Adalynn," he said, his voice rough and silky all at once, his eyelids heavy.

Her eyes met his for a split second before she caught his face between her hands, pulled him down, and pressed her mouth to his.

Merrick's eyelids drifted shut as her warmth and softness enveloped him, and the energy that seemed ever-present when they touched flooded him. He lifted his hands, slipped his fingers into her hair, and leaned over her, deepening the kiss, deepening the overwhelming sensations it produced. He'd shared kisses with other women, but this was something entirely new. Something entirely different. His mana song interwove with hers and resonated in his heart, spreading throughout his body and into hers.

A delirious thought flitted through his mind—*this is not a kiss, it is destiny.*

DELICIOUS HEAT SPIRALED THROUGH ADALYNN, coiling tight in her core. She opened her mouth eagerly and kissed him in full, savoring every detail of this moment—the firmness of his mouth, the soft bristles of his short beard tickling her palms, the solidness of his jaw, the tingling sting on her scalp caused by his grip on her hair; every stroke, nip, and lick of his lips, teeth, and tongue.

He took her mouth with an intensity that left her weak and trembling with need.

But there was something more, something powerful that swept through her and filled her with longing, with anticipation, with an unfulfilled need—like a song without an end. It coaxed her closer, enticed her, sang to her, and she reached for it willingly.

The connection was instantaneous. Adalynn shivered with delight. The sensation rushed through her like a sweeping orchestral crescendo, gaining in power until it suffused every inch of her body. She was aware of nothing except Merrick.

He groaned, tightening his hold on her hair with one hand while the other moved down her back. His fingers spread over the gentle curve of her lower spine, and he drew her against him, pressing her belly to the hard evidence of his want.

Adalynn moaned and slipped her arms around his neck, holding onto him as though he was all that kept her grounded, all that kept her from falling. But she *was* falling—into his kiss, his taste, his scent, his touch. Her body felt as though it were no longer hers.

With only a kiss, Merrick was consuming her.

Her body burned as lust surged through her. Her breasts were heavy, her nipples tight and aching, and her clothes felt too hot and restrictive, abrading her sensitive skin. All she wanted in that moment was to tear them off and feel his hands on her naked flesh. She was caught in a maelstrom of sensation, and she wanted to be lost in it forever.

Except…she didn't have forever. She had months, maybe only *weeks*.

What am I doing?

Dropping her arms, she flattened her palms against his chest and pushed away from him, breaking the kiss. Merrick's hold on her tightened for an instant, but he released her, allowing Adalynn to open some space between them. As soon as their connection was severed, as soon as those thrilling sensations halted and the strange energy he exuded no longer radiated directly into her, Adalynn felt…bereft. Like she was missing a part of herself.

"We shouldn't have done that," she said, panting softly as she reached up and touched her mouth. Her swollen lips tingled; it felt like he'd *branded* them with his searing kiss.

His tongue slipped out to slowly trail over his lips. "Why?"

Oh God, why is that one of the sexiest things I've ever seen?

"You know why, Merrick."

"All I know is that it felt *right*, Adalynn."

It did. It felt so right. It felt perfect.

That didn't change the fact that she was dying.

"We shouldn't," she said again.

Merrick frowned, and his nostrils flared with a heavy exhalation. "Do you plan to spend your last days denying yourself pleasure? Denying your desires? Denying *life*? This place is a chance for you to reach out and take whatever is within your grasp simply because you *want* to."

Adalynn stared at him, throat tight, heart heavy.

Why now? Why, when the world had changed and her time was limited, did she have to find someone like him—a man who made her feel more alive than she'd ever felt before? A man whose voice made her shiver, whose gaze made her melt, whose touch set her body ablaze.

It was…*unfair*.

Why not give in to him? Why not give in to what she wanted, to what they *both* wanted? She was immensely drawn to Merrick. But could they keep their relationship purely physical? Could they keep themselves from forming a deeper, emotional connection?

Adalynn wasn't sure she could.

What if *he* couldn't? She already knew Danny would be devastated when she was gone, and she didn't want to leave behind another person who'd be hurt by her inevitable passing.

"I need time to think," she said, turning away from him

and walking toward the piano. She pressed the *Stop* button on the cassette player, silencing the music. Picking the player up, she returned it to her pack and closed the zipper. She felt Merrick's eyes on her back as she picked up her bag and stepped into her boots.

She looked at Merrick just as a flash of lightning lit the window behind him, turning him briefly into a shadowy, featureless figure—with two intense *blue* eyes. The effect faded quickly, and he was just Merrick again, frowning as he stared at her—but not visibly upset or angry.

Thunder rattled the windows.

"Whatever you require, Adalynn," he said, "simply let me know."

She hurried across the room, her boots thumping heavily on the floor, and paused in the doorway. "Thank you again, Merrick. For letting us stay."

Merrick slipped his hands into his pockets and nodded. "It is my pleasure."

But his eyes said, *It could be your pleasure, as well.*

She left him there. Whatever had transpired between them, she didn't regret it. She would never regret the kiss they'd shared. Her only regret was that, no matter what she chose, there couldn't be many more of those kisses in the future.

Chapter Seven

The storm thankfully broke on the seventh day—if it had continued any longer, Adalynn would have been driven to harm her brother. Being cooped up indoors was making him stir crazy. He chattered, he whined, and he hounded her endlessly to talk and play games with him, desperate for something to fill the time. And, of course, Adalynn often gave in to his demands.

Fortunately, Danny was self-aware enough to know he risked getting into trouble if he didn't find productive ways to occupy himself. He understood that the food and shelter Merrick was providing were too important, that their situation was too good, for him to screw up because he was bored.

When he wasn't pestering Adalynn, he'd often sought Merrick's company. Sometimes he'd pace in front of the study, brimming with impatience, only to burst into a torrent of questions and banter with Merrick as soon as the man emerged. Danny had grown attached to Merrick fairly quickly, and Merrick, for all his potential gruffness, was patient with the boy—sometimes, he was almost *fatherly*.

Since they were officially living here, Danny had claimed the bedroom next to Adalynn's. She was proud that he was establishing some independence—they'd been inseparable for six months, and she knew how much he suffered, how terrified he was when he woke from a nightmare in the dead of night. But she couldn't help worrying about him. She'd taken comfort in his nearness, in knowing he was an arm's length away. In knowing he was safe.

This morning, the sun had broken through the clouds for the first time in six full days, bringing a welcome reprieve from the storm. Adalynn had drawn the curtains after waking, sat on the edge of the bed, and basked in the golden sunlight streaming through the window. She couldn't remember the last time she'd been able to sit and enjoy the sun. It wasn't merely a matter of the weather having shifted after the Sundering—most days were cloudy and gray, it seemed, though no less hot during the summer—but a matter of survival. It had been too dangerous to relax for so much as a moment, too dangerous to take pleasure even in these simple things.

During breakfast, Merrick had said, "It's finally time for the idle teen to earn his keep."

Danny—who'd been bouncing in his seat as though he were ready to leap out of it—had stilled, and a huge grin spread across his face.

Merrick expressed some disappointment; he'd hoped for dismay, for dragging feet, for complaints. Danny's enthusiasm had thrown the man off. Adalynn had made no effort to hold in her laughter.

They'd donned rubber boots—much too large for Adalynn and Danny, but at least they'd be dry—and thick gloves, had gathered several baskets and various gardening tools, and exited the manor through the back door in the kitchen. She'd pulled her hair into a ponytail, and both she and Danny wore baseball caps to shield their faces from the sun. Adalynn had even taken out her bottle of slightly expired sunblock and slathered it over her and Danny's exposed skin, much to the boy's annoyance.

Now, Merrick was leading them toward the towering hedge wall that had seemed so dark and impenetrable when she'd looked out the back window that first night. It was over-grown and unkept, but in her mind's eye she could picture how it must've looked while it had been neatly trimmed. Everything out here had, at some point long ago, been as well-cared for as the interior of the manor was currently.

The outward appearance of Merrick's home was inten-tional; she hadn't asked him about it, but she knew it all the same. It looked run-down and abandoned to keep people away. In hindsight, Adalynn was glad they'd ignored her instincts when they found this place. This time, it had paid off.

Merrick led them through an arched opening in the hedge. Another tall wall of shrubbery stood before them. Was this a hedge maze? She supposed that was one way to keep Danny occupied for a while, but how would this be *earning his keep?*

But she understood when they rounded the first corner. Her eyes widened and her breath hitched as she looked out over the largest garden she'd ever seen. Neat rows of crops were planted in squared patches across the entire space—all contained within the high outer hedge walls of what must've *been* a maze in the past.

There were tomatoes, cucumbers, green beans, peas, corn, carrots, a variety of squashes, raspberries, blackberries, several types of peppers—including colorful bell peppers—a few fruit trees, and at least a dozen other things she couldn't easily identify. Pipes and tubes ran in precise lines around and through the crops —irrigation, she realized after a moment. Even with the jars of home-canned goods in his pantry—all of which must've come from here—it seemed far too much for one person to ever eat.

"This is amazing," Adalynn said.

Danny swept his awed gaze over the garden slowly. "It's like a supermarket, but *outside*."

"This is a garden, Daniel. The sort of place from which a market *receives* its goods," Merrick said. "And you may now consider yourself a farmer."

"I'm hungry just looking at it all."

Adalynn laughed. "You're always hungry. And you *just* ate."

Danny grinned and rubbed his stomach before flexing his arms. "I'm a growing boy, sis. Gotta get my manly muscles somehow."

Merrick snickered. "You need to *have* some muscles before they can become *manly*. You've a long way to go." He placed the baskets he was carrying down on the muddy ground. All the vegetation glistened with droplets of moisture in the morning light.

"Hey! I have muscles!"

Adalynn picked up one of the baskets and thrust it into her brother's arms. "Good. Then put them to use and start picking squash and cucumbers."

Danny took hold of the basket's handles and trudged away through the mud, muttering to himself about bossy older sisters. Adalynn watched him with a grin before bending to pick up a basket for herself.

"It looks like the raspberries are finally ripe," Merrick said as he took up a basket and a three-pronged hand cultivator. "Would you please start there, Adalynn?"

Adalynn's grin widened; she absolutely *loved* raspberries. "Oh, I don't know. Only half of them might actually end up in the basket."

"I'll only allow that if you make sure Danny doesn't see you. He'll devour half the garden if he thinks he's allowed to eat while he works."

She laughed. "Deal."

She made her way through the garden, around batches of

peppers and rows of carrots, toward the fencing along which the berries grew. Her feet sank into the soft ground, and she had to battle the hungry mud's pull each time she lifted a leg, being careful to ensure the oversized boots didn't slide off. Still, she was glad she didn't have to put her own boots through any more punishment today.

The raspberries stood out like clusters of rubies amongst the green leaves and vines, beckoning her. She picked the biggest, plumpest one, wiped it on her shirt, and popped it between her lips. Its juices burst across her tongue when she bit down.

Sooooo good.

She worked her way from one end of the long row of bushes to the other, selecting only the fully ripe berries and remaining mindful of the thorns throughout. Of course, she couldn't avoid all the thorns, and ended up collecting a few minor scrapes on her arms, but her gloves protected her from the worst of it.

Most of the clouds dissipated as the day went on, and the sun shone hot and bright overhead. Danny and Merrick conversed as they worked. Adalynn glanced over her shoulder to see Merrick crouched down, working in the dirt. He lifted a mud-clumped root and showed it to Danny. The boy watched, attention rapt, hanging on Merrick's every word as the man explained what the root was.

It was then that Adalynn knew Danny would thrive here. Merrick would teach him, guide him, and keep the boy safe.

Merrick would do what she couldn't.

It was a bittersweet realization, but it was what Danny needed. Everything she'd done since the Sundering had been for him. They were *here* because of him.

"Well how am I supposed to know which ones are weeds?" Danny asked. "They're all green."

Even from several yards away, Adalynn saw Merrick roll his eyes.

"Because they are *different* than whatever is planted in that row. Really, Daniel, it isn't complicated," Merrick said.

"Just because you're old with more *worldly experience*, doesn't mean I'm dumb. Just means I'm inexperienced compared to you."

"I did not say you were dumb, but you *are* being deliberately obtuse."

"I don't know what obtuse means, but you're still old."

Chuckling, Adalynn carried her berries over to the baskets Danny had filled with cucumbers and squash, setting her basket beside them. As she was bending down to retrieve an empty basket, a spike of pain—as sharp as an ice pick—hammered across her temples. It came and went in an instant, but that was more than enough time for her to halt, her body tensing. She held still for a moment to await the next wave of pain, but nothing came.

Maybe I just bent down too fast.

Once her tension eased, she grabbed the basket, slowly straightened, and started toward the tomatoes.

Danny jumped to his feet and hurried over to her, his brow furrowed. He extended his arms as though to take the basket from her. "Why don't you take a break, Addy?"

She swung the basket out of his reach. "I'm fine, Danny. I want to help. I don't want to sit around being useless."

"You're not useless, Addy, you're sick."

"I'm fine. Really. It's been days since I've had a headache or any symptoms at all." She glanced at Merrick.

He was staring at her with an indecipherable expression on his face, his eyes veiled. There was an almost *guilty* cast to his features; she couldn't imagine why, couldn't be sure if it was just her imagination.

"Take a break, Adalynn," Merrick finally said. There seemed to be a hint of strain in his voice. "You, too, Daniel. There's some water in one of the empty baskets. You've both been working hard, and it's a hot morning."

Though she knew Merrick was right, she couldn't help but feel as though he was calling for a break only because of her; having Danny also stop was a way to lessen the blow. Merrick had been pulling weeds ceaselessly since they entered the garden—which felt like hours ago—and she'd not seen him stop or slow the entire time.

Adalynn and Danny sat on a stone bench in the shade of a pear tree. As soon as Adalynn allowed herself to relax, every one of her muscles protested; the longer she was still, the sorer her body felt. It was *wonderful*. She hadn't pushed herself like this in so long—at least not by *choice*—and she'd forgotten what a good workout felt like. The dampness of sweat on her skin, the fire in her muscles, and the thumping of her heart were all the sweeter because she'd *chosen* to work, to contribute. The rush of having to flee or fight for one's life was a wholly different experience—one she'd rather do without.

While she and Danny rested—mopping sweat from their faces, drinking from the water bottles, and nibbling on bits of their harvest—Adalynn found herself watching Merrick.

He wasn't dressed like a man toiling in a garden—he wore black dress pants and a white button-down shirt, the sleeves rolled up to just above his elbows. His hair was pulled back in a ponytail with loose strands hanging around his face. The strangest part, however, was that despite the smudges of dirt on his clothing and the tall rubber boots on his feet, he pulled off the outfit. He looked *dignified*.

Her eyes drifted to his strong forearms; toned muscles played beneath his skin as he worked.

He pulled off that look *very* well.

Danny elbowed her. It caught her so off guard that she nearly toppled backward off the bench and into the mud; she stopped herself only by extending her legs and digging her heels into the ground.

Once she'd regained her balance, Adalynn turned her head to glare at him. "What the hell, Danny?"

"You're checking him out."

A heat totally unrelated to the sun suffused her cheeks. "And?"

Danny's eyebrows rose in surprise. "You're not going to deny it?"

"No. Am I supposed to?"

"Well, yeah."

"Why?"

Danny shrugged. "I don't know, because you're my *sister*, and I don't need to see you checking guys out." He glanced briefly at Merrick. "I've seen him check you out, too. You guys need to at least learn to be subtle about it."

"We're grown adults, Danny." She raised the water bottle and took another drink.

Merrick hadn't pressed her any further since their kiss in the ballroom. He was leaving the decision to her. But even if he hadn't said anything directly, he'd not stopped flirting with her, hadn't stopped looking at her with undisguised want in his eyes—the same way she looked at him when she thought he wasn't looking.

Adalynn's nights had become torturous; she'd lie in bed, replaying their kiss in her head, fantasizing about it going beyond that. It was harder and harder to resist him with each passing day.

He was just so...*charming* when he wanted to be. And seeing the interactions between Merrick and Danny...

"Isn't he...*old?*" Danny asked.

Unable to hold back her laughter, Adalynn nearly choked on her mouthful of water. She swallowed it down and wiped her lips with the back of her arm. "He's not that old."

"Did you ask him?"

"No, but he doesn't *look* that old."

"You both realize I'm only thirty feet away, don't you?" Merrick asked without looking up from his work.

Adalynn ducked her head and covered her face. "Kill me now."

Danny laughed. "See! That's what I expected."

With a smile, Adalynn raised her head and looked at Merrick. Sweat glistened on his brow as he moved along his row, pulling deep-rooted weeds with practiced ease. Adalynn picked up a fresh bottle of water and stood. Dizziness assailed her immediately; she sat quickly and closed her eyes.

"You okay, Addy?" Danny asked; his voice, playful only a few moments ago, was now thick with concern.

She took in a deep breath and released it slowly. The dizziness faded, but it left a cold, heavy lump of dread in her belly. "Yeah. I just stood up too fast. I'm fine." She smiled at her brother and placed a comforting hand on his arm. "Don't worry. Let's get back to work."

Danny eyed her skeptically for a moment before finally nodding. He picked up his basket and went back to picking weeds. Adalynn walked over to Merrick; the mud was already hardening beneath the intense sun.

She stopped next to Merrick and held the bottle out to him. "Here. You need to take a break, too."

"Perhaps." Merrick turned to face her, tugged off his gloves, and accepted the bottle. He twisted off the cap and drank half the water in one go. His gaze settled upon her as he replaced the cap; his eyes narrowed slightly, and a little crease appeared between his dark, thick brows. "You're *sure* you're all right, Adalynn? You look pale."

"I got a little dizzy from standing up too fast. I'm feeling fine now."

The skepticism remained in his expression as he handed the bottle back to her. "I will finish the weeding with Daniel. You go ahead and check the tomatoes, as you'd intended."

Adalynn nodded. She returned to the bench to set down the water bottle and collect her basket before walking over to the tomatoes. Their strong, earthy scent enveloped her, but it wasn't enough to distract her fully.

She shouldn't have been irritated that Danny and Merrick were worried about her, and she wasn't, at least not toward them—but she hated feeling like an invalid.

She forced those thoughts aside and focused on her work, picking the plump red vegetables—or were they fruits?—from the vines and placing them gently into the basket.

The dizziness came and went like lazy waves rolling ashore and then slipping back into the sea. She paused each time it came on, closing her eyes and willing the sensation away before resuming her work. She didn't want to stop; she didn't want to stop feeling *normal*, didn't want Merrick and Danny to stop treating her like normal.

Before long, a throbbing headache joined the dizziness, but it didn't recede. The dread she'd felt earlier solidified.

I'm just overworking myself. I've felt fine for days. *I…I can't relapse* now.

She sensed Merrick's eyes on her with increasing frequency; whenever she glanced at him, he was staring at her, his expression troubled. After what couldn't have been more than ten or fifteen minutes, he declared their work finished for the day.

"So long as the weather permits, we will continue tomorrow," he said, setting the basket full of pulled weeds a few feet away from the other containers, all of which were laden with produce. "I think we've earned a good meal and some relaxation, have we not?"

"I'm *starving*," Danny said.

"And I am unsurprised," Merrick replied. "Young Daniel and I will carry our harvest to the porch. Would you go inside ahead of us, Adalynn, and decide on something we can cook?"

Adalynn nodded, and—not wanting to concern her brother—forced a warm smile onto her lips. "All right."

The Warlock's Kiss

The intensity in Merrick's gaze made it clear that he saw through that smile. Thankfully, he didn't call her out on it.

"Aww. We gotta carry all these? My arms are killing me, and there's no way we can get it all at once," Danny said as Adalynn turned and made her way toward the house.

"It will take several trips, undoubtedly," Merrick said. "It should be a pleasant task, as I'm sure you'll complain throughout."

"Just for that"—Danny grunted—"you won't hear anything from me."

"Curse you, boy. You certainly know how to punish me for my sharp tongue."

Adalynn's lips curled into a genuine smile despite her discomfort. She glanced over her shoulder to see Danny carrying a basket of cucumbers, lagging just behind Merrick, who had the basket of tomatoes in one hand and the basket of squash in the other. Danny's features were contorted in a scowl, while Merrick's lips were upturned in a smirk—at least until he looked at her.

His smirk fell into a frown, and that worried crease reappeared between his eyebrows.

She turned away and left the garden.

I'll be fine. It's just a combination of the heat and the hard work.

To her relief, she *did* start to feel better after entering the relative coolness of the house. As much as she enjoyed sunshine, it didn't seem to agree with her these days. She'd probably just pushed herself too hard and underestimated the heat; she'd likely been on the verge of heat exhaustion or something like that.

She made sure to drink some more water before washing her hands and face. Then she went to rummage through Merrick's pantry. "What to make for dinner…"

After sliding aside several cans of vegetables, she discovered a box of spaghetti with a jar of tomato sauce conveniently close by. *Bingo.* It'd go perfectly with the homemade bread—which was only *slightly* burned—she'd made the day before.

Grabbing the pasta and sauce, she stepped out of the pantry, nudged the door closed with her foot, and set the items on the counter. She still wasn't entirely familiar with Merrick's kitchen, but it didn't take long to find a couple pots that were the right size. She got the fire going in the wood-burning stove—the sort of large, black thing she would've thought was just a decoration people bought in antique shops when she was young—and set a pot of water atop it. She was still learning how to deal with the altered cooking times caused by baking with a wood fire, but boiling some water and heating some sauce would be easy enough to get right.

While she waited for the water to boil, she opened the sauce and dumped it into the other pot, pausing as an idea came to mind. There were plenty of fresh vegetables in the pantry that needed to be used. Hurrying back to the pantry, she grabbed a zucchini, an onion, and a carrot.

Though Adalynn's head still ached, she pushed through it. She was chopping the vegetables and adding them to the sauce when Danny came flying into the kitchen.

"Is it done yet? What's that?" Danny moved closer to her and peered into the pot. "No way! Spaghetti?"

Adalynn leaned away from him, wrinkling her nose. "Ugh, you stink. Go take a quick bath."

Danny stared at her incredulously. "Seriously? You worked outside, too. I'm sure you don't smell like roses."

"She doesn't," Merrick said as he strode inside, shutting the door behind him. "She smells like lavender." He walked to the sink, turned on the water, and washed his hands and arms.

Adalynn stared at his forearms, once again transfixed by the play of his muscles. "I do?"

"You do." He dried his hands on a dish towel and turned to face her.

She snapped her gaze up to meet his, and her cheeks warmed. She'd totally been caught staring.

Danny threw his hands up. "Can you guys at least wait until I'm out of the room? I don't need to see you hitting on each other *all* the time."

Before Adalynn could reply, Danny snagged a couple slices of carrot and left the kitchen. She frowned but didn't bother calling him out on the theft—or on his accusation.

Even if it was true, what did it matter? She *was* a grown woman. She was allowed to flirt and be flirted with, especially when the man who'd caught her attention was tall, well-built, dark-haired, and sexy as hell in that brooding, mysterious, bad boy kind of way.

They'd flirted plenty over the week, though their interactions over the last several days had been tame compared to what had happened in the ballroom. She'd told him after their kiss that she had to think, but she still wasn't sure *what* she thought about all of it. She knew he'd been right—she *did* want him—but she didn't know what to do about it. What she was *ready* to do about it.

Could it really be that easy to give in to her desire? Could it really be so simple and uncomplicated?

The answer her heart offered was brutally honest, and it was the one thing preventing her from succumbing to her desire—it would *absolutely* be simple and uncomplicated...for *Adalynn*.

Merrick was the one who'd have to carry on afterward. Merrick was the one who'd have to deal with the hurt, with the loss, unless their relationship was purely for pleasure, purely physical. And she didn't think that was possible.

But oh, she *wanted* him.

"What do you need help with?" Merrick asked, drawing her attention away from the doorway Danny had disappeared through.

"Nothing. I've got it all handled." Her eyes trailed over

him, stopping at his feet, which were now bare except for his socks. For some reason, she found that funny, and couldn't hold back a giggle. It was the first time she'd seen him without shoes.

Merrick tilted his head, leaned his hip against the counter, and folded his arms across his chest. "Is something amusing?"

"No," she said, turning back to vegetables on the cutting board, but her grin lingered. She peeked at him from the corner of her eye.

"Your lips suggest otherwise, Adalynn."

"I've just never seen you without shoes on. It makes you less...intimidating."

He arched a brow and glanced down at his black socks. "So it was my footwear making me intimidating all along? I wish I'd known that sooner."

Adalynn dumped the carrot slices into the sauce, set the knife down, and turned toward him. "Why sooner?"

"It might've saved me some trouble in the past. I could've simply upgraded my shoes, and people would've been too frightened to cause issues."

Though she knew he was making light of it, Adalynn frowned. "What happened?"

Darkness fell across his features for an instant. "A great many things over many years. Suffice it to say, my past experiences with...*people* have driven me to live here, in the middle of nowhere."

Adalynn pushed away from the counter and closed the distance between them. His eyes remained locked on hers. Slowly, she reached up and lightly touched the scar on his forehead and cheek. Faint energy hummed beneath her fingertips. "And this?"

He caught her wrist. His grip was firm, and she could feel the tension in his muscles, but he did not pull her hand away. "I received it when my parents died," he said in a low, strained voice.

Adalynn's eyes flared. His tone implied that something horrible had happened—and that he didn't want to discuss it further—but he didn't tighten his hold on her wrist or hurt her. She curled her fingers into her palm. "I'm sorry, Merrick."

He searched her face for a few seconds, lips downturned, before something in his eyes softened. "*You* were not responsible for what happened."

"Doesn't mean I'm not sorry about what happened to you, or to them."

Merrick shifted her hand to his lips and kissed her knuckles. "Thank you, Adalynn. It means more to me than I can express."

Adalynn smiled up at him. However chaste his kiss seemed, it had sent a rush of heat through her, which pooled deep in her core. With Merrick this close, she could smell the scents of dirt, vegetation, and sweat clinging to him—the latter was an alluringly masculine smell—but there was more. Hints of leather and cedar underscored the other smells; she'd come to associate those aromas with him.

She wanted nothing more than to move closer, to press her face into his neck and breathe in those scents, to feel his hands —his mouth—upon her. But the ache in her head insisted now was not the time.

"I should get dinner finished before the human garbage disposal returns," she said, taking a step back.

For a moment, he didn't relinquish his hold, and Adalynn wondered if he meant to draw her against him, to take her in his arms, to make her tell him what her decision was now that she'd had days to ponder it. But he did let go; she was at once grateful and disappointed, despite the way her head felt.

"You can go sit, Adalynn. I'll finish dinner."

Though her instinct was to object, she resisted it. Nodding, she pointed at the pot behind her. "The sauce is ready to heat up, and there's some leftover bread we can warm to have with it."

He set to work without hesitation, and Adalynn sat at the table. She found herself transfixed; even in this—a task so mundane, so simple—he moved with purpose and confidence. Once he saw to the sauce, he dumped the pasta into the boiling water, sliced the bread, and seasoned it.

"We've more than enough vegetables," Merrick said, turning toward her after he'd slipped the bread into the oven. "We'll have to make our own sauce next time."

"I'd love to learn how."

"And I would love to teach you."

As seemed the case so often, there was *more* in his expression—unspoken words gleamed in his eyes, highlighted by a fiery spark. But he simply turned back to the food, and they chatted casually as he cooked. He'd once described himself as an eccentric millionaire, but he didn't fit the image those words brought to Adalynn's mind. She would never have expected anyone with such wealth to cook for himself—much less know how to make spaghetti sauce from scratch—or tend his own massive garden.

Danny returned with his hair hanging damp around his face as Merrick was dividing the food between three plates. Danny sat in his usual spot beside Adalynn and dove into the food as soon as Merrick placed it before him, shoveling forkfuls of pasta into his mouth and slurping noodles noisily.

Merrick shook his head before walking into the pantry. He returned a few moments later with a green container of parmesan cheese. He unscrewed the lid, removed the seal, and replaced the lid before setting the container at the center of the table. He took a seat across from Adalynn.

"This is awesome. Thanks," Danny said, reaching for the cheese.

"I think we've earned it today," Merrick replied. He looked at Adalynn, and when he smiled, a hint of mischief danced in his eyes. "Of course, this *does* count against your meal allotment for tomorrow, Daniel."

"*What?* No way!"

Leaning his elbows on the table, Merrick turned his palms upward. "My apologies, but rules are rules. I suppose you'll have to do extra work if you want supper tomorrow."

Danny groaned. "I guess so."

Adalynn failed to hide her smile.

They talked amongst each other as they ate, but, as the meal wore on, Adalynn spoke less and less. Exhaustion settled over her heavily, and her headache worsened by the minute. Those symptoms were accompanied soon enough by a touch of nausea. She'd only made it through a quarter of her meal when she finally set her fork down; as much as she hated the thought of wasting food, it felt like one bite more would send her over the edge.

"Here, Danny." She slid her plate toward her brother.

Danny frowned, glancing first at the plate and then her. "You okay, Addy?"

"I'm just going to take a quick bath and go to bed. I think…I think I might have overdone it a bit."

He hurried to his feet. "What's wrong?"

"Stay and eat, really. I'm just feeling tired."

Merrick placed his hands on the edge of the table and rose, sliding his chair back as he did so. "At least allow me to help you upstairs, Adalynn."

"I'm fine. Please. Stay and enjoy dinner." She smiled; the expression felt strained. "I just need some rest."

Worry gleamed in their eyes, and she could almost sense words of protest forming on their lips, but Danny and Merrick kept quiet.

After several seconds of silence, Merrick nodded. "Please be careful. We are close, should you require anything."

Adalynn nodded, tucked a few loose strands of hair behind her ear, and stood up. "Thank you."

She exited the kitchen, made her way down the hall, and went upstairs to her room, where she gathered her things to take into the bathroom. She took a quick bath, scrubbing away the sweat, dirt, and grime of the day. She still couldn't believe there was hot water here. But, as much as she would've loved to soak in the tub and let her muscles be soothed by the heat, her body felt heavier with each passing moment, as though her strength were being drained by some unseen force. Her lightheadedness only intensified; all she wanted to do was get to bed.

Once she was dressed and back in her room, she dropped her belongings next to the bed, crawled on top of it, and slipped beneath the covers. The moment her head hit the pillow, she passed out.

She felt like she'd only just closed her eyes when a burst of agony in her skull forced them open. She cried out, lifting her hands to clamp them around her head, and gritted her teeth against the overwhelming pain. It was far worse than anything she'd ever experienced.

I'm dying. Oh God, I'm dying.

Tears streamed down her cheeks as she turned onto her back. The movement, usually so insignificant, triggered a debilitating wave of vertigo that was accompanied by a fresh spike of pain; it was like a screwdriver was being hammered into her head.

She struggled to sit up, but the room—which was much dimmer than when she'd lain down—spun wildly around her, and she toppled over the side of the bed. She landed heavily on the floor and barely had enough time to push herself up on her elbows before she vomited. The pressure in her head increased; her skull felt like it was about to split in two.

Chapter Eight

After cleaning up the kitchen with Danny's help, Merrick returned to his bedchamber for a shower and a change of clothes. He stopped to check in on Adalynn along the way; when she didn't answer his soft knock, he opened the door a crack to find her in bed, asleep.

It had been a week since Adalynn and Danny had arrived, a week since a seizure had rendered her unconscious and Merrick had used his magic to force back her sickness. He'd not seen her exhibit any signs of illness in that time, but today...today she'd seemed unwell. Though she'd insisted she was fine, he didn't believe her—her features and actions had contradicted her words.

She simply pushed herself too hard, too soon, he thought as he backed out of her bedroom and quietly closed the door.

But a strange feeling lodged itself in his chest as he continued to his room—it was an anxious, restless energy only a few steps removed from outright dread. Though that feeling remained indistinct, refusing to reveal its true origin, he knew it was related to Adalynn. To her sickness.

Without conscious thought, his mind drifted to the texts he'd studied over the last week—all of which had stated, with varying degrees of firmness, that warlock magic was not suited for healing.

He entered the shower and stood beneath the steaming spray of water for a long while, letting it cascade over him as though it could wash away his worry, as though it could silence the whispers in the back of his mind.

You made it worse.

You haven't helped her at all.

You've sped her doom.

Growling, he slammed a fist into the wall. The tiles shattered, opening a few shallow cuts on his knuckles. Ceramic shards clattered into the tub. For several seconds, all he could do was stand there, his blood flowing in watery rivulets that eventually swirled into the drain at his feet. He released a heavy exhalation and finally withdrew his hand. Magic crackled from his core and raced along his arm; he focused the power on the broken tiles. The shards floated up from below and returned to the damaged portion of the wall.

The blue glow around the ceramic faded once the pieces were in place, revealing whole, unmarred tiles.

Why could he not do for Adalynn what he could do to broken glass, to broken tiles? Why couldn't he keep her preserved in perfect health just like he'd preserved this house?

There had to be a way. There had to be a means by which he could overcome the inadequacies of his magic, a means by which he could cure her.

He left his bedroom after he'd dried and dressed himself. He paused outside her door as he passed it, stilling to listen, letting even the sound of his own heartbeat fade from his perception.

Adalynn's soft breathing was barely audible through the door, and hearing it only provided a sliver of the comfort he'd hoped to garner. Merrick continued down the hallway in quick strides. Her presence tingled at his back, growing fainter but more insistent with each step he took away from her. And that feeling in his chest, that anxiety, that dread, deepened.

Though he'd intended to enter his study, he found himself walking downstairs and along the southern hallway, not stopping until he was in the ballroom. The curtains were closed, allowing only hints of the diffused late evening light to flow in around the edges of the windows, but his eyes were little affected by the gloom. He couldn't recall the last time he'd used this room—the last time he'd even entered it—before Adalynn had come. She'd breathed life into it.

She'd breathed life into *him*.

The weight and pressure in his chest intensified as he absently retraced the path of their much too brief dance, as he mounted the stage and ran his fingers along the graceful curve of the piano.

Though the music of magic had flowed through his blood for his entire life—even while he was too young to feel it—he'd never quite deemed his talents adequate when it came to mundane instruments. He was competent enough, knew the notes and the keys, could even play many complex songs, but there had always been something missing—the *passion*, the *feeling*. For whatever reason, he'd never been able to capture those emotional cores. Everything he played sounded flat. All his focus, all his passion, had gone into *power*.

But he knew, without having heard her play, that Adalynn could instill her music with any emotion she chose, with immense, overwhelming passion. He knew music was as effortless to her as magic was to him.

He wanted to hear her play. More than that, he wanted to hear her play *for him*. And that want filled him with…sorrow.

Why, after a thousand years, had he found the one woman he desired above all others, the one person he longed to be with, the one person whose soul seemed to speak to his, only for it to come with the knowledge that she would be gone soon? Why was the greatest beauty—both inside and out—always so terribly fleeting?

Merrick stepped to the piano's front, lifted the fallboard, and settled his hand over the keys. He pressed one down gently. The soft note it played was jarringly out of tune. How had he kept the rest of his house in immaculate condition but neglected this? Had it been some subconscious reflection of the discordance within him?

Closing his eyes, he willed his power into the instrument slowly, feeling out the resonance of each individual string through its mana song. Even with magic, it was a delicate process, a time-consuming process, but it felt like the right thing to do. The piano deserved better than he'd given it.

And Adalynn deserved only the best.

Even when he was done tuning the piano, he didn't step away from it. His mind wandered toward her, always her, forever *her*. He wasn't sure how long he stood there, lost in thought, but the room was noticeably dimmer when the sound of a cabinet slamming in the kitchen caught his attention. He drew in a steadying breath, turned around, and walked toward the sound. The dread in him continued to build, making his throat and chest tight.

Something is wrong, but what? What am I feeling?

He entered the kitchen to find Danny standing at the sink, sipping from a glass of water. The anxiousness thrumming within Merrick, as powerful and consuming as his magic, only grew.

"Is your sister still resting?" Merrick asked.

She's fine. She just needed some rest. She's fine.

Danny jumped, nearly sloshing water over the rim of his glass. "Damn, man, do you always have to sneak up on people like that?"

Merrick narrowed his eyes and lowered his brows.

"I mean, *darn, sir*...you, uh...startled me?" Danny set his glass down on the counter and muttered, "I bet you cussed when you were a kid."

Cussing had been markedly different in Merrick's youth, but he had no intention of dating himself by bringing that up—especially because the English he'd grown up with was classified as a different language by modern speakers. "Your sister looked quite unwell. I know she's suffered such spells before…was the way she looked and behaved earlier normal, in your experience?"

Danny frowned and looked down at his feet. "It's different every time, but she has headaches most days. Seizures sometimes, too, like you already saw." He raised a hand and ran it through his shaggy hair, pulling it back. "Sometimes she gets really tired, or her speech might slur like she's drunk, but Addy doesn't drink." He looked back up at Merrick. "She said she worked too much today, but do you think it's her cancer?"

Merrick couldn't share his true fear with the boy—that yes, it was her cancer, and it was doing this now because of what Merrick had done to her. That it was potentially *worse* because of what he'd done. He told himself that he couldn't know for certain, that this was all wild speculation based on the dread growing inside him, that this was merely the reality of Adalynn's situation, but none of it eased him.

"I don't know," Merrick finally said. "I think—"

Something thumped heavily on the floor upstairs. Merrick snapped his mouth shut, and everything within him stilled. The sound had come from the direction of Adalynn's bedroom.

"You think what?" Danny asked.

Had the boy not heard the thump? It had sounded too much like a body hitting the floor.

Merrick raced out of the kitchen and down the hallway, ignoring Danny's confused calls. He was at the top of the spiral staircase within a few long strides and continued into the hallway without pause.

He burst into Adalynn's room to find her on the floor beside the bed, in the throes of another seizure with a pool of vomit on the floor in front of her; there was blood mixed in with it. Her jerking movements were more violent than last time, more intense, and her bluish veins were more visible than ever.

The dread that had been gathering within Merrick mutated into a toothy, primal beast that ripped his insides to shreds. In a thousand years, he'd never been more frightened than he was in that moment. He'd never stood to lose more than he did here and now.

He thrust that fear aside and crossed the room, dropping to his knees beside her. His magic roared to life within him as he reached forward and placed his hands on either side of her head. He couldn't dwell on speculation right now; she was in distress, she was in trouble, she was in danger, and he *needed* to help her, to save her.

Danny ran into the room and skidded to a stop at his sister's side. "Addy! Oh, no, no, no. Please don't die."

"She will not die," Merrick growled. He forced the connection between them open.

This time, he expected the darkness within her, the cancer; Merrick blasted into it with full force, roaring in his mind as his magic swelled to beat back the taint. Her illness would not take her. He would not allow it. Even if he didn't understand his relationship with Adalynn, even if she had not yet truly reciprocated his feelings—feelings of which he wasn't entirely certain—he knew without a doubt that she was *his*, and no one, *nothing*, would take her.

Heat gathered rapidly within him, building to a searing pain that pulsed through his entire body from its focal point in his skull. He welcomed it. Welcomed the struggle. The dark stain on Adalynn's bright, brilliant soul receded, curling in upon itself, shriveling away from his power, but not before lashing out at him in turn. Merrick growled again and pushed harder, filling his awareness with the blinding blue light of his magic.

The cancer retreated, but it would not be defeated. Not by willpower alone.

Adalynn's body went limp. Merrick sagged forward, catching himself on a hand. His head ached like it had been hewn down the middle with an ax, and his entire body trembled from the exertion, from the feedback of his massive expenditure of power. He remained beside her, staring down at the floor as he caught his breath.

A drop of blood splattered on the rug.

Merrick lifted his free hand and gently touched his fingers to his face. Blood had flowed from his nose and tear ducts. He felt more trickling from his ears and tasted it in his mouth.

If this is the price, let me *be the one to pay it. Let* me *be the one to suffer.*

"W-What just happened?" Danny's voice came from Adalynn's other side. "What...what'd you *do*? What was that?"

Merrick ignored him; he had to focus on Adalynn, had to help Adalynn. He still felt her mana song resonating in his heart even though their connection had been closed, still felt her pull on him, still felt her pain—because her pain was *inside* him now.

His vision blurred. He shook his head and pushed himself upright, forcing his arms forward and gently slipping them beneath Adalynn to turn her over and draw her against his chest.

"Merrick...what's going on? Is Addy okay? What'd you—"

"Enough, Daniel," Merrick rasped. He clenched his jaw. His head throbbed so hard that it threatened to explode at any moment as he slowly got to his feet. When he was finally standing, he leaned forward and lowered Adalynn onto the bed.

He blinked away the pink tint in his stinging eyes and

braced himself with a hand on the bedpost as the world whirled and swayed around him. Adalynn didn't stir; her breathing was slow and even, the pallor had faded from her skin, and her muscles were relaxed.

I just need to be prepared next time...need to anticipate her illness resurging.

The thought echoed in his head loudly enough to cause a sharp pain at his temples. He squeezed his eyes shut until it passed.

"Are...are you okay?" Danny asked.

Merrick opened his eyes and swung his face toward Danny. The boy looked pale and frightened, his eyes wide and pupils dilated. Merrick found himself both unwilling to lie and unable to explain; thinking was too taxing now. He swallowed the coppery blood in his mouth and shoved away from the bed.

As he moved past Danny, Merrick said, "Tend to your sister."

Merrick staggered into the hallway without a backward glance and walked to his room, keeping a hand on the wall for stability—and still stumbling occasionally, regardless. He'd never experienced such agony, such vulnerability, such weakness, in all his years, and it made him feel for Adalynn even more.

She was *his*, and he would find some way to heal her—even if he had to defy the universe to do so.

WHEN ADALYNN OPENED HER EYES, she was hit by a powerful feeling of déjà vu. She was lying in her bed, the room dark but for the flickering light of a single candle on the nightstand. She'd woken like this before—with the same disorientation, the same confusion, the same sense that she'd just been pulled from the soothing embrace of a dream she hadn't wanted to end.

There was so much pain...

She raised a hand and touched her fingers to her head. It was still whole. Thankfully, it hadn't split open despite how it had felt. In fact, there wasn't any pain at all, not even any tenderness.

She grimaced; even if her head didn't hurt, her mouth tasted like shit.

A pair of arms looped around her and hugged her tight.

"Oh God, you're okay," Danny said.

It was only then that she realized her brother had been lying beside her on her bed. He held her tight, pressing his face against her arm, and something wet soaked through her sleeve. His tears.

"Danny?"

"I thought you were going to die. I thought you were really gone." His voice was thick with emotion, and his body trembled.

Adalynn's heart broke.

It happened again, except it came hard *this time. I felt like I was dying.*

Tears welled in her eyes, and she turned slightly to slip an arm around her brother. "It's okay. I'm still here. I'm not gone yet."

"B-But you could have been if M-Merrick hadn't helped you."

Her brow furrowed. "What do you mean?"

Danny lifted his head, and his pinkened, tear-filled eyes met hers. He'd obviously been crying for a while.

How long was I sleeping?

"What'd Merrick do, Danny?"

Her brother sniffled. "I...I don't know." His frown deepened as he glanced at the door. "Do you remember what that...elf-guy did? The golden guy?"

"What about him?"

He scooted closer to her and lowered his voice. "I think Merrick's the same."

Adalynn drew back and shook her head. "No, he's not the same."

That elf-like man's eyes had been cold, empty, devoid of warmth and kindness. Devoid of *humanity*. But she'd seen all those things glimmering in Merrick's eyes, and he'd shown them with his actions.

Danny's hold on her tightened. "He has *magic*, Addy. I *saw* it."

She placed a hand on his cheek. "Shh. It's okay. Whatever Merrick did, whatever he is, he's *not* like the monsters, Danny. Merrick won't hurt us. He would have already if he meant to. Whatever he's doing to me...it helps."

I think.

"What did you see, Danny?" she asked softly, lowering her hand.

"He was touching you, and there was blue *lightning* stuff all over his arms, going up from his hands. And there were shadows coming off him...like thick, moving shadows. Like *tentacles*, Addy. They were moving up and down around his shoulders and in the air over his back—over *you*—and every-thing around them was dark." He paused, eyebrows falling low. "No, that's not right. It was almost like...like looking into the night sky. Like I could almost see *stars* in the shadows, but my eyes couldn't quite make them out. And *his* eyes were glowing blue.

"And then you stopped moving. He...stopped your seizure. I think he did it before, that first night we came here, but he was hiding it then. But this time"—Danny shook his head, and his eyes were troubled when they met hers—"he was bleeding from his face. Not just a bloody nose, but everywhere —his eyes, mouth, and ears too."

Worry sped Adalynn's heart. "Is he okay?"

"I don't know. He left and told me to take care of you. He sounded…angry."

"Stay here." Adalynn extracted herself from Danny's embrace and moved to the edge of the bed.

"Where are you going?" The bedding rustled behind her as Danny shifted. "Addy! You should be resting."

Adalynn stood slowly, testing her balance; when she wasn't hit by even a hint of dizziness or lightheadedness, she stepped away from the bed. "Stay here, Danny. I'll be right back. I need to check on him."

"But what if he—"

She turned to face her brother. "Merrick will not hurt me. Or you. Do you understand?"

He nodded solemnly.

"What he did for me… Danny, he might be suffering because he helped me. I need to check on him, okay?"

"Okay."

"I'll be back."

She grabbed her flashlight from the nightstand and left the room, closing the door behind her. Clicking the flashlight on, Adalynn made her way down the hall toward Merrick's room. The flickering light visible beneath his door suggested he was within.

Every so often she caught a whiff of vomit, and she cringed, wondering if any was caked in her hair. A glance down was enough to tell her she was in a different shirt than before she'd fallen unconscious; she had to assume Danny had changed her, that he'd cleaned her face, but it would take more than a wet washcloth to get rid of that smell. She would've liked to have taken a bath and brushed her teeth, but her concern for Merrick was foremost. Tending to herself could come after.

When Adalynn reached his bedroom door, she raised a fist and knocked. "Merrick? Are you okay?"

"Leave," he said from inside the room.

"Please, come to the door."

"I'm fine. Go back to bed, Adalynn."

"No. Not until you talk to me."

"Tomorrow. Go to bed."

That's it.

Grasping the door handle, she pressed the latch down, pushed the door open, and strode into the room without hesitation. "I'm not a child to be ordered to bed, Merrick."

His bedroom was large and surprisingly open. A wide bed —king size, at least—stood against one wall, its headboard and footboard both made of thick, dark, carved wood. It was flanked by matching nightstands. Across from the foot of the bed was a grand fireplace with a large rug and two upholstered chairs set before it. A small fire crackled within the fireplace. Straight ahead stood a pair of tall glass doors that must've led to the balcony, and two more doors on either side of the fireplace likely belonged to a bathroom and a closet. A small writing desk—piled with books and papers—was in one corner; it was there Merrick sat with his back toward Adalynn.

He didn't turn to look at her, but his voice carried clearly when he said, "I did not give you many rules to follow, Adalynn. Staying out of my study and my bedroom was the first of them."

"I don't care about your damn rules. I came to check on you. Danny said you were bleeding."

"*You* are the one who had a spell. I'm fine, Adalynn. Good night."

Adalynn remained in place, closing the door behind her. She clicked off her flashlight, tightening her grip on it, and crossed her arms over her chest.

Merrick's posture stiffened. He placed his hands on the desk and sat up straight, turning his head slightly to look at Adalynn over his shoulder. "You should be resting now."

She met his eyes. "Funny thing about that, I feel

completely fine. As though I wasn't just dying moments—no, hours—ago. What did you do, Merrick?"

He shoved away from the desk, stood up—toppling his chair over—and spun to face her. "Haven't I given you enough? I helped you when I was not obligated to do so, and I am continuing to help you! What have I asked in return but some courtesy? Now do you mean to wrench every secret from my soul?"

She could feel *power* radiating from him, could feel it tingling over her skin, and realized now that she'd felt whispers of it from the moment they'd first met—though never this clear, this strong. Yet despite his anger, she didn't fear that power. She didn't fear *him*.

Adalynn remained where she stood, holding his gaze. "Then make us leave, Merrick. Why do you put up with us when all we're doing is eating your food and intruding upon you?"

"What does it matter? You don't have long."

The words might as well have been a slap across her face; their sting caught her off guard. Adalynn flinched.

His brows, which had been slanted sharply in anger a moment before, leveled out and dropped low. A crease formed between them as the hard light in his eyes faded. His jaw muscles ticked, and he averted his gaze. His voice was raw when he said, "You're still dying, Adalynn."

The hurt from his words diminished that easily; he was angry and lashing out, but he wasn't angry at her. It was the same sort of rage she'd seen in her family after her diagnosis—an anger born of helplessness, the anger of someone who was forced to watch her waste away knowing they could do nothing to save her.

"I've *been* dying," she said gently. "I've known it and I accepted it a long time ago, Merrick. My only concern has been to find a place where Danny will be safe when I'm gone." She lowered her arms to her sides and closed the distance between them. "You're one of them, aren't you? One of the...*others*."

Only shame, resignation, and sorrow remained in his eyes when they met hers again. "I am not human."

His confirmation didn't change the way Adalynn felt about him.

"And you used something—magic?—to heal me twice now, didn't you?" she asked.

"Yes. And I will use what power I possess to save you as many times as necessary."

Her heart thumped, and warmth suffused her. His voice was hard with conviction and raw with deep emotion.

"But it does something to you, doesn't it?" she asked. "Danny said you had blood dripping from your face."

"A small price to pay."

"But it's not. It's hurting you and it's...I don't know. I think it's doing something to *me*."

Merrick's face paled, and he stepped closer to her. "What is it doing to you, Adalynn?"

Adalynn tilted her head back, frowning as she searched his eyes. "It's like my body was making up for all those days that I'd felt good. The days I didn't feel sick. Like I wasn't really any better, and it was just building up, and when it hit a certain point it just *burst*. It really felt like this one was *it*, Merrick. Like it was the end."

He lifted his hands and cupped her face between his palms. A faint blue light had sparked in his citrine eyes—and it wasn't a reflection of the firelight. "I am going to keep you safe here, Adalynn. And I am going to find a way to stop it. To *truly* heal you."

Tears stung her eyes and blurred her vision. She blinked them away and smiled softly. Raising a hand, she settled it on his jaw and brushed her thumb over his cheek. The short bristles of his beard tickled her palm. "Thank you for telling me the truth about you, Merrick...but no."

Confusion contorted his expression. "*No?* What do you mean *no?*"

"It's hurting *you*, and that's a price I'm not willing to pay. We don't know how bad it will get, but this time was enough to prove that it *will* get worse. No, Merrick. I accepted my fate. Knowing that Danny has a place here, with you, that he'll be safe, will let me go on in peace." Warm tears continued to stream down her cheeks, gathering on his hands. "I just want to live the rest of my life in happiness here, too."

The crease reappeared between his eyebrows, deeper and more worried than before. He shifted one of his hands back, combing her hair behind her ear and trailing his fingertips along her scalp. "I will take that suffering if it spares you, Adalynn. I want you to have decades of happiness. Not mere weeks or days."

There seemed to be more he wanted to say, Adalynn could hear it in the roughness of his voice, could see it in the gleam of his eyes, but he left those words unspoken.

She shook her head and took a step back, lowering her hand from his face and pulling gently out of his hold. "*I* can't have you suffering because of me."

"That's not your choice to make."

"But it is. If you can tell me it won't hurt you, that there's no risk of harming yourself, that there will be no lasting effects on you, if you can *swear* that to me, I'll agree."

He clenched his jaw and, after a few seconds, lowered his gaze again, shoulders sagging. "I have to try, Adalynn."

She smiled sadly. "Thank you for giving me a little more time. Goodnight, Merrick."

Adalynn turned and walked to the door before he could say anything more. She opened it and slipped out into the hall, closing it softly behind her. Her chest was tight, and she was on the verge of breaking down into sobs, but she held them back with deep, slow breaths.

After the Sundering had taken her one chance at beating

her illness, Adalynn had accepted her fate. She'd accepted that her time was limited. Had accepted that she was dying.

Why was it becoming *harder* to accept as time went on?

Because of Merrick.

She didn't know how it had happened so quickly, but she had feelings for the man—feelings that ran deeper than should've been possible after only a week. Somewhere in her heart, she felt like she'd known him her whole life. And it was obvious that he felt something for her, too. Why else would he endure so much to help her? Why else would he harm himself to ease her suffering?

They were two lonely people drawn together in a dark, chaotic world. Why wouldn't they seek comfort in each other? Why wouldn't they give in to their mutual desire? It was too late not to get involved with him, and there was no reason for Adalynn to tell herself *no.*

She sniffled, wiped her eyes with the back of her hand, and clicked on the flashlight before pushing away from Merrick's door. She forced herself down the hallway.

I'm not holding back anymore.

Adalynn didn't know how much time she had left, but she was going to *live* it. She would live it with Danny, with Merrick, and take whatever happiness she could grasp. She was going to live wholeheartedly until the end.

She was going to *love.*

When she returned to her room, Danny was sitting on the bed, wide awake.

"Did you see him?" Danny asked.

Adalynn closed the door and approached him. "Yeah, I did."

"And? Is he okay? Are *you* okay? What happened, what did he say?"

She turned off the flashlight, set it on the nightstand, and sat down beside Danny. "He's fine. I didn't see any blood, but he probably cleaned himself up already. I'm fine too. We…talked."

"Come on, Addy, you gotta give me more than that!"

She turned her head to meet Danny's gaze. "You understand Merrick won't hurt us, right? You trust him?"

There was conflict in his eyes, which flickered with soft reflected light from the candle. He opened his mouth, hesitated, and asked, "Do *you* trust him?"

"Yes." She reached out and took his hand. "And you know what I want most is for you to be safe, don't you?"

He nodded, frowning.

"I trust Merrick, Danny. I trust him to keep you safe, to teach you, to help you grow." She gave Danny's hand a squeeze. "He's not human, but he won't hurt you. Won't hurt *us*. Do you understand, Danny?"

Her brother's eyes flared for a moment, but he nodded again. "If you trust him, then so do I." He smiled. "I like him, anyway. He can be a hardass, but he's actually a pretty cool guy. *And* he helped you."

Adalynn returned the smile. "Yeah, he did."

For a little while.

"And what did I say about the cussing?" she asked, arching a brow.

Danny sighed dramatically. "Don't know why it matters."

If their parents were still around, Danny would've been grounded long ago—their mother had been a wonderful, caring woman, but she wouldn't have accepted the end of the world as a valid excuse to break her no-swearing rule. It was Adalynn's instinct to remind Danny of that…but what would it change? Mom and Dad were gone, the world was different, and Danny was growing up much faster than he should've had to.

"Maybe it doesn't," she replied.

"Does that mean I can cuss?" he asked hopefully.

Adalynn grinned. "I'll think about it."

"Aww, come on."

She laughed—probably harder than was warranted, but it felt good—and was reminded when she inhaled afterward that she still smelled like vomit. She cringed.

And Merrick was standing right in front of me, was touching *me.*

It was embarrassing, but it meant he'd seen her at her worst—at least the worst it could get without her dying—and still wanted her. If anything, her sickness only seemed to drive him on harder.

"I'm going to take a quick bath, okay?" Adalynn said. "We should get some sleep while it's still dark."

"Okay. Addy?"

"Hmm?"

He ran his hands over the top of the blanket. "Can I sleep in here with you tonight?"

Adalynn smiled and leaned toward her brother, hugging him. "Yeah. You can."

He hugged her back tightly. "Thanks." He sniffled. "And Addy?"

"What?"

"You *do* stink."

Adalynn pulled away from Danny and laughed, shoving him down onto the bed. "Go to sleep. I'll be back."

Danny laughed and wriggled his way under the covers. "Love you, sis."

"Love you too, Danny."

Chapter Nine

That morning, Adalynn woke alone. She wandered the house, calling for Danny and Merrick and receiving no answer; the place was empty. Guessing they'd gone to the garden to continue their work from the day before, she ate a quick breakfast, tugged on her mud-caked rubber boots, and headed outside to join them.

Her hunch proved correct; Merrick and Danny were tending the crops beneath an already hot morning sun.

And the moment they saw her, they insisted she return to the house.

No amount of arguing would sway them. They were adamant that Adalynn not overwork herself so soon after an attack. Danny was on the verge of tears—such a cheat!—while Merrick threatened to tie her to the bed.

Merrick's threat might not have sounded so bad if she knew he would've stayed with her in that bed. But his expression and tone had told her both that he'd intended no sensual innuendo and he wasn't afraid to fulfill the threat. He would have carried her to her bedroom, strapped her to the bedposts, and gone back to work without a second thought.

Rightfully pissed at them, Adalynn turned and stormed

back toward the house. She stomped up the steps onto the back porch, kicked off her boots—taking petty satisfaction in their heavy *thumps* against the wall—and continued into the kitchen through the back door. She slammed the door behind her.

Once inside, she folded her arms across her chest and seethed.

I'm supposed to be living *right now. Not…not…not being treated like an invalid.*

They're just worried about me.

The thought diffused some of her anger. What if working in the garden yesterday had triggered her attack? Maybe it had just been time; she'd certainly felt overdue for an episode after a week of feeling so good. If Merrick had used magic to suppress her symptoms, maybe it had simply…worn off.

Closing her eyes, she took in a deep breath and released it slowly.

It's still my *choice. I don't want to worry them, but they need to respect that.*

Adalynn opened her eyes and stared up at the ceiling.

"I'll just have to find something else to do, then," she muttered. She swung her gaze around the kitchen. "Like clean this already spotless house."

She washed the few dirty dishes in the sink and wiped down the dustless counters before stopping herself. It was pointless, and she was bored. It wouldn't have surprised her if Merrick used magic to keep the house clean.

I could march back out there and tell them I'm helping and that's that.

She *could*, but Merrick had been serious about his threat. It would only end up with her *more* bored, restless, and angry.

With nothing else to do, Adalynn took a long, hot bath, and read her favorite romance book—which also happened to be the only one currently in her possession—while she soaked.

The heat and steam soothed her, and reading allowed her

some semblance of an escape from her frustration, her sickness, and this broken world—but not from her *desire*. She couldn't help but think about Merrick when she came to the first sex scene. Soon, all she could focus on was the memory of his hands on her skin, of the feel of his lips against hers, of his masculine scent.

The book quickly lost its appeal; she tossed it onto the floor near her bag, closed her eyes, and slipped her hand between her thighs.

Her self-induced orgasm came swiftly, but it left her feeling unsatisfied, *hollow*, and lonelier than before.

After her bath, Adalynn dressed and brushed her hair, leaving it hanging freely around her shoulders. She slipped her book into her bag, which she returned to her room before wandering around the house again. She took her time examining the rooms and the objects within them, moving pictures and tugging on light fixtures to see if there were any hidden compartments or secret passages. Why wouldn't there be? This was a big, old house; it was bound to have as many secrets as its owner, wasn't it?

Her search turned up nothing exciting, but at least it had distracted her currently overactive imagination for a little while. She forced herself to press onward.

She paused when she reached the entrance of the ballroom; the double doors were closed today. She flung them open and stepped through. As usual, all the curtains were closed, blanketing the large chamber in thick gloom.

Time to change that.

Shutting the doors behind her, she strode across the dancefloor and went from window to window, drawing the curtains wide. With each window, more sunlight streamed inside; soon the whole ballroom was gleaming with it. Rays of sunshine struck the chandeliers' crystals, casting countless tiny, colorful points of reflected light on the polished wood of the floor, walls, and ceiling.

Adalynn hummed softly as she moved about the room, sometimes walking, sometimes dancing.

I should teach Danny to dance.

Even if it was the end of the world, even if it wasn't a practical skill, there was no reason not to teach him; people still needed to enjoy themselves from time to time. People still needed small, brief means of escape from the stresses of this new world.

When she reached the stage, she climbed up and sat on the piano bench. The fallboard was upright. She skimmed her fingertips over the keys, too lightly to produce any sound, and found herself overcome with an indefinable sense of sadness.

No, no sadness. I'm living, right?

She pressed down on a few keys.

The notes were strong, resonant, and in tune.

"What?"

Startled, Adalynn moved her other hand up to the keys and played a few bars of *River Flows in You*. Though her fingers felt stiff and a bit clumsy after so long, the music flowed from her, the notes crisp and *perfect*.

Merrick. He'd done this. For her?

She brimmed with excitement, and joyful tears welled in her eyes. She clasped her hands together and lifted them to her chest, which was tight with overwhelming emotions. It'd been *months* since she last played, and she hadn't realized how much she'd missed it, hadn't realized how big a hole its absence had left inside her, until this moment. Music—especially piano—had been the core of her life since that first time her father played her *Moonlight Sonata*.

To have it back now, while she still had some time…

It was incredible beyond words.

Unable to bear the silence any longer, Adalynn separated her hands, stretched her fingers, settled them on the keys, and played—starting with *River Flows in You* and shifting into *Moonlight Sonata*. She moved right into another song when it was done, and then another and another, smiling as the music filled the room. It didn't matter if her fingers ached; they needed this as much as she did.

The sun roamed across the sky as she played, shifting the position of the rainbow, refracted lights cast by the chandeliers' crystals.

She paused, fingers hovering over the keys, after she finished Elton John's *Your Song*. She'd heard the lyrics in her head as she'd played, and it had turned her mind toward a different song—one she'd never played before but which she *knew* all the same. She'd never *heard* it; it was a song she'd *felt* inside her heart ever since she'd come to this house. And it was always at its clearest when she was near Merrick.

Closing her eyes, Adalynn set her fingers back down and let instinct take over. The melody came as naturally to her as breathing. Her fingers danced over the keys as the haunting, yet beautiful song took form, swirling around her like a physical presence.

MERRICK AND DANNY carried their harvest—two baskets laden with produce—into the kitchen through the back door and deposited it on the floor along the wall. Between today and yesterday, they'd picked far too much for the three of them to eat before it started spoiling, but Merrick would use it as an opportunity to teach Adalynn and Daniel the canning process. Summer was speeding toward its end; now was the time to bolster their long-term stores in preparation for winter.

"Think Addy's still mad at us?" Danny asked, brushing his hands together to dislodge some of the dirt that had caked upon them.

Merrick frowned at the flecks of dirt falling to the floor in front of the boy, but the mess was less troubling than the way he and Daniel had treated Adalynn earlier. She'd only wanted to contribute, but Merrick and Danny had sent her away without listening to her protests, united in their concern for her health.

As Adalynn—making no effort to mask her anger—had stormed into the house, Merrick had recalled their conversation from last night. His worry did not grant him the right to dictate her actions, and no matter how deeply he *felt* that she was his, she was not bound to his will. Only Adalynn knew her limits.

But Merrick couldn't shake his memories of her latest episode, and that had hardened his resolve. He could not dismiss the possibility that it had been her overexerting herself —rather than a failing of his magic—that had brought on the resurgence. Even if that didn't ring true in his heart, any chance of it was one too many.

"I don't think she is. At least not as much so as before," Merrick replied. "You know her better than I do; what do you think?"

Danny shrugged and stuffed his hands into his pockets. "Dunno. Addy doesn't really get mad all that often. I think she hides a lot of what she really feels since the Sundering. But…"

"But you can still see the sadness in her eyes," Merrick said softly. A lump of regret solidified in his upper chest and sank slowly into his gut.

"Yeah." Danny looked down and absently toed the dirt he'd brushed onto the floor. "But you can make her better, right, Merrick?"

When the boy lifted his gaze, his eyes—glistening with unfallen tears—held such sadness, such hope, such desperation, that Merrick found himself being crushed under the weight of that question.

Though Merrick wasn't human, he understood the raw emotion on display. He understood, even after a thousand years, what it felt like to be young, powerless, and desperate not to lose the last person who loved you, the last *family* you had. He'd been that boy once—but in the end, no one had been there to comfort him, to care for him.

Without thinking to, Merrick drew the boy into an embrace. "I will find a way, Daniel. We will *not* lose her."

Danny clung to him for several seconds, his hold almost tight enough to hurt.

The thought of losing Adalynn filled Merrick with despair, sorrow, and impotent fury.

How had she come to mean so much to him already? Eight days meant nothing in a lifetime spanning hundreds of thousands of days. Yet the bond between them was so strong it was almost tangible. He felt it constantly, had been aware of it every moment since he'd first sensed it. No one, mortal or otherwise, should've been able to draw him in so quickly and completely.

He knew her passing would leave a massive wound on his heart—a wound that would never heal.

Even Danny had earned Merrick's affection—Danny, who always wore so brave a face despite the burden of loss, terror, and responsibility thrust upon him. Merrick didn't want the boy to suffer any more. It wasn't right, wasn't fair, wasn't acceptable. Merrick's magic could shape reality, could bend the natural laws to his whim. There had to be some way to alter Adalynn's fate.

There had to be a way to save her.

Danny sniffled and pulled away, averting his face as he lifted a hand to wipe the moisture from his eyes. "I'm gonna go take a shower, okay?"

"Don't use too much hot water, or I will have to cut your food portions."

Danny walked toward the door. "Dude, don't you use, like…*magic* to heat the water?"

While it felt strange to openly acknowledge his magic to a mortal, it was also somewhat…*liberating*, like an immense burden had been lifted off Merrick's shoulders. "I do."

"So, just magic yourself some more. No need to be so dramatic."

Despite everything, Merrick smirked as Danny hurried out of the kitchen. Though the boy's voice had still been raw, it was clear he'd been trying to lighten the mood, had been trying to push aside the sorrow and uncertainty that had suffused their brief but meaningful conversation.

With Danny out of sight, Merrick's thoughts shifted entirely to Adalynn. Merrick didn't want her anger; he wanted her joy, her passion, her *heart*. He needed to talk to her, to apologize, to explain himself, to hear what she thought and felt.

He glanced down at himself. His clothes were sweat dampened and dirty. There was no shame in it—it was proof of an honest day's work—but he didn't want to present himself to Adalynn in so disheveled a state. She deserved only Merrick's best. And regardless, a shower earned by hard work was always more satisfying.

Merrick lost himself in thought—which usually happened only when he was locked away in his study—as he made his way upstairs.

The usual no longer applies. I've been consumed by thoughts of Adalynn every day since she arrived.

Once he was in the shower, with steaming water coursing over his bare skin, his thoughts of Adalynn shifted again. His imagination conjured an image of her naked in the shower with him, water coursing over her dark hair and streaming in rivulets over her breasts and belly, and his cock hardened, immediately rousing an urgent, uncomfortable ache in his loins.

Despite the desirous fires that burned in her eyes when she looked at him, despite the way she'd melted when they kissed, she'd not yet come back for more. She'd not yet told him her decision—would she give in or not?

It was maddening.

He felt like he'd been unfulfilled for his entire life, like he'd always yearned for her, had always *needed* her, even though he'd only learned of her existence days ago. That need had always been present, but he'd only been able to identify it after her arrival. It had flared several times over the last few days, but none of those flares had been as powerful as this one.

Growling, Merrick braced one hand against the wall and wrapped the fingers of the other around his shaft. The ache only intensified. He pumped his fist up and down, each stroke building more pressure within him. Soon, his breath was short, and in his imagination, Adalynn was dancing again—dancing naked, dancing for him and him alone, brushing her bare flesh against his. For a fleeting instant, he could almost *feel* her touch, could almost feel the fullness of her mana song in his heart.

He reached a sudden, explosive climax that made his breath shaky and uneven and left him shuddering. For a long while, he stood beneath the water with his head bowed and his long, wet hair dangling in his face, chest heaving as he caught his breath.

But something had been missing, something significant. He still felt unsatisfied, still felt that deep, throbbing desire for *her*—a desire that was only greater now.

He cleaned himself and exited the shower quickly, drying off and dressing in clean clothing with equal haste. He needed to see Adalynn *now*. He didn't bother with socks or shoes, didn't bother tucking in his button-down shirt—which was damp thanks to his also-damp hair—and didn't slow down for even a moment on his way to Adalynn's bedroom.

He stopped when he arrived at her door and curbed his urge to barge in; she was upset with him, and he was here to apologize. Bursting into her room could only undermine the sincerity of his intended apology, could only make things worse between them. He lifted a hand and rapped upon the door.

When she offered no answer, he reached for the latch, only to halt his hand in midair. She wasn't in her bedroom. He would've realized that sooner had he not rushed here on a wave of overwhelming, unthinking urgency. He sensed her presence, though it was faint—she was somewhere on the opposite side of the house.

Merrick strode to the loft overlooking the foyer and stopped with his hands on the bannister. He focused on that warm, tingling sensation and reoriented himself.

Downstairs?

He descended the steps and moved into the hallway between the foyer and the parlor, where he stopped again. He turned to face the southern hallway; that was the direction from which he sensed her, though the corridor was dark, everything was still, and all the doors were closed.

But it was not silent. Music drifted down the hall from behind the closed ballroom doors, and he could *feel* the power in it this time, he *knew* it was from the piano and not from Adalynn's cassette player.

Merrick walked toward the ballroom without hesitation. As he neared it, a strange sensation settled over him, raising goosebumps on his skin and sending electric tingles outward from the base of his skull. He knew the music playing inside the ballroom, but not because he'd heard it in some concert hall a hundred and fifty years ago, not because he'd heard it playing over a staticky radio broadcast in a bygone decade; he'd never *heard* this music before.

He pushed the doors open. The song flowed over him, swirled around him, swept through him. The haunting, melancholic notes, fraught with flashes of bitterness, frustration, power, and bits of hope, spoke directly to his soul— because they already resided there. They always had.

This was a mana song—*Merrick's* mana song.

He crossed the threshold.

Adalynn was sitting at the piano. Loose, spiral locks of

hair dangled around her face as she gently swayed with the music, her fingers striking each note as though she'd practiced them a thousand times before, as though she'd always been meant to play them—as though the song had been written just for her to perform.

Merrick padded across the dance floor. He felt like he was floating rather than walking, and his magic swelled to resonate along with Adalynn's music, matching it note for note.

No, not note for note. Something was missing from her rendition, something vital—an underscoring, complimentary melody that gave his mana song new harmony, a melody that strengthened inside him with his every step nearer to her.

He mounted the low stage in front of her. Adalynn's eyes were closed. His magic thrummed, encouraged by the vibrations the piano sent through the floor, and the air felt charged with anticipatory energy. He approached the piano slowly, reverently, unwilling to startle her and break the song—she looked more passionate, more carefree, now than she had at any other moment during her stay here.

As though sensing his presence, Adalynn opened her eyes and met his gaze. She didn't seem surprised—she smiled at him and continued playing without missing a note, soft pink staining her cheeks.

Merrick walked around the bench. Adalynn slid aside, and he sat next to her. For a few seconds, he watched her fingers, so graceful and confident, fly over the keys. He'd learned to play many years ago, and, even if he was out of practice, even if he could not match her skill, he knew he could play what needed to be played now.

He raised his hands and set them in position, closed his eyes, and played the missing melody. Played *her* melody.

The two pieces came together beautifully, each unique and individual but wholly complimentary to the other, entering an intricate dance with one another.

He sensed Adalynn's gaze upon him. He opened his eyes

to meet hers, which were sparkling with joy over her wide smile. She leaned toward him, brushing her arm against his. Magic pulsed along his forearm, and fire sparked low in his belly. But that stirring of desire was nothing compared to the sound of their songs mingling in the air.

The music seemed a prelude to something larger, something deeper, something inevitable. It was like a taste of...*fate*.

He wasn't sure how long they played together—it might've been a few minutes or a few hours— but it felt like forever in the best of ways because it was so *right*, so *perfect*. They stopped in unison, and the final notes faded slowly, leaving Merrick and Adalynn's soft, panting breaths as the only sounds in the large room.

"What was that?" she asked.

"It was *you*." He lifted a hand and slid his palm over her cheek, brushing her hair behind her ear. "It was *us*."

Her dark, sultry eyes suddenly burned with undisguised need. Within the next instant, she was in his lap, straddling him, with her arms wrapped around his neck and her mouth against his. Merrick slipped his fingers into her hair and cupped the back of her head. He wrapped his other arm around her, drawing her close as he returned the kiss with *everything* inside him.

Crackling pulses of energy arced outward from his mouth, setting his every nerve ablaze, teasing him with a sampling of the pleasure she could provide. When she moaned and undulated her hips against him, he *knew* she felt it too.

Adalynn broke the kiss, keeping her mouth close to his. Merrick forced his eyes open to meet her gaze.

"I'm not denying myself anymore," she rasped, brushing her lips against his in a feathery caress. "I want you, Merrick."

His cock strained against his trousers, eager for her heat, but their clothing remained a barrier between them. Lust hazed his mind; he needed her, needed her *now*, needed to have all of her...but was this the place?

My room. My bed, where she belongs. My Adalynn.

Merrick dropped his hands to her thighs and guided her legs around his waist as he stood, sliding his palms to her backside once he was upright. She tightened her hold on him with arms and legs alike and kissed him again. He returned the kiss, deepening it, using his tongue to coax her lips apart so he could gain entry. She obliged. Heat poured through his veins, and his fingers flexed; he pulled her closer still, pressing her soft body against his hardened shaft.

Now. He needed her now.

Without breaking the kiss, he carried her off the stage and out of the ballroom, navigating primarily by his familiarity with the manor and the layers of magic he'd embedded in its walls. Adalynn rubbed her pelvis against him. He could feel the maddening heat of her core through their clothes; it nearly drove him to take her right there, on the stairs.

He climbed the steps and hurried down the hallway, everything passing in a blur. He shoved his bedroom door open, rushed through, and slammed it shut behind him, pausing only to lock the deadbolt before striding to his bed.

Merrick leaned forward, laid Adalynn on her back, and pulled away to look down at her. Her arms fell to either side of her head. Her lips were luscious, pink, and kiss-swollen, her cheeks were flushed, and her eyes were bright with desire. She was beautiful beyond words.

And she was *his*.

Chapter Ten

Adalynn was awash with desire, intoxicated by Merrick's taste and scent, and eager for *more*. She stared up at him, and her heart leapt. He was breathtaking. His long, damp hair hung around his face, his features were hard and fierce, and his eyes glowed a vibrant, electric blue.

Hands trembling in anticipation, she reached up to unbutton his shirt. She'd only managed to unfasten two buttons before he grasped the sides of his shirt and tore the garment open; several detached buttons fell away as he shrugged off the shirt and let it fall to the floor.

She settled her hands on his chest. His flesh was hot, and his heart pounded beneath her palms. She trailed her hands down, over the lean muscles of his abs, and lower still to his pants. With her fingers a bit steadier, she unclasped his pants, lowered their zipper, and shoved them down. An instant later, she grasped his hard cock.

Merrick hissed and bowed his head, placing his hands on the bed to either side of her to prop himself up. "Adalynn..."

Encouraged by his reaction, she tightened her grip and stroked her hand up and down, relishing the feel of him. His shaft was long and thick, scalding iron encased in velvet, and *oh*, it was *glorious*. Liquid heat flooded her. Her sex clenched as she imagined him entering her, thrusting inside her, filling her.

Merrick's body went taut, and he squeezed his eyes shut, his lips parting as he panted softly.

Lifting her face, Adalynn pressed her lips to his neck, trailing sultry kisses along his throat from one side to the other until she reached his ear. She snagged his earlobe with her teeth and bit down hard enough to make him growl and shudder. Something wet aided the glide of her hand as she continued to stroke him. She moved her hand up to the head of his shaft and slid her thumb over his slit, from which precum had seeped.

An irresistible urge overcame her; without thinking further, she released him and brought her hand up to her mouth to suck his taste off her thumb. His flavor burst across her tongue; sweet, potent, and *inhuman*. She moaned.

It was delicious.

Adalynn opened her eyes to find his upon her, glowing brighter than before. Blue energy raced along his skin, pulsing out from his eyes and the tips of his fingers like restless electric currents. The light he emitted was intensified by its contrast to the thick shadows forming above and behind him, which seemed to writhe and move as though they were alive, throughout which was present a *suggestion* of light—like stars viewed through a black veil.

He was otherworldly; she had the sense that his body was merely a shell, that the true Merrick *was* magic, *was* power, that he *was* that song she'd played downstairs.

Merrick wrapped his hand around her wrist, and that energy thrummed into her, so strong and pleasing that it stole her breath. He guided her thumb from her mouth to his and slipped it between his lips. His tongue swirled around it as he sucked.

His eyes flared; despite the intensity of their light, it wasn't painful, and she didn't look away from him until she realized her clothes were glowing not with his radiance, but with their own.

She glanced down to see her shirt unraveling, separating into individual threads that broke apart into tiny bits of dust before vanishing entirely. The process spread to her bra, to her pants and panties, and then to his pants, revealing their bodies rapidly. The feel of it was unlike anything she'd ever experienced—it was like a million whispered words breathed over her skin, raising goosebumps in their wake and sending a thrill to her core.

The fabric over her pelvis was gone, having disintegrated into nothingness. Before the process had reached her knees, Merrick released her wrist and shoved himself back toward the foot of the bed. There was no hesitation on his part as he dropped to his knees and lowered his face to her sex.

Adalynn gasped, eyes widening and back arching, as his tongue swept between the folds of her sex. As though by instinct, her legs moved to close, but he caught them in his hands. Dragging her closer, he shoved her thighs open and used his thumbs to spread her sex.

"Merrick," she rasped, her fingers clutching at the covers.

His tongue was unrelenting; it lapped at her, explored her, and teased her clit. Her breaths became rapid, shallow bursts of air. Her breasts felt heavy and needy, her nipples were tight, and her body was flooded with delirious heat.

Merrick's ravenous groan vibrated through her as he drank, and drank, and drank. His touch was fire and ice, and it spread the pleasure from her core to permeate her entire body. His unwavering, glowing gaze only heightened the sensations. He stared at her as though she were the only thing in all the universe.

The sensations soon became too much. She writhed on the bed, unable to keep still, with perspiration beading on her skin as Merrick brought her close to release repeatedly—only to back away each time, tormenting her. She gyrated her hips, needing his lips *there*, on her clit. He offered only fleeting brushes of lips and tongue, each sending a shockwave of pleasure through Adalynn that wasn't enough to push her over the edge. It left her whimpering with frustration—she needed *more*.

She touched her breasts and attempted to move a hand down to sate her own need, but *something* knocked it away. That invisible force pulled both her wrists over her head and pinned them on the bed, refusing to let her touch herself, refusing to let her take the release she needed.

"Merrick," Adalynn cried, *begged*, straining against the magical bonds, straining toward *him*, his mouth, his tongue.

"I will take as long as I please," he said against her sex, his deep voice alone enough to make her hips undulate.

A light, airy sensation—like a soft, sheer fabric against her skin—coursed over her legs, and she looked down to see those moving shadows spread outward from behind him and descend upon her. Their touches were ethereal, caressing her calves and thighs, brushing over her hips, so gentle and yet brimming with power. They stretched upward to circle her breasts, twining around them, and Adalynn gasped, her hips bucking as the shadows solidified and tweaked her nipples. Another rush of heat flooded her, and her sex quivered. It was like a dozen hands stroking her all at once.

"Please, Merrick," Adalynn panted, her every muscle trembling with need. "No more. I need you." She didn't expect his compliance.

When his lips closed around her clit, his tongue pressed down on it, and he sucked it into his mouth, she shattered utterly. Her cries filled the room as she drowned in ecstasy bordering on pain. He didn't pull his mouth away, didn't allow her suddenly tense body any path of escape. The pleasure was pure and explosive. And she didn't want it to stop, even though it was consuming her from within.

Adalynn was in a haze, panting with her face buried

against her arm, when he finally relented.

He lifted his mouth from her sex to place gentle kisses upon her inner thighs—but even those little kisses were charged with magic that pulsed across her skin, rebuilding the sensation at her core faster than she'd realized possible.

Merrick rose slowly, continuing to trail his lips over her pelvis and across her stomach. Shivers of delight followed in their wake. Adalynn forced her eyelids open to stare down at him as he closed his mouth around her nipple. She arched her back and struggled to raise her arms, to delve her fingers into his hair—which was now tickling her chest—but his power held them firmly in place. All the while, his shadows continued to caress her legs.

He slid a hand down and cupped her sex; the pressure alone was thrilling, but the way he thrummed with energy put every vibrator she'd ever owned to shame. He teased her nipple with his lips, tongue, and teeth, keeping his eyes locked with hers; his stare was a branding iron on her soul.

"Kiss me," she said, tugging on her arms again. "Let me touch you."

Merrick lifted his head, biting lightly on her nipple and tugging on it for a moment. "Is that what you desire, Adalynn?"

She caught her lower lip between her teeth and moaned. "*Yes.*"

He pushed himself up farther, his mouth continuing its slow, blazing trek across her collarbone and up her neck before finally meeting her lips. And in that instant, the magic holding her arms dissipated. Her senses reeled and her emotions whirled as their mouths moved against each other in a consuming kiss. She raised her knees, squeezing his hips with her thighs.

His cock was hard and heavy against her belly.

Lifting her hands, she smoothed her palms up his arms, over his shoulders, and along his neck before delving her fingers into his hair. Merrick deepened the kiss, slipping his tongue into her mouth to dance with hers. All his movements were set to that haunting, internal music Adalynn always sensed when he was near, were set to *his* song—which was now clearer than ever.

"Going to take you, Adalynn," he growled against her lips, shifting his hips.

The head of his cock pressed against her entrance. She wanted nothing more in that moment than to push up against him, to feel him sink into her. But despite floating on a wave of pleasure, she retained a degree of clarity.

She dropped her hands, flattening them against his chest, and broke their kiss. "Merrick, wait."

He lifted his head, his brow furrowing slightly. "What's wrong?"

"Do you...do you have protection? Just in case?"

"Just in case of what, Adalynn?"

"A...baby."

Though the energy coursing over his skin didn't diminish in the slightest, his expression softened. He moved a hand to her face and gently brushed the backs of his fingers over her cheek. "There will not be a baby."

"How can you be sure?"

"You'll just have to trust me a little more."

Adalynn smiled up at him. Knowing that he had magic at his command, that he could bend the rules of reality, there was no need to question him further. She lifted her head and kissed him. "I trust you."

Merrick cupped the side of her neck, positioning his thumb beneath her chin to tilt it up as he reclaimed her lips with his own. He rocked his hips forward, and his cock slid into her, stretching her, filling her inch by tantalizing inch. They moaned in unison.

Adalynn undulated her hips, urging him to go deeper. Without hesitation, Merrick pulled his hips back, withdrawing from her almost completely, and surged forward again, thrusting deep. She gasped at the sudden fullness.

His heartbeat pulsed through her, a steady, strong under-lier to the more frantic buzz of his magic, which itself was strong enough to make her toes curl. She felt it radiating from him constantly, washing through her, striking a chord within her that nothing else could. His song was inside her now—but she also sensed the melody he'd added to it. *Her* song.

MERRICK TENSED. Being inside Adalynn was the most overwhelming, impossible blend of agony and ecstasy he could ever have imagined—even while he was still, just the feel of her sex around his shaft was almost enough to send him over the edge, pushing the pressure in him well beyond what should've been his limits. She was a sampling of heaven made all the sweeter with her resonance singing within him. Magic coursed through his body freely, flowed into her and back again completely unhindered, heightening every sensation.

Their mana songs played in unison; Merrick and Adalynn were in exquisite harmony with one another, body and soul, were closer in that moment than he'd thought possible.

He shifted his hips back. The slide of her sex around his cock nearly undid him, but he groaned and held out—he wasn't willing to let this end, not yet, not so soon. She looped her legs around him, ankles crossing over his backside, and pulled his pelvis against her again with increased force. He broke the kiss and gritted his teeth as a shudder wracked him. The intensity of his pleasure was too much for him to keep still any longer; he needed to move, he needed *her*.

His shadows wrapped tighter around her legs and held her against him, their little movements producing phantom sensa-tions along his back; he could almost *taste* her through them. He'd never revealed this aspect of his magic to anyone—he'd never used them to *touch* anyone. The sensation was wholly new and utterly thrilling. Drawing in a trembling breath, he forced his hips into motion again.

They fell into a steadily quickening rhythm, his every movement complimentary to hers, each of hers complimentary to his. Their hearts pounded at the same elevated rate, their breath came in the same short, heavy gasps, and the sounds they made wove together until he could no longer tell what was him and what was her—there was only *them*, only their immense, consuming pleasure.

The pressure in him grew with every thrust; his magic carried the sensation throughout his body, but even that wasn't enough to assuage it, to ease it, to make it bearable. He needed release, needed that little death, but it would not come.

And why should it be so easy? He'd waited more than a thousand years for this, for *her*.

Adalynn's nails bit into his shoulders, and her throaty moans filled his ears. Her sex gripped his cock, and he felt the first flutters of her impending release. Her movements gained more urgency as their mingling songs reached a crescendo. Linked with her through his magic, Merrick increased his pace accordingly, and his breath caught in his throat as ecstasy seized his muscles.

He looked down at her. Adalynn's eyes were half-lidded with lust—and shone with intense blue light to match that of his magic.

It was the final thing he saw before he snapped his eyes shut against the overwhelming force of his climax, which was only increased when she cried out in her own release, her sex clamping around him as liquid heat flowed from her core.

For a moment, Merrick had the sensation that he was floating in the air outside his own body—like he *was* his mana song, intertwined with hers, more intimately connected than any two individuals had ever been in the entirety of existence. Pleasure permeated his being.

Just as quickly, he was in his body again. He sagged over Adalynn, catching himself with an elbow atop the bed, and panted to catch his breath. Their bodies were hot and damp with sweat, and her sex quivered around his throbbing cock in the aftershocks of her climax.

The air was perfumed with a new scent—*their* scent, the result of their individual smells interweaving to create something intoxicating.

Adalynn, who had been clinging to him, released him to lay limp upon the bed, breath ragged. She turned her face to the side and closed her eyes. A soft smile curled on her lips. "Mmm. I shouldn't have waited so long."

"And I shouldn't have let you," he replied with a smile of his own.

She opened her eyes to look up at him. He watched as their blue glow faded, leaving only her lovely, natural brown. She grinned cheekily and ran her fingers lightly from his bicep to his shoulder. "Can we do it again? And I...seem to have developed a thing for...*tentacles*."

Laughter bubbled up from Merrick's throat; he hadn't expected anything like that from her. "You can have as many *tentacles* as you want."

"You seriously can't just whip those out and not expect *some* kind of reaction."

"Oh, I expected a reaction. Just not *this* reaction." He moved a hand to her face and swept some of her damp curls back from her cheek. The perfection of her features, enhanced by the flush of her cheeks, struck him anew, and he couldn't help but stare in awe. His heart skipped a beat. "You are beautiful, Adalynn. More so than words can describe."

Her smile softened, and she lifted her face, brushing her lips over his in a gentle, lingering kiss. That kiss led to another, and then another—and it wasn't long before he flipped her over onto her stomach and put his *tentacles* to good use.

Chapter Eleven

Merrick sat up suddenly, eyes snapping open; he'd gone from sound asleep to fully awake in an instant. Adalynn stirred beside him, her sleep-warmed body shifting against his beneath the covers.

Something had breached the wards around his property. No, not something, but *somethings*—a group of five, moving at great speed. Though he could not determine their nature through the wards alone, he guessed they weren't human.

His bedroom was lit only by pale, yellow-tinged moonlight from outside, which flowed in through the drawn curtains. The night sky was a murky midnight blue behind a vague gray haze that left the stars obscured.

"What's wrong?" Adalynn murmured.

"Get up," Merrick replied, tossing aside the bedding as he hurried out of bed.

The grogginess in her expression quickly gave way to concern and confusion. She pushed herself up into a sitting position. The blanket fell away, exposing her pert breasts and rosy nipples; under different circumstances, Merrick would've leapt back into bed after that glimpse and put all his focus and energy into pleasing her. But entirely different instincts were at play in him now—he needed to protect her from this sudden, mysterious threat. Nothing mattered beyond keeping her safe.

He strode to the armoire, tugged it open, and pulled out a black silk robe. He tossed the garment onto the bed beside Adalynn. "Put that on and fetch your brother."

Though her confusion didn't ease—and her eyes now gleamed with a hint of fear—Adalynn grabbed the robe and pulled it on as she climbed off the bed. "What's going on, Merrick?"

"Intru—"

A deep, unnatural howl sounded from outside—too deep, too layered to have come from any normal wolf. Adalynn's face paled, and Merrick's magic flared in his chest, building to crackling heat in a flash.

"—ders," Merrick finished. "You've heard that sound before, haven't you?"

She pressed her lips into a tight line and nodded.

Merrick took a pair of pants from the armoire and tugged them on. "Get Daniel in here."

Adalynn rushed to the bedroom door as Merrick went to the windows one-by-one, scanning the grounds outside for movement as he closed the curtains. His latest uninvited guests were nowhere to be seen—*yet*—but their trajectory when they'd crossed the wards would take them directly to the house.

Five werewolves. He'd never encountered werewolves running in a pack before the Sundering, but he imagined they'd changed when the moon shattered just like so much else had.

For one, they were in wolf form—but the moon-shards were not full.

A door opened down the hall. Adalynn and Danny had a brief, whispered conversation, their voices too soft for Merrick to make out their words.

Merrick glanced through doorway to see the siblings

jogging down the hall toward his bedroom. He walked to the chest against the wall and knelt in front of it, lifting the lid to rummage through the bedding and old clothing inside until he found what he wanted tucked neatly at the bottom.

At the corner of his vision, Adalynn—holding Danny's hand—led the boy into the room, closed the door, and locked it.

Merrick removed the wool-wrapped bundle from the chest, along with the box of shells that had been nestled beside it. He unwrapped the bundle as Adalynn and Danny moved to stand near him, revealing the old but pristine pump shotgun it contained. He opened the box and fed shells into the tube.

"There's one of those werewolves outside, isn't there?" Danny asked.

A chorus of eerie howls answered before Merrick could, all closer than the first. Adalynn and Danny crowded closer to Merrick, their eyes wide with fear.

Merrick stood and worked the shotgun's slide action to chamber a shell. The sound shattered the relative silence of the bedroom with an ominous finality. "There are five of them."

"What's that for?" Danny looked from the gun to Merrick. "Don't you have *magic*?"

Merrick met Adalynn's gaze and held the shotgun out to her. "I do. But you two don't."

Only hours earlier, he and Adalynn had been in each other's arms, drifting on seas of passion, relishing the joining of their bodies and souls. During that time, there'd been no other cares—the rest of the world had ceased to exist. Future and past had faded into meaninglessness. The present was all that had mattered. *Adalynn* was all that had mattered.

Clearly, the outside world had deemed that unacceptable.

Adalynn's face paled further, but she took the shotgun in both hands. Merrick felt the trembling of her arms through the weapon before he released it. She held it against her chest, one hand on the action and the other on the stock.

"I've never used a gun," she said, her voice low but steady.

"Point and squeeze the trigger," Merrick replied. "Pump the action to chamber another round and fire again."

Adalynn adjusted her grip on the weapon, clenched her jaw, and nodded.

Merrick cupped the back of her head with one hand, leaned forward, and kissed her. Despite the urgency of the situation, he was tempted to let the kiss linger. He resisted that temptation and drew back after only a moment. "Stay here. Do *not* come outside, no matter what happens."

She released the shotgun's stock to press her hand against his chest, fingers curling as though to grab him. "What? Where are you going?"

Merrick covered her hand with his and gently squeezed it. "To greet our visitors."

"Dude, you can't!" Danny said.

"No!" Adalynn said simultaneously. "Those things rip people to shreds, Merrick."

"And you don't even have a shirt on," Danny added.

"Stay here," Merrick repeated. Magic thrummed from his core, pulsing outward in waves, each stronger than the last. He sensed several presences outside now, all similar in the feel of their mana songs—each contained a burning core of rage, as animal as it was human.

"Please, be careful," said Adalynn. She looped her arm around his neck and pulled him into another quick but passionate kiss before releasing him.

"You two are lucky we have bigger problems," Danny said, "or I'd have a *lot* of questions for you right now."

Adalynn took the shotgun in both hands again. "Danny, grab that box of bullets and stay close."

Frowning, Danny bent down and scooped up the box. "*Shells.*"

"Shells?"

"Yeah. It's a shotgun, these are shells. You sure you don't want me to hold the gun?"

"No," Adalynn and Merrick replied in unison. They exchanged a brief, amused glance before Merrick turned away and walked to the balcony doors.

The bestial presences outside remained in place, giving off their unique resonances, which were more distinct now as Merrick willed his awareness of the ley line running beneath him to life. Though he only slightly opened himself to the ley line, its sound was more a roar than a song, at once harmonious and discordant, deafening and whisper-quiet, high pitched and low-rumbling.

Merrick opened the glass door and stepped onto the porch. Just before he closed it, he said over his shoulder, "Lock it behind me."

He turned his attention forward. The air, while not cold, had a crispness that hinted at the approach of fall. Insects made their soft night music beneath leaves gently rustled by the breeze, and his ears were sharp enough to pick up the sound of the brook running about a hundred yards to the manor's north. The gray haze blanketing the sky was more pronounced out here, but the moons—two primary halves that had once comprised the greater whole—shone through it, casting their unsettling, bone-yellow light on the world below.

And none of that mattered.

Merrick walked around the porch toward the back of his home. Once he rounded the corner and the back lawn was in sight, his gaze fell on the tall, powerful figures in the grass, staring up at him. Four werewolves—two males and two females, he guessed, as the former were larger and more broadly built. They were hybrids of human and wolf; they stood upright on two legs, their bodies were covered in fur, and their fingers were tipped with wicked claws. Their lupine eyes glowed yellow with reflected light.

He stopped and settled his hands on the railing. The werewolves were displaying more control than he'd thought possible from their kind. Before the Sundering, werewolves —like anything else humans considered supernatural—were exceedingly rare, and only appeared in this form during the full moon. The few he'd encountered had been ravening, bloodthirsty beasts, no more controlled than wild animals.

These werewolves, on the other hand, had intelligent gleams in their eyes—at least as intelligent as a human's.

"We've come for food and shelter," said the foremost wolf in a growling, guttural voice—but in perfect modern English, nonetheless.

"I'm afraid I've run out of hospitality for the millennium," Merrick replied. He held back the magic bristling within him, which intensified as the tension in the air thickened. "Come back in a thousand years. I ought to have replenished my stores of generosity by then."

"Let us in or we'll let ourselves in," a gray-furred female snarled, stepping forward with claws splayed.

"Be silent," the lead wolf said, snapping his jaws at the female.

She bared her teeth and growled but backed away, lowering her lupine snout.

The lead wolf—the alpha, most likely—returned his attention to Merrick. "We don't mean you any harm, but we *will* take what we need whether you cooperate or not. This is our territory."

"Strange," Merrick replied. "I must've missed the letter from the county explaining that they'd seized my land and sold it out from beneath me."

"Come down here, and we'll see how smug you are," said the gray female.

The other male and female—both brown furred—eased back a step.

"This place smells unnatural," the brown female said. "We should leave."

"The old rules don't matter anymore," the alpha said. "This land is ours now. It belongs to my pack. Accept that and cooperate, and we'll leave you in peace."

"More like *pieces*," the gray female said.

Adalynn's presence tingled on Merrick's back; she was still inside his bedroom, but sensing her was a powerful drive for him—it enhanced his protective instinct and meant the wolves' threats sparked greater rage within him. A threat to Merrick's home was a threat to Adalynn and Danny—because Merrick and the manor were what would keep those two humans safe in this dangerous new world.

Though he was outnumbered, though the wolves were physically stronger, faster, and tougher, Merrick would not tolerate threats. Especially not threats to his Adalynn.

Merrick drew in a deep, slow breath and opened his conduit to the ley line a little more. Its song increased in strength, and its power—infinite and unfathomable—trickled into him, making the hairs on his arms stand on end.

"Where's your remaining companion?" Merrick asked, reaching outward with invisible tendrils of magic to seek the animalistic resonance of the fifth wolf—*five* had broken his wards—but he couldn't look very far in that manner without shifting his full attention to the task.

Clearly, it was a skill he'd have to improve upon over the years to come.

With Adalynn at my side throughout.

The alpha shook his head from side to side and snorted. The other werewolves exchanged questioning glances.

"Scouting ahead," the alpha replied.

Wispy, ethereal clouds drifted in front of the moons, further diffusing the light and deepening the darkness beneath the trees bordering the lawn. It seemed a fitting precursor to what was likely about to happen.

"Disrespect, threats, *and* lies." Merrick tightened his grip on the railing. He'd been wrong for all those years—the flaws and shortcomings he'd attributed to humankind were evident in people of all species. To think human cruelty was unique had been a mistake. "You've failed to ingratiate yourself to your would-be host."

Merrick vaulted over the railing. He slowed himself with a release of magic just before his feet touched the ground, landing easily in the grass while remaining upright.

The wolves recoiled slightly, nostrils flaring; whether they'd seen or sensed his magic, they'd *noticed* it.

Good.

For once, Merrick wanted it to be known that, despite his appearance, he was anything but human—and that these wolves did not intimidate him.

This was an unquestionably risky move; he was outmatched physically, and he doubted the more aggressive pair of wolves would be dissuaded by his display of bravado, but at the very least it meant he'd be able to steer the fighting away from the house—away from Adalynn and Daniel.

"See yourselves off my land," Merrick said, "and I'll leave each of *you* in one piece."

Keeping his yellow eyes on Merrick, the alpha lowered his snout and peeled his lips back, baring his fangs.

"So we kill him and take it all anyway," the gray female said.

The alpha grunted. Somehow, the sound echoed what he'd said before—*the old rules don't matter anymore.*

Merrick wrenched open his connection to the ley line. Magic, rawer and more powerful than he'd ever felt, surged through him, suffusing his entire being. The heat within him built to a near unbearable degree—but it could not match the heat of his anger.

"Kill him," the alpha growled.

Merrick swept his arm in a wide arc, unleashing a wave of unshaped magical energy.

The front wolves, who'd been mid-leap already, were struck head-on. The energy swept back their fur for a fraction of a second before it blasted them both backward. Despite their size, the wolves flipped end-over-end in a pair of arcs that saw them crash down only a few yards away from the garden hedge.

Using that power was a thrill; it came effortlessly, without depleting Merrick's magic, without drawing from his own energy. Heady as it was, he recognized the danger of it—this power would destroy him if he tapped into it too fully. But he *had* to use it. This was the surest way to keep Adalynn and her brother safe. No risk was too great to protect them.

And the ley line offered more than just raw magical energy. Merrick's senses were opened wide, expanded beyond reason—he was acutely aware of the mana songs, no matter how faint, of *everything* around him, even the blades of grass, the tiny pebbles, the dirt under his feet and the worms burrowing through it. He held those senses in check. He knew instinctually that, should he choose to, he could expand that awareness to any point along the line. That he could sense *everything* along its entirety.

He also knew that to do so would mean losing himself— his *self*—forever.

The alpha and the gray female staggered to their feet and shook away their disorientation. Faint wisps of smoke rose from their fur. The brown werewolves had retreated several feet from their original positions, eyes wide and breath ragged.

"For the pack," the alpha snarled.

Those words seemed to jar the reluctant pair. Their features hardened, and they moved in unison with their companions, fanning out to form a wide half-circle in front of Merrick. Though they hung nearly ten yards back, Merrick didn't lower his guard; they could close that distance incredibly fast if they chose to do so.

He didn't intend to give them that chance.

He acted without allowing himself another moment's thought, lashing out with invisible magic coils to latch onto the sources of the various mana songs around him—clumps of grass and the far-reaching roots of trees older than the house behind him. As one, the wolves' hackles rose. Their fur shone in the blue glow Merrick was emitting, which was cast by the magic coursing freely over his skin like dancing forks of lightning, brighter and more intense than ever before. He forced energy through his connections with those plants, altering their resonances, amplifying them.

Merrick swept his arms upward, and the grass and roots surged from the ground, growing and expanding in the blink of an eye. They writhed and whipped like angry tentacles, grabbing at the wolves.

The werewolves reacted with superhuman speed, but it wasn't enough; they only managed a few feet before the magic-infused vegetation caught all four of them, halting their advance. The wolves snarled and struggled, snapped and growled, shredding the plants with fangs and claws. Their strength and ferocity saw them gradually gaining ground.

"What is he?" asked the gray female.

"Doesn't matter," the alpha replied. "He's about to be dead."

Merrick split his focus, pouring magic into his hands to form pulsing spheres of raw energy. His hold on the plants slipped slightly. The alpha lunged forward, gaining a full two yards before a thick root coiled around his neck and stopped him.

The alpha roared. The powerful sound swept over Merrick—it was so primal, so rage-filled, that it sparked a hint of fear deep in his gut. Merrick cast that aside; he would not let fear consume him, would not let himself be afraid of these brutish creatures who'd come to take what was his, to threaten his home, his *woman*.

The fury that had already been stoked in Merrick erupted. He let out a roar of his own—it rumbled with magic, quaked with rage, thundered with protectiveness, possessiveness, and love—and unleashed the magic from his hands.

Blue-white energy sprayed from his palms and ignited the magic-enhanced vegetation, enveloping the wolves in a blinding column of raw power. He knew immediately it would not be enough; the grass and roots disintegrated within a second, but the werewolves were made of tougher stuff than that. Freed of their bindings, they all leapt clear of the supernatural blaze, crashing to the ground to the left and right of the blast zone—all but the gray female, who leapt directly at Merrick.

She emerged from the blaze with singed, smoking fur and raw burns all over her body, but her eyes were bright and filled with bestial fury. Her black claws, each more than an inch long, gleamed in the light of his magic. They could rend Merrick's flesh as easily as a razor could slice a sheet of paper.

And *immortal* did not mean *invulnerable*.

Merrick released his hold on the magic and jumped aside. The wolf soared past him, her claws opening a set of shallow gashes on his shoulder as she twisted to account for his movement. Hot blood trickled down his arm, seeping ethereal blue wisps of magic, as he turned to face her.

She hit the ground hard, rolled, and sprang back to her feet. Smoke wafted from her damaged body, but her wounds —despite their severity—showed signs of healing right before his eyes.

Apparently, the werewolves' already accelerated healing factor had only been enhanced by the Sundering.

Her gaze met Merrick's, and she leapt forward to attack again.

Through the ley line, Merrick sensed the other wolves

moving, but he didn't look away from the charging female. He lifted both arms and shaped his magic into solid, pointed shafts—like spears of glowing blue glass—and extended the weapons out from his palms.

The points struck the female in the chest and burst out her back. Her momentum carried her along the shafts, closer to Merrick, with arms and legs thrashing wildly and jaws snapping.

Merrick growled and channeled magic through the spears —magic directly from the ley line. The surge of unbridled energy tensed his every muscle and resonated through his bones, threatening not merely to drown out his mana song but to unravel it entirely. He held on, wrapping himself in a cocoon of willpower and fury to maintain his assault.

The magic flared inside the wolf. She opened her jaws wide and released a cry that was part agonized scream and part bloodthirsty roar. Her flesh split and cracked; arcane energies poured out of the widening wounds.

In his mind's eye, Merrick saw the other werewolves advancing, their forms depicted in the flickering crimson of their mana songs.

The female wolf shattered, the pieces breaking smaller and smaller until nothing of her body remained. The magic snuffed out, and the glass-like spears dissipated. The alpha howled in rage and grief, a sound that pierced Merrick but could not give him pause; he'd offered them a chance to resolve this situation in a different way. This was *their* choice.

Merrick clenched his jaw and squeezed down on his connection with the ley line, struggling to stifle some of that dangerous flow. It was only as he spun to face the remaining werewolves that he felt what he'd originally sought—the fifth intruder, who had just entered the range of Merrick's magical senses.

Another wolf, at the north end of the manor—the same side as Merrick's bedroom.

Fear reintroduced itself to Merrick, cold and slithering through his insides, but it wasn't fear of the wolves or for his own safety—this was fear for Adalynn, for Danny. For the only precious things Merrick had to lose.

All three of the wolves in front of him attacked.

Merrick folded himself in magic and twisted his mana song, phasing his physical body into a different state. For an instant, he was only energy, was only the magic he'd always harbored within himself, and the mana song of the ley line became deafening.

Join me, it sang. *Become one with me. Become power.*

Slashing claws and gnashing teeth swept through the space his physical body had occupied. He felt them only distantly, as though they were the phantom caresses of ghostly entities. The wolves' muscular bodies collided. Merrick forced his incorporeal form aside. He flowed through the air effortlessly, but something pulled him farther along than he'd intended, pulled him *down*.

One with the power, whispered the ley line.

The notion was tempting. He could be a part of the lifeblood of magic, could flow in its source, could cast aside all his worries, all his bitterness, all his pain. Even now, he could feel his concerns falling away, could feel his form growing lighter and more indistinct even as the ley line's magnetic draw strengthened.

Adalynn.

Her name jolted through him, and he latched onto it. Merrick couldn't go—Adalynn needed him, and he needed her.

Merrick cast off the ley line's call and willed himself *back*, rematerializing his physical body a few feet away from the confused wolves. A shudder ran through him from head to toe, and his muscles tensed, each threatening to cramp at once. Piercing pain, as sharp as a knife, lodged itself deep in his skull.

Best not attempt that *again.*

Despite their initial confusion, the wolves spun toward him quickly; the brown-furred pair were closest. They lunged together, one to each side of Merrick, and he had no choice but to backpedal frantically to avoid their claws.

With a growl, he thrust another blast outward. The force of it lifted the brown wolves off their feet and high into the air. Before they could fall, he wrapped them both in invisible clouds of magic, halting them in midair, where they hovered in place, slowly spinning—too high up to reach the ground.

Another of Merrick's wards broke—the ward to the balcony doors leading into his bedroom—accompanied by the sound of shattering glass.

Merrick's heart seized, and for an instant, he couldn't even feel his magic anymore. All that remained were his feelings for Adalynn—his love for her, his need to protect her.

The alpha charged in Merrick's moment of hesitation.

A gunshot boomed in the bedroom and echoed across the night sky.

Huge, black claws sliced through the air an inch from Merrick's face. He staggered back from the wolf, whose jaws snapped close enough to Merrick's throat for him to feel spittle splatter his skin. He'd only barely managed to keep the other two wolves aloft in his sudden fear; his concentration was still too jarred to mount any meaningful defense now.

The sound of Adalynn's terrified scream—"Merrick!"— from inside the bedroom sharpened his focus instantly.

A fresh surge of power flowed through Merrick—not the ley line's power, but his own, drawn from somewhere deep inside that he'd been unaware of before that moment. The alpha's claws raked across Merrick's chest, but he didn't feel any pain, not even distantly. He was beyond that now.

Crackling blue energy coalesced around Merrick's hands and spread upward to sheathe his arms, intensifying the light he emitted. He lashed out with his left hand, catching the alpha's extended arm at the elbow. The magic flared, shifting closer to white than blue, and Merrick's fingers sank into the wolf's suddenly sizzling flesh. The alpha growled in pain. Before the wolf could retaliate, Merrick thrust his other hand forward, unleashing a raw burst of concentrated magic that flowed out in a wide, short cone.

When the light faded, the upper left half of the alpha's torso was gone—including most of his head. The body fell aside, landing heavily on the charred ground. Merrick poured more power into the corpse, blasting it to dust within a few seconds. He couldn't risk it getting back up again.

Need to get to her…

He glanced up at the remaining wolves, who were hovering ten feet off the ground. The threat to Adalynn was more immediate; these two weren't worth the time or energy it would take to dispatch them right now—but he couldn't risk losing hold of the magic keeping them aloft.

Merrick focused on the mana song of the dirt; it was a simple thing to alter it and make the ground intangible, no more solid than a ghost, as malleable as water. He released the magic holding the brown wolves in the same instant.

They dropped into the ground; Merrick returned the dirt to its solid state when only their heads were still above ground level. He willed the dirt to pack tight, as solid as stone, creating a rock-like prison around the wolves as he ran toward the house.

Coming, Adalynn. Hold on.

Chapter Twelve

The sounds from outside—bestial, preternatural snarls, growls, and roars, and strange *whooshing* noises almost like bursts of flame—were terrifying, but Adalynn couldn't help looking. Merrick was out there *alone*, facing down a pack of werewolves; she had to know he was still okay. She peeled back a curtain to peek out into the back yard.

Fiery blue energy—Merrick's magic—had scorched a huge patch of the lawn, but the wolves were still alive, still moving. She couldn't see Merrick due to the angle and the balcony in the way. Her fear mounted with each passing second, and her heart lodged in her throat.

Just a glimpse of him. That's all I need. That's all I need to see to know he's all right.

"What's going on?" Danny asked. "Is he okay?"

Adalynn knew Danny was trying to be brave, trying to be strong, but there was a slight tremor in his voice.

She looked at her brother over her shoulder. "He'll be fine. *We'll* be fine. He's…powerful."

Danny's features hardened, and he nodded.

A sense of pride filled her at the sight of her brother's

resolve, but it wasn't without a touch of sadness—he shouldn't have been forced to grow up in a world like this.

She turned back toward the window, and crippling terror seized her muscles. Glowing amber eyes stared at her through the windowpane—a *werewolf's* eyes. The wolf's lips drew back in a predatory grin, baring sharp fangs.

"Danny, go! Hide!" Adalynn cried as she stumbled back, releasing the curtain. It fell, obscuring her view of the beast.

Heavy footsteps sounded along the balcony, moving around the corner and stopping at the glass doors leading out. The thin line of light below the long curtains was suddenly blocked out. The doors rattled violently.

Adalynn's breath hitched. She raised the shotgun.

The balcony doors exploded inward with a cacophony of shattering glass and snapping wood, the shards glittering momentarily in the faint moonlight that streamed in through the opening. The werewolf was huge—he had to duck to fit through the doorway, and his shoulders were almost as wide as the double-door entry. But despite his size, he moved with lightning speed.

Adalynn pulled the trigger. The shotgun boomed, and the butt kicked back, slamming against her shoulder, but she was too scared to feel any pain.

The werewolf darted aside; Adalynn's shot hit the upper doorframe, blasting a chunk out of it.

"Merrick!" she screamed. She tugged the shotgun's grip back, ejecting the spent shell.

With another powerful leap, the werewolf was in front of her. Before she could finish pumping the weapon, he grabbed its barrel—it looked tiny in his massive fist—and tore it out of her grasp, tossing it aside. His other hand lashed out and wrapped around her throat. He lifted her off the floor like she weighed nothing and slammed her back into the wall.

Choking, Adalynn clawed at his hand and forearm in a desperate but meaningless battle against his hold.

"What've we got here?" the werewolf rumbled. He leaned his face closer, stuck his snout into her hair—close to her ear—and inhaled deep. A low, hungry growl rose from his chest. "You smell like sex." He loosened his grip on Adalynn's neck just enough for her to draw breath.

Adalynn dug her fingernails into his hand. "Let me go."

The beast laughed—the sound was oddly raspy—giving her a whiff of his breath; there was metallic hint to it, reminiscent of blood. "When I'm done with you, woman."

He licked her cheek, neck, and chin before shifting closer to settle his other hand on her thigh—her *bare* thigh. It was then that Adalynn realized the robe she was wearing had parted. His thickly calloused palm slid higher, but it didn't hold her attention for long; something else grazed her inner thigh, something hot and thick that nonetheless sent horrified chills up her spine.

Releasing a growl of her own, Adalynn simultaneously slammed her fist into the side of the werewolf's head and rammed her knee into his groin. She opened her fingers to grasp the fur near the wolf's ear and tug it sharply.

The werewolf grunted, swatted her hand away, and retightened his grip on her neck. "Lively one. I like that. But you're gonna have to learn your place, bitch."

Adalynn continued her struggles, kicking, clawing, and hitting the werewolf, but it only seemed to arouse him further. When he finally released her neck, she fell to the floor, her legs crumpling beneath her. She sucked in several deep, gasping breaths. A second later, pain stabbed across her scalp as he grabbed her hair and dragged her away from the wall, forcing her onto her hands and knees.

Realization of what he intended to do struck her hard.

"No!" she cried, turning, drawing back her foot, and kicking the beast's chest. It was like kicking a brick wall—the wolf didn't budge. Adalynn managed only to scoot herself back on the floor a foot or two, pulling her robe taut beneath her. She flipped over and crawled away, but the werewolf caught her ankle and dragged her back beneath him.

His weight pressed down on her back. "I'm gonna get off whether you fight or not," the wolf growled, "but it'll hurt a lot more for you if you don't knock it off."

"Get away from my sister, you fucking asshole!"

Adalynn's throat constricted, and everything within her stilled, frozen in icy terror.

No, no, no. No! Danny was supposed to go!

Adalynn turned her head to see her brother charging the wolf, his ridiculous bowie knife raised overhead. His lips were pulled back in a snarl that bared his teeth, and his face was contorted with more hatred and rage than she'd ever thought possible from him.

Danny brought the knife down, plunging it into the werewolf's back.

The beast snarled and reared back, dragging Danny—who clung to his knife with furious desperation—along with him as he swung around, lashing out to reach for the boy. Danny grabbed a fistful of the werewolf's fur, pulled his knife out, and stabbed the beast again.

"Danny!" Adalynn cried, scrambling out from beneath the wolf.

One of the werewolf's groping hands caught Danny's shirt. The beast plucked the boy off his back like he was pulling an insect from his fur and threw the boy across the room. Danny hit the wall and fell to the floor in a heap.

The wolf stalked toward Danny. "You little shit, you're gonna pay for that!"

Adalynn pushed herself up to her feet and lunged at the werewolf. She grasped fistfuls of fur on his back and forearm, planted her feet on the floor, and wrenched back with all her strength. "Leave him alone. Don't you fucking touch him!"

He shook her off effortlessly. Adalynn stumbled backward and fell, landing hard on her backside.

"I'll deal with you in a minute, little bitch," the werewolf said.

Gritting her teeth, Adalynn braced her hands on the floor to either side, meaning to get back up. She paused when her fingers brushed something cold and hard. She turned her head to see the shotgun on the floor next to her.

Slapping her hand down on top of the weapon, she picked it up, swung it around, aimed it at the werewolf's torso. She slid the grip forward, producing a loud *click* as a new shell loaded into the chamber. "I *said*, leave him alone, *dog*."

The werewolf spun around. His reflective eyes flared, and he opened his toothy mouth wide to release a roar. Adalynn pulled the trigger just as he leapt off the floor. His roar died in a snarl of pain as the shot struck him in the groin, shredding his flesh and spraying blood on the floor.

Adalynn rolled aside as the wolf crashed down nearby. She shifted the shotgun and tugged the grip down to eject the spent shell.

"You fucking cunt," the werewolf wheezed, pushing himself up from the floor and cupping his bloody groin. He grimaced and snarled before launching himself at her again.

Adalynn braced for the impact, for the inevitable pain, tightening her grip on the shotgun. She wouldn't get it reloaded in time, wouldn't be able to get another shot off— and she didn't think it would make a difference even if she could.

A blast of roiling blue, fire-like energy struck the werewolf with enough force to lift him off the floor and send him crashing into the wall. The plaster cracked and crumbled, and wood snapped inside the wall itself. Adalynn flicked her gaze to the open doors.

Merrick stood in the open doorway, his body wreathed in crackling blue energy that both flowed like fire and scintillated like electricity. It burned in his eyes, and wisps of it poured from the claw wounds on his arm and chest. Behind that energy was a darkness far too deep to be natural, from which shadowy tendrils writhed and whipped.

Adalynn dropped the gun and crawled across the floor toward her brother. She swept her hands over him quickly but gently, checking for wounds. Danny groaned and opened his eyes. Adalynn helped him sit up; he seemed unsteady even in that position.

Danny's eyes rounded as they fell on Merrick. "Oh *shit*."

Those two words sent a wave of relief through her.

Adalynn clutched the sides of her robe together and turned to look at Merrick.

The wolf struggled to get up. Merrick stalked across the room, trailing blue energy and star-flecked shadow behind him, and stopped to stand over the beast. With a grunt, the werewolf lashed out and buried the claws of both hands in Merrick's sides.

Merrick didn't flinch, didn't make so much as the slightest sound of pain. He clamped his hands on the sides of the werewolf's head. The energy sheathing Merrick flared, and the shadows swarmed around it, swept *through* it, to envelop the werewolf and pierce him with their tendrils.

The brightness intensified; Adalynn turned toward her brother and squeezed her eyes shut, throwing her body over Danny to shield him. The light was so bright she could see it through her eyelids, even while facing away. The only means she had of marking the passage of time were her own rapid, thumping heartbeats, which were too fast to count.

When the light finally faded, Adalynn straightened and opened her eyes, blinking to rid them of the dark afterimages skittering across her vision. She looked at Merrick over her shoulder.

He was standing over a pile of ash that had been the wolf only moments before. A thin, slowly dissipating cloud of ash hung in the air in front of him. Though the magic on his skin had faded from its height, it still crackled and pulsed like constantly shifting veins in a marble sculpture, casting a blue glow throughout the room. He turned his head to look at her, and his eyes burned a little brighter.

Adalynn turned toward Merrick as he walked over to her.

He sank into a crouch in front of her. There was fury on his face, but also a strange hint of wariness and uncertainty. He reached for her, but stopped before he touched her, lowering his hand. "Are you two all right?"

Adalynn launched herself at him, throwing her arms around his neck to embrace him tightly. Somehow, she *knew* the magic flowing around him, over him, and through him would never hurt her. That magic whispered over her and permeated her body as she touched him; it *sang* to her.

Merrick wrapped his arms around her and held her just as tightly. His magic made her skin tingle in the most delightful way; it brought her every nerve ending to life despite all that had just happened.

"Wow," Danny said, his voice strained. "You obliterated him."

Drawing back from Adalynn, Merrick flicked his gaze between her and her brother. "Are you okay? Are either of you hurt?"

Adalynn shook her head. "Just some bruises. It would have been worse, but you got here in time."

He raised a hand, settled it on her cheek, and brushed his thumb across her skin. "It was too close. I should've just stayed with you."

"You didn't know." She looked down at his body and gently touched the skin just below the glowing claw marks on his chest. "What about you? You're...not bleeding, but you're hurt."

"I am fine, Adalynn. I will heal." He took hold of her wrist and guided her hand away. "There are two more outside

I have to deal with. Grab the shotgun and stick close to me."
His eyes flicked to Danny again. "Both of you."

Knowing that there were still more werewolves nearby
sent a fresh jolt of fear up her spine, but Adalynn nodded and
went to retrieve the gun. On her way, she pulled the sides of
her robe together and tied it tight.

Once she had the shotgun in hand, Merrick led them into
the hallway. His magic gave everything an ethereal blue glow
as they walked along the silent corridor and descended the
spiral stairs. Adalynn might've thought this place haunted had
she seen a light like his when she'd first arrived.

Danny kept close to Adalynn's side throughout, and she
walked only a couple feet behind Merrick, unwilling to get any
farther from him than that. They walked into the kitchen and
through the back door, stepping onto the porch.

The devastation wrought by his magic was even more
apparent from this closer vantage. A wide swath of the back
lawn—at least ten yards across in all directions—was scorched
to ash and dirt. Half of a tree had been in the blast zone, and
was now a charred mess with faint blue energy glowing
through the cracks, a harsh contrast to the other half that was,
for now, still green and alive.

Merrick led them to the wide steps and down onto the
lawn. As they walked forward, movement ahead—at ground
level—caught Adalynn's attention. Her eyes widened as she
realized what she was staring at.

Two werewolves, both with brown fur, were *in* the ground,
only their heads visible. They were buried up to their cheeks,
their eyes wide with fear and their breaths shallow and ragged.

"Whoa…" Danny said.

Adalynn seconded that sentiment.

Merrick strode up to the wolves and crouched in front of
them. "I found the last member of your group." He slapped
his hands on his pants, producing a small cloud of dust.

206

Not dust. Ash.

The smaller of the two werewolves sputtered and coughed as she breathed in the ash.

"I suppose that makes one woman he got inside tonight," Merrick said.

Adalynn looked at Merrick. For all the hardness he'd shown her and her brother when they first arrived here, he'd never sounded so cold, so callous, so unforgiving as he did in that moment. She realized then that Merrick really *was* a monster. He was dangerous, and his power was terrifying. But he was *her* monster. She knew he'd never hurt her and Danny —because there was a *man* within that monster, and that man had given himself to her.

"So, who here feels the burning need to avenge their fallen comrades?" Merrick asked. The energy around his hands intensified, casting long shadows behind the wolves' heads.

Their eyes widened farther, bright with reflections of his magic.

"We submit," the male said, lowering his snout as far as possible and averting his gaze.

"Please," the female replied. "We…we didn't want this."

The male nodded—at least as best as he could. "My sister and I joined this pack for protection, that's all. To survive, not to kill people."

Adalynn clutched the gun against her chest. Her eyes flicked to Danny. She understood the driving need to protect the ones you love, understood the need to do *anything* to keep them safe.

Merrick glanced back at Adalynn over his shoulder, his brow low over the one glowing eye she could see. He turned back to the wolves.

"Please," the female said, "Colin is gone, and we don't have ties to any of the others. The pack is dissolved."

"I cannot tolerate any threats to *my* pack," Merrick

growled as he stood up. "I gave you all a chance to leave. Now this must end." He lifted his hands, and spheres of blue fire sparked into existence on his palms.

Adalynn closed the distance between herself and Merrick and placed a hand on his back. "Merrick, stop."

She felt the energy radiating from him, felt its vibrations, sensed the dissonance in his mystical song, which raged faster and stronger now than ever before. The black, shadowy tentacles which writhed around him shuddered and calmed, dropping to caress her arm.

Once again, he looked at her over his shoulder. This time he didn't turn away.

"Let them go," she said.

"After all that's happened, Adalynn? They are a threat."

Her attention shifted to the werewolves. The female met Adalynn's gaze, eyes desperate, sad, and pleading, glimmering with a hint of hope. This female and her brother were just like Adalynn and Danny.

Adalynn looked at Merrick and slid her fingers up his back to rest on his shoulder as she moved closer to him. His shadowy tendrils embraced her, and she welcomed their feel. "They're people. They got caught up with someone bad, but they're just *people*. They're just trying to survive, same as everyone else."

He released a heavy exhalation and pressed his lips into a tight line. Adalynn saw the struggle on his face, could almost *hear* it in the song of his magic. And she understood. His dilemma was a clear—what was best for *his* people? If he let these wolves go, would they return later and cause more trouble? Would they come back with *more* of their kind to seek revenge?

Right now, all she could see in the wolves' faces was fear. That *could* turn to anger and resentment, but she didn't believe it would in this case. She believed what the wolves had said.

"Let them go, Merrick," she repeated, softer, before pressing her lips to his shoulder.

Some of the tension in his body eased, and the energy radiating from him diminished. He curled his fingers, and, after a few seconds, the magic around his hands wavered and changed. It went from flamelike to fluidlike, shifting and wobbling in the air like oil in water.

The ground rumbled, and then it, too, rippled like the surface of a lake. Eyes wide, Adalynn stared as the wolves rose out of the ground as though riding an unseen elevator. Once they were fully free, the ground solidified, but the wolves kept rising until they were at least five feet above the ground.

"You've seen what happens to those who trespass and threaten me," Merrick said. "Leave my land. If you come back, you'll wind up like your fellows—and I will use your ashes to fertilize my crops. Do you understand?"

The werewolves whined and nodded quickly.

"We swear," said the male.

Merrick lowered his arms, and the wolves dropped along with them, crashing onto the ground mere feet away from him. "You have thirty seconds before I change my mind again."

They scrambled to their feet. The male ran, but the female hesitated, her gaze flickering between Merrick and Adalynn.

"Thank you," she said before following her brother, who had paused at the edge of the woods.

The werewolves were gone a moment later, vanished amid the darkness between the trees.

That quickly, the tension left Adalynn's limbs, and she lowered the gun to the ground. She could feel every bump and bruise she'd suffered, every hurt; the pain had been swept aside by terror and adrenaline.

She shifted her attention to Merrick. The magic around

him faded until all that remained of it was a lingering afterimage, which itself was gone in a few seconds.

He turned to face her. His wounds were already sealed—in fact, they looked like they'd been healing for two or three weeks—and his eyes still glowed blue. "We should get back inside. I'll tend to this mess tomorrow."

Adalynn stepped up to him, cupped his cheeks, guided his head down, and kissed him. She pressed her mouth hard against his, tasting the magic on his skin. It tingled on her lips, as arousing as it was soothing.

Merrick submitted to her kiss, but his body was tense, as though he were holding himself back. She didn't want him to. She didn't care about what he was, didn't care about her own pain; all she wanted was to feel his arms around her, to feel *him*—all of him—alive and well, against her, holding her.

She met his gaze when she pulled away. "Thank you."

The hardness that dominated his features since he'd woken her smoothed away. His tongue slipped out and flicked over his lips. "For what?"

"Everything."

"Gross," Danny said from behind her. "Dude. Are you having sex with my *sister*?"

Adalynn's cheeks warmed, and she pressed her lips together in a failed attempt to contain the laughter bubbling up within her. She dropped her hands to Merrick's shoulders and let her head fall against his chest as she quietly chuckled.

Merrick slipped his arms around her and held her close. "It's well past your bedtime, young Daniel. I think it's time we remedied that."

"Oh, no way. I am not a little kid," Danny replied. "I think I have the right to know what your intentions are. She's my sister."

"And you're what, ten, eleven? Ask again in twenty years and we'll decide if you're mature enough to know."

"Dude, I'm thirteen! And I stabbed a werewolf tonight! I think I'm mature enough."

"And I *killed* three werewolves, dude. You have a way to go, I think."

"That's not the point. What are you planning on doing with my sister?"

Adalynn glanced up at Merrick, who shook his head and rolled his eyes.

"You do realize, Daniel, that it is incredibly rude and inappropriate to be asking those questions of a lady?" Merrick said. "Especially your sister."

"Nope. Don't care," Danny said. "And stop sounding so *old*."

Adalynn stepped away from Merrick. She felt his hesitation, but he released her, his arms falling to his sides. She turned toward her brother. Danny wore a very unhappy frown on his face, his expression a blend of upset and frustration.

Her heart ached. She walked over to him and enfolded him in her arms. He hugged her back without delay.

"Danny, I'm old enough to make decisions for myself. You don't need to worry about me." She pulled her head back and met his gaze as she lowered her voice to a whisper, though she knew Merrick would likely hear her anyway. "You trust him, right?"

Danny glanced at Merrick over her shoulder. "Yeah."

"Then you have nothing to worry about, because I trust him too."

Danny shuffled his bare foot in the dirt, looking down for a moment. "Do you like him?"

"Of course I like him."

"No, I mean, do you *like* him like him?"

Adalynn's breath caught. It was strange that a phrase like that—one she probably hadn't heard since she was about Danny's age—could cut so directly to the core of what she felt. Just the thought of Merrick made her heart quicken and her body react, filling her with the need to be close to him, to feel him, to touch him and be touched by him in return. Her *soul* called out to him.

But those weren't things she could admit out loud—not to Danny, and most especially not to Merrick. Those feelings were hers to harbor. Because despite the intensity of those feelings…she hadn't really come to understand them yet. She didn't know how deep they ran, or what they *really* meant.

And because she was dying. She didn't want to encourage anything more than a physical relationship with Merrick, didn't want him to get so involved that he'd be crushed when the inevitable came to pass. But she couldn't stop what she already felt for him—and she would embrace it, cherish it, and cling to it for as long as she could.

She smiled softly. "Yeah, I *like* him like him."

"Okay, well…just don't let me hear or see anything, okay?" His face screwed up in an exaggerated a look of disgust. "I'm not a fan of puking."

Adalynn chuckled, pecked a kiss on his cheek, and released him before turning back to Merrick. There was a smirk on his lips, and though it was a tender expression, it could not conceal the mixture of relief and concern lingering in his still-glowing eyes.

"If you vomit on my floor, Daniel, you'll be sleeping outside for the foreseeable future," Merrick said.

"Can't you just"— Danny waved his hand vaguely— "*magic* it away? And don't you know it's *rude* to eavesdrop?"

"It's a bit difficult not to overhear when you're standing five feet away, and it doesn't matter whether I can *magic it away*. I don't want my floors soiled. They've been pristine for a century, and I don't need a ten-year-old mucking them up."

"Bet you don't care if Addy does," Danny muttered.

"I would rather she not," Merrick replied, "but for entirely different reasons." He gestured at the house. "Now let's get inside before anything else slithers out of the night to say hello."

Danny sighed and turned toward the manor. "Gotta admit, though…you were pretty cool, Merrick. You're like a badass superhero."

Merrick leaned down to pick up the shotgun. "I'm just going to assume all that was a compliment." He led them back up the porch steps, opened the door to the kitchen, and stood aside, looking at Adalynn. "We can move into one of the guest bedrooms for the rest of the night. I will repair the master bedroom in the morning."

Danny released a dramatic sigh and moved ahead of Adalynn, walking past Merrick and into the house.

"*We?*" Adalynn stopped just inside the kitchen, glancing at Danny as he turned into the hallway.

Merrick stepped through the doorway and tugged the door closed behind him, pausing directly in front of her, leaving barely a few inches of space between them. "I would prefer to have you back in my bed, but I fear there'd be something of a draft in there tonight."

Adalynn lifted her hand and lightly ran her fingertips over the new scars on his chest. "So, you want me to sleep with you?"

She wanted to be back in his arms, lying next to him, feeling his hands and lips on her skin; she wanted more than anything for him to erase the memory of the werewolf's touch with his own.

He leaned slightly closer. Even though magic no longer pulsed along his skin, he still radiated that thrilling power. "Is that not what we were doing before this interruption?"

"I just…didn't know, now that we're awake, and we're not…you know?" The heat in her cheeks intensified.

"You think I would use you for pleasure and set you aside?" He took hold of her wrist and guided it to his chest, flattening her palm over his heart. "What we've shared runs *much* deeper than that, Adalynn."

I know.

She wanted to say those words aloud but couldn't; her throat constricted around them. Instead, she slid her free hand up into his hair and pulled him toward her while rising on her toes to kiss him. She let her lips convey what she felt as they caressed and nipped his, and, when he opened his mouth to return the kiss fully, fervently, she used her tongue.

His mouth covered hers hungrily. He set the shotgun on the counter behind Adalynn and slid his arms around her, seizing control of the kiss. He kissed her with a soul-searing desperation that left her breathless and needy. His hands roamed over her, sliding down to her ass. He cupped her backside, pulling her against him, against the hardness of his erection; she was separated from it only by his pants. Desire burned in her core and flooded her veins, and her inner thighs slickened with arousal.

Merrick groaned appreciatively. He broke the kiss and rasped, "Guess we're not going to your bedroom."

Adalynn opened her eyes and met his glowing gaze. "No. Here. Now. I need you now."

He grinned and tightened his grip on her ass, lifting her and sitting her on the edge of the counter. Moving quickly, he reached between them, released his cock from the confines of his pants, shoved her legs apart, and thrust inside her.

Adalynn gasped, her eyelids fluttering but not closing, as Merrick's power—that song from his soul—arced into her. She slid her arms around him, clutching at his back as he pushed deeper into her, stretching her. His way was made easier by her wetness, her arousal. Clasping her hips, he pulled back and thrust into her again, burying himself completely inside her.

Perfect. This is perfect.

She raised her knees and wrapped her legs around him,

wanting to hold him inside her forever. She longed to be in this moment forever, hearing their songs intertwine, feeling *him* through this magical connection they shared.

Merrick tilted his head back as he bared his teeth and growled. His features were contorted with agony—the agony of longing, of yet-unfulfilled desire, of pleasure already building beyond what one person could bear. Blue trails of energy blazed along his arms and flared in his eyes, and the air behind him darkened as his supernatural shadows coalesced.

The shadowy tentacles swept forward and brushed over Adalynn's skin, their touch at once cool and electric, soothing and thrilling. When one of them slipped between her legs to stroke her clit, pleasure shot straight through Adalynn. She cried out and undulated her pelvis against Merrick.

He groaned deep in his throat and moved his hips, pulling back and pushing forward repeatedly in a quickening rhythm. The slide of his hard cock sent waves of bliss through her that only built in intensity with his momentum. He kept one hand on her backside, holding her exactly where he wanted her as he pounded into her. He tore open her robe with his other hand.

Leaning his face forward, he cupped her breast in his palm and squeezed it, kneaded it, and pinched her nipple to send sharp jolts of pleasure-pain right to her core.

"Ah, Adalynn," Merrick rasped. His lips roamed over her chin, her jaw, and her throat before moving to her mouth. "You are *mine*, and I will keep you no matter what we face. I will *never* let you go."

Then his mouth claimed hers as punishingly as he'd claimed her body. He devoured Adalynn, consumed her, and she was enveloped by his magic as spirals of ecstasy rushed through her. She succumbed to it, to *him*, and she soared higher and higher, her cries muffled by his kiss. Her nails bit into his back as she tried to draw him closer. She couldn't get enough; she needed *more*.

His dark tentacles caressed her, leaving no place untouched as Merrick surged in and out of her, pounding harder and harder, deeper and deeper, each thrust producing a burst of pleasure that created a maelstrom of sensation deep inside her, coiling tight around her center.

Suddenly, that intense pleasure unfolded within her, and she reached her peak. Her body shuddered, locking tight, as she was racked by powerful spasms. Every muscle quivered, and her sex clamped around his cock.

Merrick's climax came on the heels of hers. He arched his back as he tensed, and with a final thrust, buried himself deep inside her. His magic surged in time with the eruption of hot seed within her, its intensified thrum engulfing her from head to toe and rocketing her to another orgasm. Merrick growled out his pleasure and shifted his hips in erratic motions, pushing the two of them just a little further.

As the urgency of their lovemaking faded, Adalynn sagged in his arms, pressing her face against his neck. She panted softly, breathing in his scent—leather and cedar. Sweat slick-ened their skin, and she could feel both his seed and her wetness seeping out of her. She and Merrick were completely exposed in the middle of the kitchen, but Adalynn didn't care.

She was exactly where she wanted to be.

She kissed his neck.

Merrick lifted his hand from her breast and moved it up to delve his fingers into her hair. His other arm wrapped around her, drawing her tighter against him.

I love him.

I love *him.*

The realization wasn't surprising. It didn't matter that they'd only known each other for so short a time, she felt it without question—in her heart, in her soul, in the song that played in her mind and thrummed within her. As soon as she had opened herself up to her emotions, it hadn't been hard to fall in love with Merrick. How could it have been when everything about him felt so *right?* Being in his arms was like being home; safe, protected, sheltered.

If only I had more time with him.

As though he sensed the discord in her, his hold on her tightened further, and he tipped his head forward to rest his cheek atop her hair. "Whatever it takes, Adalynn. I will find a way."

Chapter Thirteen

The next several days passed with a lightness and joy that outshone the darkness of the werewolf attack. Adalynn, Merrick, and Danny settled into something of a routine during that time; they'd have breakfast together—which always included snappy banter between Danny and Merrick that made Adalynn laugh—and, once everything was cleaned up, Merrick would take Danny outside to tend the garden. While they saw to the crops, Adalynn would work in the kitchen, preparing food for canning. She found the process relaxing, and often lost herself in the task. Merrick and Danny would come back in for lunch in the early afternoon, and Merrick would help her finish canning.

That would signal the end of their workday. After that, Adalynn and Danny were free to do as they pleased. Merrick took them out back a couple times and taught them some basics with the shotgun. Danny's enthusiasm for the lessons was a bit alarming to Adalynn, and he seemed little deterred by Merrick's attempts to ease them into using the weapon—he'd only allowed Danny to fire a few shells. Still, Merrick brought Danny hunting with him early one morning. They returned well before noon with a fat turkey slung over Merrick's shoulder.

For the rest of his free time, Danny, who'd never been much of a reader before the Sundering, had taken to enjoying the stacks of books and old magazines Merrick had provided —many of them old pulp adventure and fantasy stories dating back to the twenties and thirties.

While Danny occupied himself, Adalynn would sneak away with Merrick to his study or his bedroom—which looked as good as new after his repairs—to satisfy their mutual desire for one another, often for hours at a time. They couldn't keep their hands off each other once they were close. Unfortunately, her illness always loomed in the backs of their minds; it was something neither of them spoke about, seemingly both unwilling to shatter the happiness they'd found.

When Adalynn wasn't spending her free time with Merrick—the occasions upon which he reluctantly isolated himself in his study for research—she danced or played the piano.

Today, Adalynn and Danny decided to change things up while Merrick was shut away with his old books. They explored parts of the house they'd not had access to when they first arrived. So much had changed since that night; this was their *home* now, and Merrick had opened every door to them to make it true in every possible way.

After some wandering, they found themselves in a surprisingly clean attic—which *shouldn't* have been all that surprising considering how Merrick kept the giant house magically dust free. Adalynn couldn't help a bit of disappointment, however, after the expectations set by dozens of horror movies featuring musty attics full of cobwebs and ghosts.

Instead of restless supernatural entities, they found boxes upon boxes of books, some dating back hundreds of years. Any bibliophile would've gone crazy over the hidden collection. All the books were in perfect condition, their pages as crisp as though they'd just been printed. Adalynn knew magic had a hand in it. There were also old toys and trinkets —an entire nursery all packed away—antique furniture, stores of candles, and mounds of like-new, Victorian-era clothing.

"Where'd Merrick get all this stuff?" Danny picked up a black disc and pushed on the middle; it opened into a top hat with a *pop*.

Adalynn stood before a tall, antique floor mirror, holding an elegant, royal blue ballgown against her body. It had a square neckline, long sleeves that flared at the elbows, bows on the bodice, and delicate lace trim. It was absolutely gorgeous, and she could just imagine wearing it as she spun around the ballroom downstairs.

"I don't think any of this was his. I think it came with the house, left here by whoever owned it before him," Adalynn said, running her hands over the satiny dress.

"Huh. Probably. How old do you think he is?"

Adalynn glanced at Danny's reflection in the mirror as he picked up a cane and attempted to twirl it. It promptly slipped out of his hand and clattered loudly on the floor. He winced and bent to pick it up, peeking at Adalynn with a sheepish grin.

She smiled and shrugged, shifting her gaze back to the dress. "I don't know. Old."

"And you don't mind doing it with an old guy?"

Adalynn twisted to look at her brother, mouth agape. "Danny!"

He laughed. "What?"

She jabbed a finger at him. "*That* is none of your business."

Danny laughed and set the cane down. He lifted his chin toward her. "You should try it on."

Adalynn looked back down at the dress. It really was pretty. What could it hurt playing dress up for a little while?

"Why not?" She grinned and gestured to the suit hanging in the armoire. "Are you going to dress up, too?"

"Nah."

"Oh, come on. Please? For *me*?"

He pointed at her. "That isn't fair."

"It's not every day that I get to see my little brother in a fancy top hat and suit."

Danny's lip curled. "Fine. But you owe me."

"You can have my share of peanut butter."

"Deal!"

Adalynn laughed and glanced around the attic, her gaze falling on the folded-up privacy screen leaning against the angled ceiling. Laying the dress over her arm, she picked up the matching slippers, walked to the screen, and opened it up. She stepped behind it and bent down to remove her boots. When she straightened, she was hit by a wave of dizziness. She stumbled, catching herself before she fell over, and closed her eyes until it passed.

A flash of fear followed the brief episode, and Adalynn waited with bated breath for something more to happen, for a twinge of pain, a flaring headache, a hint of nausea, but nothing came.

Only vertigo. Slow down, Addy.

She was okay. She felt *fine*. Better than fine. It was nothing like before, and she wouldn't let fear ruin her day.

She removed her shirt and pants, leaving on her bra and panties, and stepped into the dress, carefully pulling it up her body. The slippers came next. The bodice sagged, so she held it to her chest to keep from giving her brother a heart attack as she stepped out from behind the screen.

"Come help me with the laces," she said.

Danny, who was buttoning up the double-breasted vest of his suit, looked up at her. "Wow. You look great, Addy."

"You're looking pretty handsome yourself."

A dark blush stained his cheeks. He moved toward her,

and Adalynn turned, facing the screen. She swayed slightly as he pulled the laces tight and tied them off.

"So…do you think there'll be others?" he asked.

"Others?"

"People."

"There are still a lot of people, Danny."

"No. I mean, like…people like us. *Good* people. Do you think they'll come here? Do you…do you think Merrick would let them stay?"

A pang of regret filled her chest. She could understand how he'd feel lonely here, even with her and Merrick; he probably craved the company of someone closer to his age. And once she was gone…

Adalynn turned to face her brother, placed her hands on his shoulders, and gave them a gentle squeeze. "I can't say what Merrick would do. But he took us in, didn't he?"

Danny nodded.

"The supplies here are abundant, but they're not unlimited. So long as the crops continue to produce, and so long as there's game in the woods, you'll never be hungry. But the more people there are, the faster those resources will be used up. Merrick couldn't open his doors to every person who might come here, but I believe, in time, he'd allow *some* people to stay. But we are his priority—our safety is his priority."

"I know." He inhaled deeply and released the breath in a rush. "I just…"

"You're thinking about the future."

"Yeah."

Adalynn leaned closer, and her lips stretched wide into a smile. "And about getting a girlfriend?"

Danny's face turned bright red. "No! I'm just…*no*! It's not that."

"Mmhmm."

"Shut up and let me finish tying your stupid dress."

Adalynn laughed, but gave him her back once more.

Once he'd finished, she helped him don the suit jacket and a pair of white gloves, then pulled on a long pair of lady's gloves herself. They stood side-by-side before the mirror.

"Check us out!" Danny said. "It's like we went back in time." He curled a finger beneath his nose like a moustache and pursed his lips, deepening his voice. "Hello, m'lady."

Adalynn curtsied. "Hello, kind sir."

Peals of laughter flowed freely from Adalynn and Danny as they posed and acted out the parts of fancy, well-to-do people from some vague, bygone era.

It was times like these during which Adalynn could forget about her illness, forget about the Sundering, forget about how broken, terrifying, and dangerous the world had become, if only for a little while. She was simply living in the moment, having fun with her brother. Nothing else mattered. Seeing his smile, hearing his laughter, and knowing he was *happy* filled her with joy.

Her only goal now that Danny had a safe place to live was to fill every second she had left with this joy, this happiness.

MERRICK CLASPED his hands behind his back and stared at the scorched patch on the back lawn through one of the rear windows of his study. Though everything else had been cleaned up, he'd made no attempt to regenerate the grass—the land would heal on its own, given time. But for the last four days, that spot had bothered him, and he found himself looking at it more and more often.

It was a reminder of his near failure.

Even with his property warded, even with the fore-warning of approaching danger, he'd come close to failing to keep Adalynn and Danny safe. If he'd been more prepared, if he'd been more decisive, more *aggressive*, he might've been able to prevent any harm from befalling them. Only luck had saved Danny from serious injury. Only seconds had saved Adalynn from being violated by that beast.

But he'd spent little time in bolstering the estate's defenses. He wasn't entirely sure *how* to do that without extensive research into the proper magic-shaping techniques, and his research was spent on something even more important lately —searching for a permanent cure for Adalynn.

He knew the measures he'd taken were only temporary, and they'd proven quite taxing—on himself in the short term, and on Adalynn in the long term. Days had passed; her second relapse loomed ahead of them, potentially only minutes away. Would he be able to save her this time?

Even if he could, it would eventually prove too much for one of them; it was unsustainable. But today, he'd made his first breakthrough, had found the first real possibility.

Merrick glanced down at the yellowed scroll laid on the windowsill before him. Though it was preserved by his magic —as was most everything in his home—it had already been quite old when he'd obtained it. In all likeliness, it had already been old before he was born. But this seemed to be the key. The best chance of saving her. The only option he'd found so far.

And it came without even a modicum of certainty.

Soul binding. That's what it all came down to—the interweaving of two lives, of two souls, forever. The text was vague on what exactly that entailed, but it gave hope in the mention of mortal being made immortal. If he could share his immortality with her...would that be enough? Could that overcome the ailment that was killing her, or would it simply spread her illness to him and make him susceptible to its ravages?

Would it prevent her from being killed by her cancer but allow that illness to continue worsening, thus lengthening her suffering into eternity?

There were no answers to find here.

"Written in a different era," he muttered to himself.

And it had been. Even in his youth, there'd been more of his kind than now—and that was after millennia of decline for *all* supernatural beings. In the centuries before his time, there'd been more still, and they'd maintained a collective knowledge of their magic and its uses that, unfortunately, only existed in fragments today. Twelve hundred years ago, there would've been someone alive who could explain this *soul binding* to him, who could tell him what it would and would not accomplish, who could guide him through all this.

Merrick shook his head and growled in frustration. "To be a thousand years old and still know so little…"

Something about the information on the scroll, something about the magic it described, spoke to him on a deep level. It was familiar, though he knew he'd not given it more than a cursory glance since obtaining it a great many years before. But he couldn't place *why* it was familiar, and his mind was too preoccupied to determine the reason.

The spell was *something*, which meant it was a great deal more than he'd had a day ago. And if nothing else came up before her next relapse—which could well be her *last* relapse—he would take the risk. He knew already that he could not continue on without her. The world, his own life, would be too empty with no Adalynn. It seemed mad that she should mean so much to him in so short a time, but it was the truth of his heart.

He *loved* her. That was more than he'd felt for anyone in his entire life—there'd been love between himself and his blood kin, of course, but that had been far more muted, and they'd all been taken from him by the time he could've been considered a grown man.

Nothing would take Adalynn from him.

With great care, he rolled up the scroll and returned it to its case. He'd spent enough time pondering it, enough time fretting over how jarring the werewolf attack had been, enough time brooding. Each moment of research was a moment apart from Adalynn, and he didn't want to waste any more of those than was necessary to save her.

He set the scroll case on his desk and strode out of his study without allowing himself another moment to pause in contemplation.

Once he was in the hallway, he followed the muffled sound of laughter to the attic staircase. The door leading to the staircase was open, and he could clearly hear Adalynn and Danny above. His steps were silent as he ascended, and the lightness of their laughter, the joy, eased Merrick's worries along the short journey.

He'd only taken a few steps away from the stairs before the siblings came into view. They were dressed in some of the old clothing that had been stored up here—a blue dress for Adalynn and a slightly over-sized suit with a double-breasted vest for Danny, the boy's outfit capped by a top hat. It was clothing that had already been here when Merrick purchased the property, slightly outdated even then, and he'd not given it a second thought in over a hundred years.

Adalynn and Danny were standing in front of a tall mirror, posing, speaking in silly voices—using terms and accents they must've thought old-fashioned—and giggling. It was endearing. Adalynn was beautiful all the time, but now, with that dress on—which fit like it was made for her—and all the worry smoothed from her face by laughter, she was utterly radiant.

The things I'd do to her right here, right now, if her brother weren't nearby…

Imaginings of Adalynn against the wall, caged by Merrick's body, with her lips parted, her eyes hooded, and her skirts raised flitted through his mind.

He shook them off; this was innocent fun. He could let it be simply that.

Merrick moved closer, unable to keep a smile from his own lips. "Seems you two are putting on the Ritz."

They both started and spun toward him. Adalynn's surprise quickly transformed into delight. Her smile widened, and her eyes sparkled—but there was something deeper in her gaze, something grounded, powerful, and potent.

Merrick's heart thumped a little faster, and a flare of heat raced across his skin. Perhaps it was too much to hope for, but that look in her eyes seemed to perfectly reflect what he felt for her.

Danny's brows furrowed. "Why are you talking about crackers?"

It took an immense amount of willpower for Merrick to shift his attention from Adalynn to Danny. "I'm not talking about crackers, and I've not the slightest idea why you'd think I was."

Danny gave him a droll look, as though Merrick had lost his mind. "Ritz? The crackers?"

Merrick put on an equally droll expression. "No, *Ritz*. The hotel. The song. What does that have to do with crackers?"

"I have no idea what you're talking about, man."

Adalynn burst into laughter, covering her mouth with her hand. "Merrick, I'm sorry to say it, but you're showing your age."

Merrick frowned at her. He knew human culture changed quickly—he'd been around for a thousand years of it—but the rapid advancement of technology over the last half-century or so seemed to have left him further behind than normal. "I assure you both that the reference, however dated it may seem to you, is timelier than the clothing you're currently wearing."

Danny turned his face toward Adalynn, brows raised. "*Old.*"

She punched him in the shoulder.

"Ow!" He slapped a hand over the spot she'd hit, rubbing it with a pout.

"And you seemed so happy a moment ago," Merrick said dryly.

"You gonna play dress up with us?" Danny asked.

"I've been *dressed up* the entire time you've been here." Merrick spread his arms to the sides and glanced down at his vest, dress shirt, and slacks—the attire he wore most days. He'd thought his clothing, despite having been designed and purchased many, many years ago, had something of a timeless quality to it, at least through to the modern day.

Danny plucked his top hat off his head and tossed it to Merrick.

Merrick caught the hat by its brim and held it upside down. "I suppose you expect me to pull a rabbit out of this or some such nonsense simply because you know I can use magic?"

Danny rolled his eyes. "Put it on."

"Can I see a rabbit?" Adalynn asked with a grin.

With a sigh, Merrick dipped a hand into the hat. He knew Adalynn was teasing, but he found himself unwilling to deny her request. He called up just enough magic to shape into the appropriate form—a glowing, translucent blue rabbit, its details somewhat vague—and lifted his hand to make the illusory creature rise above the brim.

Danny and Adalynn's eyes widened, and their lips parted in wonder as the magical creature leapt out of the hat and hopped around the floor. It darted between Danny's legs, beneath Adalynn's skirt—*lucky bastard*—and around the furniture before it dissipated.

Danny's face was lit up with excitement when he turned back to Merrick. "That was so cool!"

Adalynn closed the distance between them, the swaying of her hips sweeping the fabric of her skirt from side to side as she walked. She plucked the hat from Merrick's hand, placed her free hand on the back of his neck to tug him down, and pecked a kiss on his cheek before placing the hat atop his head. "Thank you."

He tipped the hat, unable to prevent himself from grinning. "My pleasure, madam."

She chuckled and looped her arms with his. "You're finished early. What brings you here to visit with us?"

"I spend enough time cooped up in that room. Livelier company seemed in order." He adjusted the lay of the hat atop his head. "And, since we're already dressed up, might I suggest a stroll around the grounds? There's far more to my estate than you've seen thus far."

"Can we bring lunch?" Danny asked.

Adalynn's excitement was palpable as she beamed at Merrick. "We could have a picnic."

"Anything you'd like, Adalynn," Merrick said. "Do you still have the shotgun?"

"It's in my room."

"I want you to bring it along. Any time you're outside, even on the estate grounds, keep it with you."

Danny raced toward the stairs. "I'll get it!"

Merrick's eyes widened slightly as he swung his gaze from Danny to Adalynn. He'd already been adept at using several potentially deadly tools by the time he was Danny's age, but modern children seemed so much less mature in comparison. Certainly, this world had forced Danny to grow up faster than normal for his generation, but he was still a boy—and a gun was amongst the *deadliest* of mundane tools.

"Tell me I'm not the only one uncomfortable with the notion of him *running* to fetch a shotgun," Merrick said.

Frowning, Adalynn stared at the open entryway through which Danny had disappeared. "You're not. Let's go make sure there's no tripping involved."

Chapter Fourteen

Large, slow-drifting clouds of pure white provided ample shade from the afternoon sun as Merrick, Adalynn, and Danny walked past the garden's walls and onto a wide footpath leading into the woods. Their lunch was split between two wicker baskets—Adalynn had declared them *perfect* for picnicking—with Danny carrying one and Merrick the other. Adalynn had a folded blanket tucked beneath one arm and the shotgun in her opposite hand.

Fortunately, Danny had managed not to hurt himself in his somewhat reckless race to collect the weapon from her room.

Birds sang in the trees, and a light, warm breeze rustled the leaves. Everything was green and alive, but there was still a hint of approaching fall—a hint of eminent decay. Summer was rushing to its end, and this winter would likely be a harsh one in too many ways.

Merrick moved a little closer to Adalynn and plucked the blanket from beneath her arm, tossing it atop the basket. When she looked at him questioningly, he answered by taking her now-free hand in his and squeezing it gently.

Nothing will ever harm you again, my Adalynn.

Danny glanced over his shoulder and rolled his eyes before increasing his pace, putting a little more distance between himself and the couple. Merrick smirked.

"Does the wall go all the way around?" Danny asked.

"It rings the entire property, yes," Merrick replied.

"No wonder there haven't been any revenants around," Adalynn said. "Was there always a wall?"

Merrick shook his head. "The wall in front was in place when I purchased the property. The rest was somewhat more rudimentary in nature—just piles of stone, really, running through the woods in a few places. I've extended and upgraded it extensively over the years."

"Did you know the Sundering would come?"

He'd not been aware they'd planned on conducting an interrogation during the trip, but he found himself oddly unbothered by it. When Adalynn and Danny had first arrived, he'd been loath to answer questions, and even ones as simple as these would've annoyed him, but now…it just felt good to talk to people he trusted. It felt good to not have to hide himself, hide his truth.

"I knew *something* was coming. I could feel it in the months and weeks beforehand. The forces of magic that run through this land, that run through everything, changed. It was both ominous and exhilarating."

"Did you have magic before it happened?" Danny asked, swinging his cane back and forth, smacking long blades of grass and overgrown weeds. It was preferable to have him carrying a cane over a firearm, but the cane *almost* seemed just as dangerous in his hands.

"Yes, though it was but a shadow of what it is now." Even now, without being connected directly to the ley line, Merrick could sense the mana of everything around him— the trees, the undergrowth, every rock and clump of dirt, and all the little creatures scurrying about through it all. But all of it was faint compared to *her*. Her song had only strengthened in his perception, had become a steady accompaniment to his own.

Danny turned around to face them and walked backward, his brows raised high. "Can *I* use magic?"

"There's mana in you—in everything—but no. You do not have that capability. The magic in you is a small, dormant force that will only be roused when it is released from your body." Merrick didn't add the *upon death* to that statement—he'd no desire to speak with a thirteen-year-old about his inevitable demise. "Very few humans are born with mana powerful enough to wield in the way my kind can...and for those who do possess it, it is often more a curse than a gift."

"Why would it be a curse?" Adalynn asked.

"Because magic is *energy*, and it's never quite still. Many humans have no idea how to harness that energy, how to channel it, so it builds and builds. Think of it like...a pressure cooker without a release valve. All that pressure, all that steam, keeps growing and growing, but it has nowhere to go. Eventually"—Merrick released her hand to flick all his fingers outward, pantomiming an explosion—"it bursts. With magic it's more of a consumption from within, but it's a similar enough process."

"Do you feel that kind of pressure?"

Merrick shook his head. "No. My body is adapted to it. Magic flows easily in and out of me. It's possible to overload, but I can withstand far more than any mortal."

Danny glanced behind himself occasionally, altering his course to keep on the path, as he continued to walk backward. "So, what are you?"

"I suppose there are many names for it. Mage, sorcerer, wizard. I prefer warlock, because people tended to use it with the highest degree of fear and hatred in ages past."

"Was Merlin a real wizard?"

"He was quite real. Even while our magic was limited, he was immensely powerful."

Danny grinned wide, and his eyes sparked with excitement. "That's so *cool*! I knew it! I knew he was real." He turned around and strode forward, brandishing his cane like a baton as he sang, "*Hockety pockety wockety wack…*"

"And what exactly is that gibberish he's spouting?" Merrick asked.

Adalynn chuckled. "Danny's favorite cartoon as a little kid was *The Sword in the Stone.*"

Merrick took Adalynn's hand again. "I'm afraid I'm not familiar with the film. I imagine it's some retelling of the Arthurian legend?"

"Yeah, it is. Just with more singing."

"Ah. Because I'm sure singing adds to its historical accuracy."

She laughed and nudged him with her shoulder. "It's entertainment for kids."

"Most of the stories are utter nonsense, at any rate. Humans don't have a particularly long or accurate memory, as a whole."

"Then you'll have to tell us the stories…" Her smile faded, and she looked away—but not before Merrick caught sight of the darkness clouding her eyes. "How old are you, anyway?"

He chose not to comment on that hint of despair; Adalynn seemed at her happiest outside of such conversations, and he couldn't blame her for that. This was a fine afternoon, despite the state of the world. Merrick wanted it to remain a fine afternoon.

"One thousand and fifty-three," he replied. "Or fifty-four. It was harder to keep track of the years while I was young."

Adalynn snapped her face toward him, eyes wide. "*How* old?"

"One zero five three."

"Do *not* tell Danny that. I'll never hear the end of it." Her cheeks pinkened, and she turned her face down, her expression taking on a decidedly shy cast. "I knew you were older, but I never imagined you were *that* old."

Something about the look on her face heated Merrick's blood and roused his hunger. "If it makes any difference to you, I'm sure I don't look a day older than however old it is I look."

She laughed and peeked at him from the corner of her eye. "At least thirty-five."

"I'll assume that's good, then. I've had more and more trouble gauging the age of humans as time has gone by—especially in the last few decades. I dare not guess your age."

Adalynn grinned. "Why not?"

"Because I will either guess too high or too low, and either direction can be taken as an insult."

"I'm twenty-five."

"That's a rather large age gap between yourself and your brother, is it not?"

"A bit larger of an age gap between you and me, don't you think?" Her warm, humored smile made it clear she wasn't concerned about their age difference. She looked at her brother, who continued marching on ahead of them, still singing his gibberish song. "But yeah, it is. Danny was both an accident and miracle baby."

"Oh? It seems you've a bit of a story to tell, yourself."

Up ahead, the gap in the trees created by the path widened; the ground beyond was open and bright, free of the shadows cast by the woods currently stood to either side of Merrick and Adalynn.

"No way!" Danny shouted from up ahead. He ran forward, into the wider opening, and turned to his left. Just before he darted out of sight, he added, "This is *awesome!*"

Adalynn turned her wide, worried eyes toward Merrick. "What's ahead? Is it safe?"

"As safe as anywhere else, though I'm sure that means little these days. And you'll have to see for yourself if you want to know what's up there."

A moment later, Danny's voice echoed over to them. "Woooooo!" It was cut off by a large splash.

Her brows rose. "Water? Is there a pond?"

"A pond, Adalynn? You should know by now I don't do things small on my estate."

She quirked a brow, grinning. "A lake?"

When she quickened her pace, Merrick matched it. Her grin widened as the first hints of the lake became visible through the trees to their left. Within a short while, they had reached the open area along the shore, which had long ago been cleared as a private beach for the estate's previous owners. Merrick had maintained it with a bit of magic only because he found it pleasant to sit beside the water from time to time.

Adalynn stopped when the lake was in full view. "This is beautiful!"

The blue sky was reflected on the lake's mirror-like surface, albeit darkly; the scene was made only more beautiful by the tall reeds and thick trees along much of the shore. The water was disturbed only by a gentle breeze, a flock of water-fowl a couple hundred yards away, and Danny, who'd stripped out of his suit and leapt into the lake without any sign of hesitation.

Merrick set the basket down and spread the blanket over the sand. "This spot will do, yes?"

Adalynn turned back toward him, smiled, and moved to the basket, placing the gun on the ground nearby. "It's perfect."

He collected Danny's basket and the pile of discarded clothes and brought them back to the blanket as Adalynn set out the food, all of which had been collected from the garden save for the peanut butter and the cold turkey; the meat he and Danny had brought home two days before had given Merrick a reason to power the ice box with some magic.

Once everything was arranged, Adalynn sat down, and Merrick seated himself across from her. Danny, seemingly oblivious to the food, continued to splash, swim, and hoot in delight.

"So, you were saying about Danny?" Merrick asked.

Adalynn smoothed her hands over the satin skirt of her dress. Merrick's attention caught on her low bodice and the delectable way the tops of her breasts rose and fell above it with every breath. His fingers itched to tug the dress down, to bare her breasts to his gaze, to his mouth and tongue; more than that, he wanted to bury his face elsewhere—somewhere warm and sweet.

She chuckled, calling his eyes back to hers; the same heat he felt was evident in her gaze. Leaning forward on hands and knees, Adalynn brushed her lips lightly across his, and, surprisingly, scraped her nails along the hard length of his shaft through his pants. Merrick jolted as fire blazed inside him; he was sure he'd seeped from the tip of his cock.

"Later," she promised as she pulled away and sat back down.

"You are a tease, Adalynn. You've no idea the amount of restraint I'm exercising to keep from throwing up those skirts and taking you right here. To keep myself from shoving my tongue between your thighs and licking—"

"Merrick!" Her cheeks burned red as she glanced toward her brother.

He loved it when she blushed, loved the shy, yet aroused gleam in her eyes.

"*Anyway,*" she said, glancing at him from behind her thick lashes, "my parents had trouble conceiving after me. They tried for years, but it just never happened. I guess they even consulted a few fertility specialists, but after her first miscarriage, my mom couldn't go through it anymore. They stopped trying. Then, years later, out of the blue, there was Danny, a complete and utter surprise."

"Their accidental miracle," Merrick said.

A soft smile touched her lips, and she glanced toward Danny again. "Yeah."

"And how did young Adalynn handle his arrival?"

"I was ecstatic. I always wanted a little sister to play with growing up, but by then, I didn't care. A brother was just as good. He was the cutest little thing ever, all squishy cheeks and pudgy thighs. I bragged about him all the time at school and showed him off to my friends."

Merrick turned his head to glance at the boy playing in the water—a boy with a good, brave heart. He didn't doubt that Adalynn had a hand in shaping Danny into the person he was now. "That must feel as though it was so long ago now."

"It does and doesn't at the same time, you know? I look at him, see how tall he's gotten, see how much he's changed, but I can still see the little boy he was as if it were yesterday."

"My perspective is different than yours, but I believe I understand. For me...time seems to go by faster and faster with each passing year. These days with you have been the first time I find myself wishing it would slow down, wishing I could stretch out every moment."

She smiled up at him. "Me too."

Adalynn picked up a piece of turkey and took a bite, turning her face toward the lake with a wistful light in her eyes. He knew she was thinking about her future—her *lack* of a future—but this didn't seem the time or place to discuss the spell he'd found with her. She'd already said she didn't want Merrick to harm himself to help her, and he couldn't guarantee the soul binding was without risks.

He plucked up a strawberry and bit into it, relishing the sweet juice as it ran over his tongue. It was enough, for a little while, to simply sit here and enjoy the food, to sit here and enjoy the mana song radiating from Adalynn's core.

"Did you…have a wife?" she asked.

The question jarred him from that brief sense of serenity with its unexpectedness. He looked her over briefly; there was a new tension in her posture, and one of her hands had caught the fabric of her skirt, knuckles paling as she squeezed. Was she jealous at the very thought of him having had a spouse?

That notion gave him a strange sense of satisfaction; it meant she might've felt as possessive of him as he did of her.

"No wife. I've had fleeting relations with women over the years, but none of them ever awoke anything in me like you have."

A flush spread along her skin, and her lips fell into a small, contrite frown. "I'm sorry. I…I know it's stupid to be jealous. You're…*old*." She winced. "That sounded worse than I meant it to. But what I mean is, I can't expect you to have never been with anyone else, and it's sad that you never had anyone meaningful in your life—despite my being so relieved by your answer. I know that's wrong…"

"Nonsense," he said, shaking his head. "The only reason I haven't asked about your past romances is to spare myself a bout of jealous rage."

Adalynn laughed. "Maybe I shouldn't feel so bad, if you feel the same way."

He gritted his teeth, struggling to keep his lips from curling into a sneer; now that he'd said it aloud, he couldn't help but wonder who she'd been with. She was lovely, and kind, and a joy to be near—he had no doubt she'd had many men interested in her, and he hated them all. He *refused* to ask. She was with Merrick now, until whatever end they reached, and that was enough. She was his.

Danny joined them shortly after. Water dripped from his hair and glistened on his skin, and his feet and legs were covered in sand. He plopped onto the blanket between Merrick and Adalynn. "That was amazing."

"I would appreciate it if you could avoid dripping lake water all over the food," Merrick said.

"I'd eat it anyway." Danny flashed Merrick a grin. As though to prove his point, he snatched up a chunk of bread with his wet hands and shoved it into his mouth.

Conversation dwindled as they all ate, each seemingly content to enjoy the food. Merrick took his time to relish the flavors; he'd been eating much more than he normally would have because he'd been sharing so many meals with Adalynn and Daniel, and though he wasn't hungry now, he had no problem with delighting in the taste of their bounty.

Once they'd eaten their fill, Danny ran his hand through his damp, floppy hair, shoving it back, and leapt to his feet. As he ran toward the lake, he called over his shoulder, "Come on, guys! Join me."

Adalynn chuckled and packed the leftover food.

"The boy is nothing if not enthusiastic," Merrick said.

"I hope he never changes." She closed the last wicker basket, turned her face toward Merrick, and smiled wide. "Shall we?"

Before Merrick could answer, Adalynn got to her feet, tugged up her skirt—baring her feet, ankles, and lower shins —kicked off her slippers, and ran toward the water.

A smile crept to Merrick's lips as he watched her. Despite his age, he'd never *felt* old, but being around her…it made him feel young in the best ways. When was the last time he'd gone for a swim just for the fun of it? When was the last time he'd loosened up and *enjoyed* himself?

He couldn't recall many occasions like this—at least not before Adalynn had come into his life.

Merrick pushed himself to his feet and strolled along the trail she'd blazed through the sand, approaching the water's edge with as much leisure as he'd taken in eating the bit of food he'd consumed—though his full attention remained on Adalynn.

Adalynn stopped at the beginning of the dock and reached behind her, awkwardly unfastening the ties of her dress. To Merrick's surprise, she shoved the dress down once the ties were loosened. The whole of her tantalizing body— apart from the skin covered by navy-blue bra and black panties—was exposed to him in the bright summer sun.

That was more than enough to pour heat into Merrick's veins and reawaken that too-familiar ache in his groin. He gritted his teeth. Once again, he knew that, were it not for Danny's presence, he'd be unable to keep himself off her.

"Come on, Addy!" Danny yelled from the water.

"I'm coming!" Adalynn stepped out of the dress and padded down the dock. Her steps picked up speed; she was running, brown hair streaming behind her, by the time she neared the end of the dock. She leapt off the edge and disappeared into the water below with a splash.

Merrick maintained his slow pace as he stepped onto the dock and walked to the end. With Adalynn almost naked, he couldn't guarantee his own restraint once he was in the water…so perhaps, this time, it was best to avoid the situation and stay on dry land.

Her head broke the surface, and she swept her hair out of her face as she treaded water. "Woo! Oh my God, this feel so *good*." She closed her eyes and titled her head back. Refracted sunlight sparkled in the water droplets on her skin.

Danny swam to the dock, grabbed hold of the edge, and looked up at Merrick. "Let's go Merrick. Get in here!"

Adalynn opened her eyes and moved toward them. "Come in with us."

Merrick turned his palms upward and lifted his hands slightly. "I'm not dressed for swimming."

"Neither were we."

Adalynn's coy smile certainly wasn't making it easy for him to resist.

He drew in a slow, steadying breath. He'd spent a thousand years in control; he would not let that self-discipline falter now. "Would it not be more prudent for me to maintain vigil while the two of you enjoy yourselves?"

"I didn't realize you were such a prude," Danny said.

Adalynn burst out laughing.

Merrick parted his lips to run his tongue across the upper one. "A prude? Now who's talking like an old man, *dude*?"

"Learned that from Addy's romance book." Danny winked and smirked. "You sound a lot like the guy with the big—"

A wave of water hit Danny in the face, causing him to cough and sputter.

"Danny!" Adalynn admonished, a hint of embarrassment in her eyes.

Danny laughed. "Okay! Jeez. Just saying."

Scowling, Merrick lifted his hands and unbuttoned his vest. "I can assure you, Daniel, that your sister has no need of any romantic *fantasy* any longer."

"Oh, that's *gross*." Danny shuddered and gagged. "I don't need to picture that!"

"No, you *really* don't," Adalynn said, but her eyes were fixated on Merrick.

Merrick dropped the vest onto the dock and untucked his shirt, unfastening its buttons with a deliberate appearance of forcefulness now that she was watching. "Anything inappropriate in *your* imagination is a result of your own tainted mind, boy. There's nothing *gross* about my relationship with Adalynn."

"No, it's just that she's my *sister*." Danny shuddered again and ducked under the water, swimming away.

Once his shirt was off, Merrick divested himself of his shoes, socks, and pants, leaving his clothing in a pile. Standing only in his boxers, he took a moment to steel himself and focus on the feel of the warm air against his bare skin, on the scent of vegetation and fresh water drifting around him, on the bird songs sounding from the trees—on *anything* but Adalynn's coy smile and her current state of undress. It was hard for Merrick to maintain his composure while she was staring at him so intently, and Danny really *didn't* need to see anything inappropriate.

Merrick tipped his head back and scanned the lovely blue of the sky and the soft white tufts of cloud dotting it. These dying days of summer would mark the end of an era for him, and would stand out as unique in his long, long life, no matter what happened before the next summer arrived.

Adalynn chuckled softly, and Merrick knew the reason for it. She knew her effect on him, knew how hard it was for him to resist, and he would make sure she paid for it later.

Fortunately for her, she'd enjoy the price he would exact.

He stepped off the dock and plunged into the water.

The initial chill was exhilarating, rousing him to move his body to combat it. He swung his arms and kicked his legs to tread water—the lake reached a surprising depth near the end of the dock—and filled his lungs with fresh air once he broke the surface. It felt *good*. How had he let himself forget this?

Merrick turned his head toward Adalynn to find her already approaching him. With a smirk, he swam to meet her. Once she was within reach, he looped his arm around her waist and drew her against him.

She wrapped her arms and legs around him instantly, her gaze locking with his. Droplets of water shimmered on her eyelashes, hair, and skin, and desire burned in her eyes. Merrick groaned at her heat, the softness of her body, the slide of her limbs. His struggles a few moments earlier had done nothing to prepare him for this all-out war against his yearning; it took everything in him to keep from taking her right then.

"So, what's this *romance* book your brother spoke of?" he asked.

"What do *you* think it is? I think it's pretty self-explanatory."

"I've never been jealous of a book before. I think you'll need to dispose of it."

She chuckled and leaned her face closer, brushing the tip of her nose against his. "You don't need to be jealous. I have my very own hero right here. And"—she slipped one of her hands between their bodies and grasped his cock—"he's *quite* well endowed."

Despite releasing another groan, despite the intensifying ache deep in his belly, despite the delectable torture of her touch, Merrick grinned. "Is that all you want me for, Adalynn?"

"No." She released his shaft and pecked a quick kiss on his lips. "Though I am craving it something fierce right now. However"—she let go of him completely and pushed herself away from him—"now is not the time." She grinned cheekily, turned, and swam.

"I'm going to remind you of all the torture you've put me through tonight," Merrick said as he swam after her. "You'll be begging for release long before I'm through."

"I'm looking forward to it," she called behind her, laughing.

Merrick was, too.

"Guys!" Danny sent a splash toward Merrick. "Knock it off! Let's keep it family friendly!"

Smirking, Merrick halted his pursuit of Adalynn. That pause gave him enough time to ask himself a question more profound than he'd realized possible—was this what it was like to live a normal life alongside family and friends? He'd been younger than Adalynn when the last of his known blood kin had died, and he couldn't recall any moments like this from before they were gone.

If he could've traded the thousand years he'd lived for the chance to have met Adalynn sooner, to have experienced *this* sooner, to have lived one mortal lifetime in happiness with her, he would've done so without hesitation.

Realizing the fullness of his powers paled in comparison to this. He'd never known it, but Adalynn always would've been enough for him.

Chapter Fifteen

Adalynn lay against Merrick's side with her eyes closed. Night had fallen a couple hours ago, Danny—who'd been yawning almost uncontrollably—had put himself to bed, and there was a warm, cozy fire crackling in the fireplace. The sofa she and Merrick were relaxing upon wasn't the most comfortable seat in the house, but she wouldn't have moved for anything. His arm was around her, strong and secure, and his soothing scent enveloped her. This was exactly where she wanted to be.

Today had been a good day. Today had been the best day Adalynn could ever have asked for.

She took in a deep breath, took in Merrick's aroma, and released it slowly as she curled up against him.

"I never realized how empty this house felt before you and your brother came," Merrick said, his voice deep but soft.

Adalynn opened her eyes and tilted her head back to look up at his face. He was staring into the fire, his eyes glowing a faint blue.

"You've reintroduced me to being *alive*," he continued, his words growing heavy with solemnity. "You've shown me that the Sundering wasn't the end of the world. It was a new beginning."

"Were things really that bad for you before all this?"

He turned his face toward her and offered a sad, under-stated smile. He shook his head slightly. "I didn't think so. In hindsight, it wasn't *bad*...just *lonely*. I never realized how much so before you. Mortals lived and died around me and I simply lingered. Even if I trusted them, what point was there to building relationships? What questions would I have had to answer as they grew old and I remained the same? Now I know what I've missed all this time...but I don't think anyone other than you could've shown it to me."

The sorrow in his tone washed through her, and she lowered her eyes before he could catch sight of it in them. What was she doing? She was being so...*selfish*. It was stupid to believe she could embrace these moments with Merrick while keeping everything between them purely physical, stupid to believe that no deeper, stronger connection would be forged between them.

She was *dying*. She knew it, Merrick knew it—even if he refused to accept it—and it was just so...

Unfair.

Adalynn couldn't regret their time together, couldn't view it as wrong, no matter how selfish she thought she was being. Everything about Merrick felt *right*. But he...he would live on. *He* would have to carry the burden of grief and loss. Forever.

It felt like a knife twisting in her heart when she thought of what she was doing to Merrick and Danny. Every day, she made new memories with them, happy memories. But at the same time, it felt like she was just deepening the eventual wounds they would suffer.

What if...what if I left? Before it's too late. Before he comes to...love me.

Could she leave? Her very soul screamed *no*. But to force them to watch her suffer when her next attack came on, to force them to watch her die? To force them watch her...*change* into one of those things knowing they'd have to kill her?

The thought made her sick.

She couldn't let that happen. She didn't want Danny and Merrick's last memory of her to be of an undead monstrosity that was ravenous for their blood. Seeing her parents that way had already been too much.

I can't stay.

It was a depressing, gut-wrenching, heartbreaking thought.

Merrick's fingers squeezed Adalynn's upper arm, calling her back into the moment.

"What's wrong, Adalynn?" he asked. "I can sense your unease."

Adalynn held him just a little tighter, rubbed her cheek against his chest, and shook her head. "Nothing. Tell me about your past."

"I shouldn't let you dodge my question that easily."

"Nothing's wrong."

"You don't need to lie to me, Adalynn."

Adalynn lifted her head and met his eyes, careful to keep her thoughts from affecting her expression. She smiled softly and brushed her lips over his. "I'm happy. The happiest I've ever been. I want to know more about you. About your past, about why you live in this big old house all by yourself, and how you got this." She lifted a hand and lightly traced the scar from his forehead down to his cheek.

Merrick eased back on the sofa, letting out a soft sigh. "My past is long and largely uneventful. Survival in a hostile world necessitated as much—keeping suspicions to a minimum was vital. I was born in what was at the time called Mercia, though the name ceased to mean anything not long after my birth. It is part of central England in modern times, though I suppose those names may well change again, given the current state of the world.

"I was young during a time of unrest. The king was considered ineffective and was despised by many. The Danes were fighting the Saxons, power was shifting...it was a messy era, and my perspective during that period was that of a child with a very limited world view. Few humans ventured more than a few miles from the towns of their birth, in those days. My parents were careful with their magic, but anything outside of what people considered wholly natural in those days—even the use of natural remedies to cure ailments—was often a target of suspicion.

"They were dragged out of our home when I was eleven or twelve and lashed to a stake to be burned. Being a child, I had little understanding of what was going on apart from there being an angry mob seeking to harm my parents. I'd not grown into my magic yet, but even if I had, I know now there was nothing I could've done. This"—he touched his fingertip to the top of the scar and slashed downward along its path— "is what I received when I tried to help them. The mob spared me because they deemed me yet innocent, but the owner of the dagger I lunged for was unappreciative of my attempt to take his weapon. I was able to pull back before I lost my eye, but I wasn't fast enough to avoid his blade completely."

Adalynn's eyes widened. She'd learned about the witch trials in school—though they'd occurred several centuries after his childhood, with him being over a thousand years old—had seen movies, read books, but she'd only understood the cruelty with which those people had been treated as a distant thing. It was something that she'd never thought could've happened in the modern world; it was something by which she'd never be affected. But such things *had* affected Merrick. That had been his *life*.

"Did you have siblings?" she asked. "Did they…"

"Two. A pair of older brothers. They'd been sent off on an errand—I can't remember what—and arrived only after the fire had burned down to embers and there was nothing left. They dragged me away from the pile of ashes, and we fled that evening. My kind is far more resilient than yours, but we are by no means invulnerable, and there was no magic at our disposal that could've saved my parents from that fate."

Icy horror spread through Adalynn; even having seen the aftermath of the accident that took her parents, she couldn't imagine how traumatizing it must've been for Merrick to watch his parents burned alive. "I'm so sorry."

"You don't need to be. It was a very long time ago, as I said, and you were not one of the people who took part in it. My brothers and I traveled for a time afterward, taking work where we could to keep from going hungry. With my magic not yet unlocked, and without having reached my point of immortality, I was essentially human. My brothers, though in possession of their magic, had not yet reached that immortal state either.

"It was a difficult existence. Most people were distrustful of outsiders, but we managed as best we could. Within two years, both my brothers were dead. Killed in a scuffle over food." His hold on her tightened a little, and she could sense the discordance in the song of his soul. "Perhaps they'd been overconfident in their blossoming power, or perhaps it was merely desperation to keep our bellies from feeling so hollow. I've been alone since then."

"How did you survive?" Adalynn laid her cheek on his chest and grasped the fabric of his open vest.

"I just...*did*. In that case, I was just young enough that men saw it as beneath them to kill me. If there had been a war raging, it would've been different, of course...but a lone child was easier for folks to trust, and I worked hard enough to earn my meals. In some ways...it was *easier*, on my own. No one had to worry about me, and I didn't have to worry about anyone else.

"That's how it was for centuries. I pressed forward, interacting with mortals only as much as was necessary—though, unfortunately, that necessity only increased as time marched on. The world around me changed, the people changed, but I stayed the same…so I took to moving around every decade or so to avoid questions and suspicions. I learned new trades, I learned new languages, and, eventually, I began to discover bits of information about what I was and what I could do. I'd learned so little from my parents because I'd not been able to use my power before their deaths."

Merrick extended his free arm and held it with his palm up and fingers slightly curled. A small blue orb coalesced in the air just over his hand, pulsing and swirling. "This seemed so difficult back then. Nearly impossible. It took me years to build up to being able to produce something like this. After the Sundering, it's as effortless as breathing."

Adalynn reached for the orb. Touching it was like touching one of those plasma balls that were always sold in novelty shops; it produced a thrum that flowed through her fingertips and up her arm, tickling rather than painful. The tiny hairs on her forearms stood on end.

"Amassing wealth over the centuries has been both simple and increasingly complicated. I'd grown into my immortality some time during my thirties. My magic felt fuller, and my need for food and drink dwindled. That made it easier to survive, easier to save what I earned. I started scouring the world for anything I could find that would grant me insight into my magic, gathering a massive collection of texts with bits and pieces of information from around the world—some of them containing what I might call *spells*. That collection is in my study currently."

"Did you ever find anyone else like you?" She turned her hand over, trailing her fingers across the orb before lowering her hand onto his palm.

The magical sphere vanished. Merrick laced his fingers with hers and lifted her hand to brush his lips over her knuckles. "A few. But the need for discretion and secrecy has only amplified with the passage of time, so my interactions with them were brief. It seems most of us who were left have survived as loners and had grown distrustful even of each other."

"Is that why you never…had a relationship?" *Ugh*, why was she torturing herself by asking this question?

"I've never had a relationship because the only draw I've felt to anyone was superficial. The few times I've forced myself out into human society, I've had *relations* with women, but nothing came of it other than fleeting mutual pleasure."

Adalynn's jealousy reared within her and roared. It was furious; it was consuming. Her brow furrowed as she glared at the dancing fire. She'd known even when she'd brought up the subject earlier today that she had no right to be jealous, but *damn it*, she *was*. She hated every single faceless woman who'd ever touched him, who'd been touched *by* him, who'd experienced even a fraction of the pleasure Adalynn experienced when she was with him.

Merrick's chuckle was deep, rumbling, and rich; Adalynn felt it as much as she heard it.

"Is my little Adalynn *jealous*?" He slid his hand from her arm to her hip, trailing it up her side until his fingers brushed the underside of her breast. "No one has *ever* made me feel like you do."

Her hold on his hand tightened involuntarily, and her breath hitched. The raging flame inside her intensified and became a different kind of heat—a heat fueled by her desire, a heat that stoked her need to a feverish degree.

He leaned his head toward her until his mouth was near her ear and whispered, "If I've not made it clear by my words, I suppose I'll have to show you." Dipping his head farther, he pressed his lips to the place where her shoulder and neck met. The light scrape of his teeth against her skin sent a thrill directly to her core.

He released her hand to settle his on her right breast, cupping it through her shirt. His fingertips brushed over her nipple briefly before he moved both his hands down, over her stomach and to the waistband of her pants.

Her breath quickened. "Merrick..."

"You are the first to be *mine*, Adalynn," he rasped. "The *only*."

That thrumming, tingly sensation spread across her entire body as he unbuttoned her jeans.

"And you are the first and only to receive *all* of me," he continued.

Adalynn's eyes widened, and her heart fluttered as her body floated up off the sofa as though she were weightless. Her position remained unchanged, but she was now hovering several inches above the sofa cushion; it felt like his hands were her only anchor, the only thing keeping her from drifting all the way to the ceiling.

Merrick hooked his fingers beneath the waistbands of her jeans and panties and slowly slid them down her hips and past her ass. Something unseen tugged on her underwear and the cuffs of her jeans. He spread his fingers, running his fingertips over the small patch of hair on her pelvis, and guided her back down effortlessly as her pants seemingly removed themselves. The rasp of their material against her sensitive skin left delicious fire in its wake.

He stopped her before she was fully down and moved his hands upward, slipping them beneath the hem of her shirt. Tiny, thrilling electric arcs pulsed off his fingers, sending pleasurable jolts straight to her sex as his hands trekked over her stomach, followed the swell of her breasts, brushed over her hardening nipples, and finally settled on the backs of her arms. She lifted them up instinctually.

His hands returned to her breasts as another unseen force drew off her shirt, obscuring her vision for several seconds. Merrick's fingertips moved slowly, deliberately, dancing around her nipples without quite touching them.

Adalynn grasped his forearms and squeezed as a moan

escaped her. She arched her back. It felt strange to be floating above him, to be uncertain of what to do with her limbs, to be naked and ungrounded, wholly exposed. But those thoughts were fleeting in the face of the desire suffusing her, could not stand against the liquid heat gathering in her core.

Merrick hummed appreciatively, squeezing her breasts. "Hungry, aren't you?" He moved his hands down again, cupped the insides of her thighs, and parted them. One of his fingers dipped between her folds, sliding over the sensitive flesh to sample the wetness gathered there. "Mmm. Yes, you are. So am I, Adalynn."

Slowly, he lifted that finger to his mouth. She turned her head to watch as he slipped it between his lips and sucked on it for a moment. A satisfied rumbling rose from his chest. It only turned her on more. She wanted his hand back between her thighs, wanted his fingers stroking her, his *tongue* licking her.

"But I can wait to sate *my* hunger," he said, returning his hand to her thigh. Both his hands drifted away from her core, away from her *need*, to trail over her skin. "I believe I owe you from earlier, don't I?"

"What?" she asked breathlessly, eyes locked on his hands.

The energy of his touch only intensified with each passing moment, and little blue arcs of it crackled over his flesh, but he didn't move faster, didn't touch where she needed him to. Instead, he continued to explore her with his hands, running his fingertips across the backs of her knees and along the backs of her thighs.

A flash of blue engulfed his body for an instant, creating delicious heat along her back and bottom. He pulled her down once the light had faded—down onto his *bare* lap and chest, his clothes having seemingly vanished. The hard length of his erection throbbed against her lower back, teasing her with its warmth.

Setting his hands on the tops of her knees, he spread her

legs wider. Despite the heat radiating from the fireplace, the air touching her exposed sex was cold in the absence of Merrick's touch. A moment later, there was a hum of energy, and Adalynn gasped when several shadowy, subtly starlit tentacles appeared on either side of her. They brushed her arms, her hips, her stomach, and thighs, and one slithered toward her sex. Their touches were both cool and hot, vibrating with power.

Merrick lowered his head to her shoulder, pressing his cheek against hers. His beard rasped over her skin, enhancing the sensations fluttering through her. His hands moved back up and settled over her breasts, leaving the tentacles to caress the flesh near her sex—still teasing her, taunting her.

"You're going to feel more pleasure tonight than you've imagined possible," he said, "but it will be only at my whim." He squeezed her breasts and caught her nipples between his forefingers and thumbs, pinching and twisting just enough to blast her with another wave of pleasure that made her sex clench.

Adalynn gasped louder. Her pelvis undulated, and she caught his wrists with her hands but didn't pull him away.

The tentacle between her legs swept through her wet folds and touched her clit. It stopped in place as though it had latched onto her, and its vibration intensified.

"Oh, God. *Merrick!*" Eyelids fluttering closed, she caught her bottom lip between her teeth and tilted her head back. Little sounds of pleasure escaped her, and she writhed upon him, panting as the sensation grew, forcing her closer and closer to her peak until suddenly...it stopped. Her eyes snapped open. "*No!*"

Merrick chuckled and pinched her nipples again, making her hips buck, the movement driven by an instinctual need for *him*.

"It's not going to be *that* easy, Adalynn."

She released one of his wrists and reached toward the

apex of her thighs; she needed to touch herself, to keep the sensations going, needed to *feel*.

One of Merrick's shadowy tentacles coiled around her arm, halting its motion, and Merrick clucked his tongue. Despite looking so insubstantial, so wispy—no more solid than smoke—that tendril was impossibly strong.

"You are cruel," she breathed, forcing her eyes open and turning her head to look at him.

His eyes glowed bright, and his cock twitched against her back as though in response to her gaze. "As were you when you teased me without a modicum of remorse and left me without release."

The tentacle between her legs latched onto her clit again and resumed its vibrations. Adalynn held Merrick's gaze as her limbs trembled, as she panted, as her eyelids fluttered once more. He swept her rapidly toward a climax, but she knew, oh she *knew*, that he wouldn't give in to her.

Adalynn cried out in frustration when the tentacle trailed away and caressed her thigh as though in apology. She wanted to curse the thing, to curse Merrick, just as much as she wanted to beg him for more. She was so damn turned on, so wet, so aroused, that she was sure she'd come if that tentacle so much as tapped her clit again. Her slick was running down to her ass, but she didn't care. All she wanted was for him to *touch* her. The torment he was subjecting her to was equal parts pleasure and pain, each as maddening as the other.

His other tentacles continued their dance over her limbs, leaving her skin abuzz; she was aware of every point of contact, no matter how faint. Her every muscle quivered with anticipation—with that consuming need for release.

Merrick's hands eased on her breasts, and he gently stroked his thumbs back and forth over her hard, sensitive, abused nipples. "You are so beautiful, Adalynn. So wild, so passionate." He trailed his lips over her forehead, her cheek.

The tentacle on her thigh glided back toward her sex; instead of returning to her clit, it delved *inside* her.

Adalynn arched her back at the sudden fullness, at the fire and ice swirling within her, and moaned as the tendril drew back and pushed in again.

"You're going to give me *everything*, Adalynn."

The tentacle thrummed inside her as it thrust in and out, and Adalynn rocked her hips with it. She clutched Merrick's wrists as the pleasure at her center wound tighter and tighter. A shudder spasmed through her.

The tentacle slipped out fully.

"No! No, no, no!" she cried, squirming as her sex pulsed and clenched around *nothing*. She was *right there*. "Merrick, please! Stop teasing." She turned her face toward him, her chest rising and falling with her quickened breaths, and met his eyes.

As much as she wanted to come, she didn't want it to be from his magic, no matter how corporeal it could be. She wanted *him*. Just him. And she knew he wanted her, too. She could feel the tension in his body behind her, around her. Could feel the slickness on her back from his seeping pre-cum. Could see the need brimming in his glowing eyes.

"No more," she begged. "Just make love to me."

MERRICK CAUGHT his lower lip between his teeth and released a slow, shaky breath. His entire body thrummed with arousal and magic. Unfulfilled desire raged through him, threatening to consume him despite his struggle—and now she was begging him to give in. Begging him to stop fighting.

And he couldn't deny either himself or Adalynn any longer. His cock ached with a deeper pain than he'd ever experienced, having been teased by her warm flesh and writhing body, and his abdomen was wet with his seed.

Magic flared along his arms, racing from his fingertips

toward his shoulders in ever changing, lightning-fork paths, but he wasn't going to use it on her now. No, he wanted to touch her with his own hands. He wanted to pleasure her with his own body. As much as he saw the power dwelling within as a part of himself, it was not the part he longed to use right now.

He dropped his hands to her hips and lifted her off his lap, spinning her to face him; she swung her legs to the sides, straddling him, and looped her arms around his neck. Merrick looked up into her face. Her cheeks were flushed with passion, her gleaming eyes half-lidded, her lips parted with her quick, shallow breaths. Her mana song flowed high and strong, weaving itself through his, emanating from every inch of her delectable body.

With her knees on the sofa cushion to either side of Merrick, she held herself over him. Her eyes repeated her plea from a moment before—*just make love to me.*

Merrick dropped one hand from her hip and grasped his cock around its base. He angled his shaft to press its head against the entrance of her sex. Slowly, *so* slowly, she lowered herself upon him. Merrick's hand returned to her hip. It took everything within him not to pull her down, not to thrust up and bury himself inside her warm, wet sheath. Her inner walls gripped his cock, and he groaned as she rose and eased back down, working him steadily deeper and deeper until she was fully seated upon him.

He tightened his hands on her hips and held her down, throwing his head back as he fought the immense surge of pressure threatening to make him spill his seed. Adalynn dropped one of her hands to his shoulder and smoothed it down to his chest. She trailed it back up again, along his neck, and cupped his jaw. Her hair brushed over his skin as she leaned forward to slam her mouth against his.

Lifting his hand to bury his fingers in her hair, he pulled her deeper into the kiss. Her lips parted without hesitation, and he slipped his tongue between them to meet with hers in a dance that followed their twined mana songs perfectly.

Adalynn lifted herself again and dropped down, repeating the motions over and over. She moaned softly against his mouth, not breaking the kiss even as her tempo increased. Each slide of her sex blasted Merrick with pleasure and thrilling flares of magic, intensifying the energy crackling over his skin, but he was aware of its increased brightness only through his closed eyelids. His world was Adalynn now—nothing else made a difference but her taste, her feel, her scent.

Adalynn's muscles tensed, her breath sharpened, and she was wracked by sudden shivers. Her sex clamped around him. Her mana song swelled to a crescendo as her nails dug into his skin, the little pricks of pain only heightening Merrick's pleasure.

Taking hold of her hips with both hands again, Merrick seized control, continuing what she'd started in pushing their pace faster and faster. He pulled her down to meet his rising hips, a little harder with each thrust, and she cried out against his mouth as she shuddered in bliss.

"Merrick," she breathed between moans, her arms slipping around his neck to cling to him.

He clenched his teeth and battled the inevitable explosion in himself, struggling to hold on, to keep moving, to prolong this as much as possible—he never wanted this moment, this *intimacy*, to end. But between the movements of her body and the power of her mana song, he'd never stood a chance.

Even with his eyelids closed, his vision was filled with electric blue as he climaxed. The pressure that had been building in him for most of the day finally burst, and his body trembled with the force of it. Pleasure assailed his mind, annihilating conscious thought to leave only pure sensation. His fingertips pressed into the flesh of her hips, his back arched, and he released a ragged, desperate growl as he pumped his seed into her.

Finally, Merrick sagged against the sofa's backrest. Adalynn went limp atop him, her cheek resting on one of her arms, her soft lips settling against his jaw. Their ragged breaths gradually eased, and a bit of the heat from their bodies faded. The lingering pleasure was slower to diminish; every tiny movement of her sex was nearly enough to rouse him back to action, but he didn't allow himself to move. This was another part of the intimacy he craved—holding one another through the aftermath with bodies, hearts, and souls still connected.

She drew in a deep breath and released it with a soft, contented hum.

His own contentment was disrupted as his mind wandered to a jarring thought—this moment could be the last they shared together. *Any* moment from this point forward could be the last. Fate had brought Adalynn to him, and fate would take her away whenever it pleased, with or without forewarning.

Unless Merrick *changed* her fate.

He trailed his fingers absently down her spine. She'd opposed him the last time he'd raised the subject, and they'd avoided it in the days since. Things had been happier that way, but he knew it loomed, dark and ominous, in her mind, just as it did in his own. Merrick had no idea how much time she had left—but he was acutely aware of it dwindling with each passing moment.

"What if there was a way to heal you, Adalynn?"

Her body went rigid. "Merrick, don't. Don't ruin this."

"If not now, then when?" he demanded. "Am I supposed to wait until it's too late?"

She pulled away from him and slipped off the couch. The cool air blasted his skin—his now exposed cock—with arctic force. As much as he regretted bringing up the subject in that moment, as empty and alone as he suddenly felt, he would not back down. They *had* to address this. It couldn't be left as an unspoken thing lurking between them.

Adalynn snatched up her shirt and pulled it over her head. "This was supposed to be purely physical," she said quietly.

"It never was. We both knew that."

"It *can't* be more."

His nostrils flared with a heavy exhalation, and he clenched his jaw before shoving himself off the sofa and onto his feet. He closed the distance between them and caught her by her upper arms. "Don't tell me it can't be when it already *is*. Denying the truth doesn't change it, Adalynn."

Her features tightened as her eyes met his. "You're denying the truth just as much, Merrick."

He held her gaze, unable to contain the emotions swelling inside him—many of which were too intense and jumbled to sort. "The world does *not* operate based on the rules you knew before. This is *my* world, now. And you were mine from the moment I laid eyes upon you."

"That still doesn't change the fact that I'm dying! I'm on borrowed time, Merrick, time you've given me!"

"And I may be able to give you *eternity* if you'd stop being so damned stubborn!"

Adalynn pressed her lips together. She was quiet for several moments, her gaze unwavering, before she finally spoke. "At what cost, Merrick? How badly would it hurt you? How much damage will it do to you?"

"I will be fine, Adalynn. I always am."

"*Swear* to me that it won't hurt you."

The words gathered on the tip of Merrick's tongue, but they refused to come out; he couldn't lie to her now, even if he felt he should. "It doesn't matter, so long as it saves you."

"No."

Merrick clenched his jaw. "I'm not giving you a choice anymore."

Her eyes hardened even as they filled with a sheen of tears. "It's not your choice to make." She pulled away from him, snatched her pants off the floor, and marched toward the entryway. "I refuse to pay the price, and I refuse to let *you* pay it for me."

Merrick strode after her and grabbed her arm before she made it out of the room, spinning her around to face him again. "I will *not* let you die. I'll pay *any* price a thousand times over before that."

"I won't let you." She pulled her arm free of his grasp. "I knew what was coming, Merrick. I accepted it. It's time that you do, too." Tears trickled from her eyes. "Let me go."

"*Never.*" Rage—sparked by an overwhelming sense of helplessness—roared to life within him. "I've already told you, Adalynn, you are mine. I will *never* let you go. You're going to live no matter what I must do to make it so."

That hardness in her eyes only strengthened, as though her resolve were carbon being squeezed into diamond. If he hadn't already known it, he understood it then—she would not budge on this. She would not back down. She would not allow him to perform the soul binding.

All because he couldn't guarantee what it would do. All because she didn't want him to come to harm for her sake.

Without another word, she turned and left. The sound of her bare feet on the floor as she stormed away held a crushing finality he could not accept.

Merrick's fury would not be contained any longer. It locked every muscle in his body and triggered a surge of wild, bristling magic that engulfed him in blue energy.

Let her go? *Let her go?* Did she truly not understand the depth of what they shared, the intensity of their connection? No, she just wanted him to *think* she didn't understand—that she didn't feel the same way. But he'd seen it in her eyes. He'd sensed it in her song as clearly as he could see the blue of the sky or feel the warmth of a fire.

That fury collided with his frustration to create a firestorm within him, hazing over his rational thought and leaving only a powerful, irresistible compulsion toward destruction. He was aware of nothing else as he tore apart the parlor with a combination of magic and his bare hands, breaking the furniture, tearing the wallpaper, and shattering the light fixtures.

An inhuman roar joined the cacophony of the destruction, rising above all else. In his rage-induced haze, he didn't recognize the sound as his own.

Chapter Sixteen

Adalynn strode out of the parlor toward the spiral stairway, clutching her pants to her chest. She could feel Merrick's seed dripping down the inside of her thighs. Tears blurred her vision, and she blinked them away, letting them spill down her cheeks. She clenched her jaw to keep her bottom lip from trembling—and failed miserably.

Her throat worked, constricting further with each passing second. A crash of furniture sounded behind her, followed by shattering glass, and a *whoosh* of power. Her steps faltered, and she caught herself against the wall as a great, heaving sob escaped her. She pressed her forehead against the cool wood as she cried, listening to the chaos, the destruction, and the pain coming from the parlor behind her. Her legs nearly crumpled beneath her, but she managed to remain upright.

There was a tightness in her chest, formed around a well of hurt that went soul-deep.

This was her fault. She'd allowed herself to get too close, had allowed him to care about her too deeply, when she'd *known* what the outcome would be. And now Merrick was hurting. They both were.

Adalynn squeezed her eyes shut, forcing out more tears.

Pain, sharp and piercing, flared in her head. Her cry was drowned out by Merrick's deafening, inhuman roar, which seemed to make the entire house shake. Unable to look back, Adalynn pushed herself away from the wall and rushed up the stairs.

I have to go. I need to leave. I can't...I can't do this to him any longer.

Adalynn knew what it was like to be willing to sacrifice oneself for a loved one—she'd been ready to do so for Danny ever since the Sundering, and she wouldn't have hesitated to at any point during which it became necessary. But her time had always been limited—she was already *dying* when hell came to Earth. Merrick was not. And each time he'd fought back her cancer, it hurt *him*. When would it become too much? When would it *kill* him?

I can't let him hurt himself again.

Adalynn reached her room, grasped the handle, and threw the door open. Inside, she leaned down and grabbed her bugout bag—which she hadn't moved since Merrick said they could stay indefinitely—and tossed it onto the bed. Shaking out her pants, she shoved her legs into them, pulled them up, and fastened their buttons.

She still felt him inside her, still felt the lingering ache of her orgasm, felt the evidence of what they'd shared. That moment, this day, had been so *perfect*—like a dream. But that was all this could have ever been for Adalynn—a dream, a fantasy, a wish, so ephemeral that the wind could've swept it from her grasp and carried it away at any moment. It was something she never could've held onto.

After wiping her face with the back of her hand, she reached for her boots, which stood beneath the window. Another bolt of agony pierced her skull, and for a moment, her vision wavered. She dropped to her knees and clutched her head between her hands, curling her fingers to grasp fistfuls of her hair. The stinging pain on her scalp only made everything worse.

It's coming.

"No," she rasped. "No, please. Not now. Not yet. Please just *wait*, just give me a little longer."

But she knew her pleading would change nothing—something inside her, something dark, told her this would be the end. It was more than pessimism, more than acceptance of her inevitable fate. The specter of death had been following her for months, and now it was right on her heels, reaching out to touch her shoulder.

Once the pain finally ebbed, Adalynn took in a deep, shaky breath, grabbed her boots, and tugged them on. Standing slowly, she returned to her bag and paused. She didn't need any of it— the clothes, the emergency energy bars, the tools, the supplies. They'd serve Danny better, if he ever found himself in need.

"Addy? What's going on?"

Adalynn started at the voice behind her and turned to find Danny standing just inside her room. His hair was mussed, as though he'd just woken up, and he was wearing was a pair of long athletic shorts and a tank top.

His brow furrowed as he searched her face. "What's wrong? And what's wrong with Merrick?"

Adalynn ran to her brother and threw her arms around him. She held him tight as a fresh flood of tears fell from her eyes. "I love you, you know that, right?"

Danny embraced her. "Yeah, of course I do. I love you, too. But what's going on? You're scaring me."

Adalynn couldn't speak for a time; all she could do was hold her brother, breathe in his scent, and feel his warmth, his solidness. He'd grown so much just in the short time they'd been here. She tightened her hold on him.

Another crash—and another roar—sounded from downstairs.

Danny started and pushed away from her. "Addy! What's going on? What's wrong with Merrick? Why are you crying?"

Adalynn forced herself to release her brother. Her arms fell to her sides, and she took a step back. She needed to be calm for Danny. He didn't need to see her fear, didn't need to worry about her.

Taking another deep breath—and trying to ignore the insistent, throbbing ache in her head—she met her brother's gaze. "It's coming."

At first, confusion contorted his features, but realization dawned swiftly. His eyes widened, his eyebrows rose high, and a panicked gleam overpowered the concern that had been in his gaze. "I'll go get Merrick."

"Danny, no!" Adalynn reached out and caught her brother's shirt as he turned to leave. Her fingers clutched the fabric, bringing him to a stop.

He turned to face her again. "What do you mean, *no*? We need him to stop it!"

She shook her head. Her skin prickled, tingling and numb all at once, and her heart raced. "No. We're not stopping it."

He scowled and tugged easily out of her grip, taking a step backward into the hall. "What the hell, Addy? Why not?"

"Because it can't be stopped, Danny! We knew that. We've always known that. It was only a matter of time."

"But Merrick—"

"*No!*"

Danny flinched; it added to the worst of Adalynn's pain—the pain in her heart.

"I don't want Merrick to help again," Adalynn continued, lowering her voice. "You saw what it did to him. We don't know what more it will do. It could *kill* him, Danny."

"So…so what are you going to do? Just…*die*?"

Adalynn stared at her brother, but for a moment, she didn't see him. Her mind went blank as her stomach cramped and a feverish flush swept through her body, carrying with it a fresh wave of fear and anxiety.

On its heels came an icy certainty.

"Addy!"

She started, blinked, and focused on Danny. There was fear in his gaze.

"It's happening, isn't it?" he asked, tears filling his eyes.

"I need to go."

She stepped around him and strode down the hall. Everything around her was a blur, a haze, as it spun and shifted without regard for the laws of physics.

A hand closed around her wrist as she reached the top of the stairs, dragging her to a halt. She looked back to find Danny behind her, his eyes huge and awash with tears, his skin pale.

"What the fuck do you mean *go*, Addy?"

"I need to leave here. Now."

He tightened his grasp on her, adding his other hand to her arm. He didn't seem to notice when a massive crash from downstairs shook the floor beneath them. "You *can't* go, Addy. We can take care of you. Merrick has *magic*. He can help!"

"Not without hurting himself. No, Danny. I won't let him do that. I...I *love* him. I don't want him to die because of me. Please, just let me go, while there's still time, and promise you'll stay *here*."

Danny's tears spilled down his cheeks. "I'm not letting you go out there by yourself. People can't just...let go, Addy, that's not how it works. You *know* that."

Adalynn faced him and placed her hands on his shoulders. She squeezed, harder than she intended, as her stomach cramped, and nausea made her unsteady. She doubled over slightly, holding onto him for support as she struggled to keep her breathing slow and steady in the hopes of pushing the nausea back. "You *have* to. Do you remember what happened to mom and dad? Do you want that to happen again? It won't be *me* anymore, Danny! I won't be able to stop myself from hurting you once I change. I need to get far away from you."

Danny shook his head. "No. No, I won't let you go. You need to be here."

"Danny, please. I don't——"

Crippling pain blacked out her vision. Adalynn screamed, hands slipping from Danny's shoulders. Only his arms looping around her prevented Adalynn from tumbling down the stairs.

He laid her on the floor as her every muscle contracted and spasmed; her body was no longer hers to control. Something warm seeped from her nose, and she tasted blood in her mouth, but the agony in her head demanded her attention above all else. It felt simultaneously like her skull was being split in half and crushed in a vice, and the pain spread outward to permeate her entire skeleton, dominating every inch of her body.

"Merrick!" Danny screamed. His trembling hands smoothed over her. "Hold on, Addy. You're gonna be okay. Please, just *hold on*." His hands lifted away; she was only vaguely aware that he'd left when he called for Merrick again and his voice sounded distant.

Adalynn clawed at the carpet with stiff, curled fingers, battling the pain. She was used to feeling it in her head, in her stomach, but this was *everywhere*, like her sickness had forced its way into every cell of her body in response to Merrick's attempts to eliminate it. The room spun, and her vision faded, but she was still aware—aware of the blood, of the agony, of everything she wished she could have said and done, of her fear of what she'd become once she died.

RAGE-INFUSED MAGIC SWIRLED AROUND MERRICK, enveloping him in electric heat. It insulated his fury, allowed those uncontrollable, untethered emotions to echo and amplify, to feed into themselves and expand the mana storm surrounding him. Blinding blue energy had become his world, dominating all his senses. Nothing remained but magic and rage.

No, that wasn't right. It wasn't that simple; he could still recognize the truth of it, even in this state, though his thoughts were sluggish, hazy, and dampened. His rage was underscored by quieter but more powerful emotions—sorrow; loss; pain. Helplessness. But those emotions constantly sank under waves of rising magic, each of which was stronger than the last.

Magic...

Yes, there was only magic. Nothing else mattered.

Merrick's magic flared, tearing apart another chunk of the room. Deeper, more potent energy crackled through it, ancient beyond imagining, charging him with explosive force. It was thrilling to feel that power, to *use* that power, thrilling to unleash his fury and frustration.

And that power seemed to thrill in being used.

Merrick opened himself to it further, expanding the channels torn open by his overwhelming emotions. The power flowed through him, crackling across the fibers of his being. His heart sped, but it seemed to pump blood no longer—it pumped *mana* through his veins, pure and exhilarating.

Let go. No troubles. No pain. Only power.

He could become one with that energy. He could be free of pain, worry, frustration, and rage. Free and powerful.

Let go of yourself. Embrace magic in its purest form. Become *magic.*

A fresh surge of mana rose within him, spreading outward from his core to race along his limbs and arc from the tips of his fingers and toes. His consciousness expanded; mana songs from everything around him sparked in his mind's eye with stunning clarity, even the objects he'd already destroyed in his rage, and he knew that with one thought he could connect himself to any of them, to *all* of them. As that awareness increased, his fury diminished, and all the emotions behind it faded further.

Let go.

Two of the mana songs were stronger than the rest, their volume amplified by their familiarity. Merrick knew them both —the one moving toward him and the one holding still. The latter was *intimately* familiar; it called to him like a siren's song, coaxed him to approach despite the discordant notes disrupting its melody.

Let go.

That whisper was more insistent now, more forceful.

"Merrick!" someone yelled from far, far away, from another world—an inferior, physical world.

Let go!

He'd been told that before. Before now, before he'd been consumed by magic and fury, before the ley line had once again buried its claws in him. Adalynn had said *let me go.* That's what the whispers were demanding of him—to let everything go. To let *her* go.

The power, the thrill, the *magic* didn't matter. Only she did. He'd gladly let go of all the rest so long as he could hold onto her for the rest of his days. So long as he could keep her.

No, he shouted in his mind, blasting the thought outward.

The magic surrounding him rippled, but he could feel it building again, could feel it preparing to oppose his will, to overwhelm him.

Let go and embrace the power, the voice in his mind screamed back.

Nothing will take her from me. Nothing!

Merrick's mental roar gathered in his chest and burst from his throat, raw and primal. It exploded across the room like a rush of air, snuffing out the roiling, ravenous blue magic, cutting off his connection to the ley line and plunging the room into darkness.

He sucked in a ragged, burning breath and fell to his knees.

"Merrick," Danny called from behind him. "Oh, man, are you okay?"

The boy's hand came down on Merrick's back, icy compared to the lingering heat of the magic that had enveloped him until an instant ago.

Though Merrick's connection to the mana songs around him had been closed, he still sensed Adalynn's—still sensed the distress in it, the discord.

"Where's Adalynn?" Merrick rasped, turning his head to look at the boy.

Tears flowed freely from Danny's eyes, and his face was pale with worry and fear. "She's upstairs. It's bad, Merrick. You need to help her. *Please.*"

No. No, death cannot have her. She is mine*!*

Merrick rose, turned, and stumbled toward the staircase. His body, his flesh and bone, felt heavy, awkward, and worn now, but he couldn't let that stop him. He *wouldn't*. His muscles would obey his command and carry him to his Adalynn.

And he would do whatever was necessary to save her.

As he neared the steps, his awareness of her song increased exponentially, and he knew immediately the damage he'd done to her. When she'd first arrived, the darkness tainting her resonance had been concentrated, had been a dangerous but self-contained entity—like a rock frozen in a block of ice. Now it suffused the entirety of her song, staining her whole being with its maliciousness.

His already labored heart quickened, pounding in his chest like thunder breaking over a deep valley. Pulsating prickles of fire and ice trailed along his limbs.

Merrick had done that to her. He'd *caused* that. In his attempt to alleviate the worst of her symptoms, he'd taken whatever time she might've had—weeks, perhaps *months*—and turned it into days. Because he knew this was it. This was her end.

But he would not let it be.

He didn't care what price he had to pay; he would give up *everything* for her. Nothing would take her...and she wasn't allowed to go.

Grasping the bannister with desperate strength, he dragged himself up the stairs, forcing his legs forward faster than they were willing to move. Adalynn came into view as he rounded the spiral staircase and neared the loft. She lay at the top of the stairs, her limbs tight and trembling, her face contorted in agony. Her resonance sang to him sorrowfully, longingly, reflecting the pain evident in her body. Blood trickled from her mouth and nose, and her eyes were red with strain.

Merrick fell to his knees on the top step and bent over her, scarcely aware of Danny's presence as the boy slipped around him to kneel on Adalynn's other side. Merrick placed his hands on her cheeks, cupping her face. Her skin was cold and clammy.

"I'm sorry, Adalynn, so sorry," he said. "I did this."

Her eyes, so filled with pain and tears, met his. Despite her agony, there was awareness in her gaze. She shook her head slightly, the movement so infinitesimal and erratic that he might've thought it involuntary if he hadn't felt her response through their song.

"I'm making it right," Merrick continued. "Whatever the price, I gladly pay it. You're mine, Adalynn, and I'm not letting you go."

She squeezed her eyes shut, forcing out fresh tears, and released a harsh, clipped breath as the tension in her body intensified.

Soul binding.

That was the only option now, the only possibility. There was no more time for research, no more time to fight back her illness; after a thousand damned years, he was out of time.

Reluctantly, he lifted his gaze from Adalynn to Danny. "Daniel, there's a scroll on my desk, in the study. Fetch it. Quickly."

The boy nodded rapidly and scrambled to his feet, rushing across the loft. One of Adalynn's hands caught Merrick's wrist. Her fingers curled around it with iron strength, digging her nails into his flesh.

Merrick looked down at her again and brushed his thumbs over her cheekbones. "Hold on, Adalynn. *Hold on.*"

"Merrick?" Danny's voice quavered with fear and uncertainty.

Lifting his gaze once more, Merrick looked toward Danny —and his heart froze in place. The door to the study was open wide, and the room beyond was a charred mess—his magic from the parlor below had come up through the floor and reduced his desk to ash.

"No, no, no," he muttered. "No!"

His heart started beating again at an impossibly fast pace, and his rapid, shallow breaths couldn't draw enough air into his lungs. The scroll was gone. The key to saving her was gone.

Not letting go. Can't let go. I refuse to let go.

Adalynn released a choked breath. Her back bowed and her eyes opened to slits, displaying only whites, as her body seized.

He didn't know what to do to help her now. Didn't know how to proceed. In his arrogance, in his foolishness, he'd both thought himself capable of changing her fate and had ruined his chance of doing so.

Merrick gritted his teeth, closed his eyes, and wrapped his arms around her, drawing her against him. She shuddered, her body rigid rather than pliant and soft like it usually was.

He was losing her.

"I *love* you, Adalynn," he rasped. "I cannot lose you."

As he clung to her, he latched onto her mana song, letting it wash over him, willing it to mingle with his own, to create that beautiful duet he'd come to appreciate so much. Her tension eased, and she went limp in his hold. Her resonance flickered and sputtered…but a hint of it remained. Weak and delicate, it was barely a spark—the sort of spark that lingered briefly as a person died.

He swallowed thickly and forced his eyes open.

I don't need the scroll.

In that moment, he realized that he *knew* what to do, that he'd always known—it was an instinct buried deep within him, deep within the primal mana at his core. He'd felt it every time they'd joined their bodies, every time their mana had sung together, every time their souls had spent precious seconds intertwined.

The scroll simply detailed something natural, something he didn't have to understand to perform—because it was the *right* thing. Because she was the *right* one. The *only* one.

He lifted his head to find Danny, distraught, kneeling on the floor in front of him. "Do you have your knife?"

Eyes wide, Danny shook his head.

"Get it, boy. Now! Hasten, damn you!"

Once again, Danny scrambled away, racing down the hall.

Seed. Blood. Mana.

One of those things had already been shared—he could sense it inside her still. Along with the other two, the binding could be completed.

As gently as he could, Merrick moved up off the stairs and laid her on the floor. He pressed a hand over her chest; her heartbeat was muted, weak, slow.

"No," he growled, easing magic into her, fanning that little spark inside her. "Just a little longer, Adalynn."

The darkness surrounding that spark lashed out at him, sinking its tainted claws into his resonance, but he did not relent. He hadn't allowed himself to be consumed by the ley line, and he would not allow himself to be overcome by any disease—mortal or otherwise. Not while she was at stake.

Danny's feet thumped along the hallway as he sprinted back to Merrick. The boy fell to his knees, catching himself on one hand, and handed over his sheathed bowie knife.

Merrick tugged the knife out of its sheath. "Whatever you see, boy, whatever you hear or feel, do not interfere. Stay back."

He didn't allow Danny time to respond; he could only keep Adalynn's spark alight for a short while, and he couldn't waste even a fraction of a second. He lifted her hands one-by-one and cut her palms. Blood oozed from the wounds. Once he was done, he cut his own palms and dropped the knife onto the floor beside him.

Shifting to straddle Adalynn, he hurriedly twined his fingers with hers. A soft, rasping exhalation escaped her; she drew in a shallow, labored breath afterward.

Their blood mingled, and Merrick felt the first hints of her mana song in his veins. He latched onto that sensation, clenched his jaw, and *pulled*.

He acted purely on instinct, with little conscious understanding of what he was doing. The air between him and Adalynn glowed as snaking tendrils of glimmering magic flowed out of him—and out of *her*. Merrick's mana was a familiar blue—strong and bright, building rapidly in front of him. Adalynn's was a muted green, thinner, weaker, and slower to form, but no less real.

The still flowing magicks met in the air between their chests and swirled around each other. They moved sluggishly at first, but as Merrick tensed his muscles and poured his concentration toward it, the tendrils of magic sped until they were so fast they could no longer be distinguished from one another. The two mana sources coalesced in a vibrant teal orb. Adalynn's mana song rose to match Merrick's, becoming louder and stronger than he'd ever sensed it, taking its place not just as a piece of his own but as its equal.

A sense of euphoria spread through Merrick as he stared at that wispy, pulsating orb—at their combined essence. There was nothing more intimate than *this*. No way to be closer.

The magic split in half. One piece flowed into Merrick's chest, the other into Adalynn's. It rocketed his euphoria into unbearable ecstasy, making him shudder and growl as though he'd just reached a climax.

Adalynn's back arched. She sucked in a deep, gasping breath, eyes suddenly opened wide, only to sag back down once the glow of magic had faded. Her eyes fluttered closed and her head lolled to the side as Merrick fell forward, catching himself on his elbows without releasing her hands.

Panting, Merrick stared at Adalynn's face. It was relaxed, free of strain and pain; for one fleeting moment, he feared he'd lost her, that it hadn't worked.

But he could *feel* her, could feel her *inside* himself, suffusing his every cell, singing within his mana—their mana.

He knew she was alive just as certainly as he knew he was.

And she was *his*. She'd always been his. Though he'd not understood what that meant at the time, he'd known it from the first moment he'd seen her.

"M-Merrick?" Danny asked. "Is she…is Addy…"

"She's alive," Merrick replied, his voice hoarse. "She's *alive*."

Danny crawled closer, placed a hand on the side of Adalynn's face, and kissed her forehead. When he pulled away, he wiped the tears from his cheeks, sniffled, and looked up at Merrick. His eyes were red from crying, but there was immense relief and gratitude within them. "Thank you."

Merrick slipped off Adalynn and gently gathered her in his arms, drawing her close to his chest so that her head lay on his shoulder. He stood up and carried her toward his bedroom. His heart only gradually slowed, and his breath remained ragged as he walked.

She was alive, but was she all right? Her mana song was stronger than ever...but he could sense that her body still wasn't well, that her illness still lingered. Had he only extended her suffering?

No, he sensed that dark taint weakening, receding; he sensed her body healing. Relief flooded him.

Danny hurried ahead to open the door to Merrick's bedroom, and Merrick stepped inside. He crossed to the bed and laid Adalynn atop it. Blood continued to ooze from the cuts on her hands.

"Bandages," Merrick said.

"Okay." Danny's hurried footsteps faded down the hall.

Delicately, Merrick brushed Adalynn's sweat-dampened hair out of her face, tucking the strands behind her ears.

"Come back to us, Adalynn. Come back to *me*."

Danny returned a short time later with a wet cloth and his backpack, which he dropped heavily onto the floor next to the bed. A moment later, he produced a packaged disinfectant wipe and a roll of gauze, handing them—along with the cloth —to Merrick.

Merrick quickly cleaned her palms and bound her wounds, gently settling her hands atop the bedding when he was done. Adalynn remained unmoving but for the steady rise and fall of her chest.

"She's going to be okay, right?" Danny asked anxiously.

"She doesn't have a choice but to be okay," Merrick replied.

Chapter Seventeen

"When do you think she'll wake up?" Danny asked. He was seated at the foot of the bed, just beyond Adalynn's feet.

"I cannot guess," Merrick replied.

Danny had slept sporadically over the last three days, usually on the bed beside his sister, unwilling to leave her when it wasn't absolutely necessary. He'd only eaten because Merrick had forced him to, often protesting by pointing out that Merrick wasn't taking time to sleep or eat, so he didn't see why he should have to.

The boy looked exhausted. Though his skin was tanned, it had taken on a pale, almost sickly undertone, and he had deep bags beneath his eyes. Whenever Adalynn did wake up, she was likely to have a few things to say about Danny not taking care of himself while she was out—and some choice words for Merrick for not taking care of Danny well enough.

And those would be amongst the sweetest words Merrick had ever heard.

Merrick himself hadn't slept or eaten since he'd bound their souls together. He couldn't. Even though he sensed that everything within her was fine, she'd shown no signs of waking. Her mana song, still inexorably twined with his, had only strengthened, and he couldn't detect even a hint of that darkness in her anymore. Merrick had tended to her at every moment—he'd bathed her, dressed her in more comfortable clothing, had trickled droplets of water into her mouth to ensure she'd had *something* to drink.

She was the same Adalynn as always, but she was *more* now, too. He wasn't entirely sure what it meant, but it didn't alarm him. It might even have been comforting were it not for his worry; it would've been comforting if she'd already woken.

"When was the last time you ate, Daniel?" Merrick asked as he turned his attention back to Adalynn. Her face was so serene, so beautiful…but her peaceful expression now couldn't compare to the brightness of her smile, which he missed more and more with each passing hour.

"I'm okay," Danny said.

"When, boy?"

"Uh…yesterday, I think."

"Go eat. Then you will take a shower and get some sleep."

"I'm *fine*, Merrick. I don't want to leave in case she wakes up."

Merrick turned his head to glance at Danny. "If she wakes, I will alert you. But if she wakes while you are sitting there, looking—and smelling—more like one of those undead creatures beyond our walls than her younger brother, how do you think she will react?"

Danny slouched, his eyebrows falling low and his mouth turning down in a deep frown. "You promise you'll call me?"

"I promise."

The boy sighed heavily. He glanced at Adalynn for a moment before standing. "*Fine.*"

"If we don't keep ourselves healthy for her, Daniel…what was the point of all this?"

"*Okay*, I get it." Danny walked toward the door, stopped,

turned his head, and narrowed his eyes on Merrick. "I mean it. *Call me.*"

"If you're still here in three seconds, I'm going to throw you in your room and magically seal the door."

"All right, all right!" Danny's steps were heavy as he finally exited the room and walked down the hallway.

Merrick shifted his full attention to Adalynn. One of her arms lay outside the blankets that were draped over the rest of her body; he took that hand in his, lacing their fingers together. The bandages were gone—the cuts on her hands had vanished by the second day—allowing their palms to meet skin-to-skin. He gently stroked her cheek with the fingertips of his other hand.

"If this is even the barest hint of what things would be like were you gone, neither Daniel nor myself would last long, Adalynn," he whispered. "Your brother needs you. *I* need you. I never realized how empty my life was before you came into it."

He leaned forward and raised her hand to his lips, letting his soft kiss on her knuckles linger for a long while. "Come back to me, love. *Please.* As foolish as it may sound after so short a while…I don't know how to live without you anymore. There's nothing for me without you."

Just like every other time he'd spoken to her over the last three days, Adalynn offered no response, made no indication that she'd heard him. But she was in there; he could *feel* it, could sense her consciousness.

"If you don't wake up soon, Adalynn, I *swear* I will find some way to go in there after you and drag you back out."

He'd been tempted many, many times to use his magic to latch onto her mana song and force her awake…but he'd learned his lesson by now. He understood that such things exacted prices far too high, caused more damage than he was willing to knowingly inflict.

Merrick squeezed her hand a little tighter. *"Please."*

Her finger twitched. Merrick's heart skipped a beat.

"Adalynn?"

Her fingers twitched again, and her eyelids fluttered.

Merrick sat on the edge of the chair he'd pulled beside the bed, cupping her cheek in his palm. "Yes, wake up. Pull yourself out of it. Waking up is the easiest thing you've had to do since you arrived here."

Her resonance flared—both within her and within Merrick—and he sensed her struggling, fighting, clawing her way up from unconsciousness.

"Wake up, Adalynn," he growled. His magic crackled to life on his skin, thrumming along his limbs, and he rose, knocking the chair back as he did so. "Come back to me. *Fight.* You are not to waste another moment, do you *hear* me?"

Excitement and desperation swirled in a chaotic storm within his chest, which felt like it would burst if the pressure continued growing. She needed a jolt, a push, but he dared not use magic. He dared not risk harming her.

Merrick leaned forward and slammed his lips over hers. Their mana song surged, sweeping through him to set his body ablaze with heat, lust, and need and forcing his eyes closed. Her lips were warm and pliant beneath his, and he ravished them, claimed them, *devoured* them. And she...parted them.

Something touched the side of his face—her free hand.

He drew in a startled breath and began to pull away, but the air was flavored with her taste, with her essence, and the rightness of it lured him back in. He shifted his hand into her hair and deepened their kiss, slipping his tongue between her parted lips.

Every moment he'd spent with her was dear to him, each bit of intimacy they'd shared was powerful, special, and memorable, but that kiss was the sweetest he'd ever experienced by far.

It took all his willpower to break that kiss after several

euphoric seconds; he had to see her face, had to look into her eyes, had to *know* she was okay. He opened his eyes and met her gaze.

Merrick's breath hitched; Adalynn's eyes were glowing a soft teal, the same color that had been produced by their combined mana songs, the same color his own magic had taken on since the soul binding.

She smiled up at him, her thumb brushing over his cheek and rasping through his beard. "I'm alive."

He couldn't stop himself from laughing, and it felt so, so good. "Glad you finally noticed, Adalynn. We've been waiting awhile."

Her smile slipped as fast as it came, and the glow faded from her eyes, returning them to their normal beautiful brown. "Did you...did you do it again? Did you push it back?"

He would gladly stand here and stare into those eyes for three whole days after being denied them that long. "No. No, I didn't push it back. But it is gone now."

Her brow furrowed. "How?"

"I bound our mana songs together. Our souls. They are now one. *We* are one."

Her features smoothed out with blossoming wonder as she searched his eyes "I hear it. I *feel* it. I mean, I've always felt it before, coming from you, but now...it's in *me*."

"As it was always meant to be. Your song was a part of mine before I even met you, Adalynn." He released a shaky breath and tucked a rogue lock of her hair behind her ear. "You were meant to be mine."

She raised her other hand and slipped her fingers into his hair, tugging him into another kiss. "I'm sorry. I didn't mean what I said. I...I don't just want a physical relationship."

He tipped his forehead against hers, shaking his head slightly. "And I told you it was *never* just that. It never could've been just that. I love you, Adalynn. That's what it was always meant to be."

Her fingers tightened in his hair, producing a light sting on his scalp that only heightened his need to pull her closer, to gather her in his arms and never let her go.

"I love you, too," she said.

He pulled his face away and stared down at her; that glow had returned to her eyes again, so different from what he was used to seeing there, but so *right*. "I think you may be immortal, Adalynn."

Her breath hitched, and her eyes widened. "What?"

"Your soul is tethered to mine. Your *lifeforce*. My immortality…I believe it's part of you now, too. I cut your palms three days ago, but look at them." He leaned back, took hold of her hands, and gently guided them down from his hair, turning her palms toward her. "Not a trace. The wounds were healed completely by yesterday. And I can no longer sense any trace of your cancer."

Adalynn stared at her palms. She closed her fingers and opened them again. Merrick could see her thoughts racing, could tell she had many questions—and he would answer them, as he was able. But that wasn't what mattered now.

He caught her chin and turned her face back toward him. "We are bound, Adalynn. Forever."

She covered his hand with hers. "Forever is a long time."

Merrick smiled softly. "Adalynn, forever isn't nearly long enough."

Her lips turned up in a wide smile. "Don't men usually get cold feet when they think about forever? About being tied down? Being *bound* sounds more permanent than the ole ball and chain."

"There will be no cold feet here, save perhaps on winter mornings before we stoke the fire."

Adalynn laughed; between that sound and her shining smile, he couldn't resist releasing her arm and kissing her again. She returned the kiss just as fervently, wrapping her arms around him.

Danny would be upset, but he could wait a few minutes—the boy needed to eat and rest, anyway. But Merrick...he had found his forever, his soul song, and he was going to relish this new beginning without interruption.

Epilogue

Four Months Later

ADALYNN LAY upon Merrick's chest, listening to his rapid heartbeat and the swirling symphony of their mana songs as they came down from the heights of ecstasy. Their skin was coated in perspiration, their breath ragged, and her sex pulsed around his cock in the aftermath of her climax. She closed her eyes, smiling softly, as Merrick lightly trailed his fingertips up and down her spine.

Delightful heat radiated from the blazing fireplace across from the foot of the bed, chasing away the chill. The fireplace had seen frequent use over the last few months as summer had given way first to autumn and now winter.

During those months, Adalynn hadn't suffered a single attack—but she *had* suffered from numerous bouts of random nausea. At first, it had frightened her, and she'd wondered if her illness had returned, but there'd been no other symptoms. It hadn't been long before she'd begun to suspect something else—especially after she realized she hadn't had her period since arriving at Merrick's four months ago.

TIFFANY ROBERTS

Opening her eyes, Adalynn inhaled deeply and lifted her hand away from him, settling it on the side of her neck. "Do you remember the first time we made love?"

"Yes, quite clearly. And every time afterward. Also quite clearly."

Adalynn grinned. "Do you remember what I'd asked you?"

He rubbed his palm over his short beard. "You asked if I had *protection*."

She raised her head and looked down at him, her hair falling over one shoulder. "And I recall you saying something in reply to that."

Merrick smirked. "There was no chance of conceiving. *That* time."

"You *know*?"

"I'm attuned enough to our mana songs to tell when there's a change. There's been another melody forming beneath ours—a more perfect blend of them. I've suspected what it meant for several weeks."

Adalynn half-heartedly slapped his shoulder. She couldn't be angry with him, not when she was so overjoyed by what they had created together. "That was cheap, Merrick. That's something pretty major we should have discussed *together*."

He rolled her onto her back and propped himself over her, hands braced on either side of her head and hips pinning her to the bed. His cock was still inside her. He dipped his head and pecked a quick kiss on her lips; most of her largely feigned anger slipped away. Merrick slowly worked his lips—and his body—lower, withdrawing his shaft from her sex as he kissed along her neck and between her breasts to finally stop at her stomach.

"All the times we've made love, I made sure my precautions were in place," he said, looking up at her with his glowing teal eyes. He cradled her stomach—her slightly

290

rounded stomach. "I think it happened when I performed the binding. Seed, blood, and mana...those are the required components. My seed was already within you, and whatever protections I had woven must've been unraveled during the binding."

Adalynn smiled and raised a hand, tracing the scar cutting across his eye before brushing the backs of her fingers over his cheek. "We're going to have a baby."

"We are," he replied, his smile mirroring the joy in hers.

When she'd first come here, when she'd first met Merrick, she hadn't even thought him capable of smiling, and never would've imagined how much a smile could transform his face.

Her smile faded slightly, the joy of sharing this moment overshadowed by thoughts of the future.

Merrick lifted his head, propping himself up on his elbows. "What is it, Adalynn?"

"Are you worried?" she asked. "About the future? About having a baby...in *this* world?"

His eyes blazed like twin fires. "Nothing will harm our child, just as nothing will harm you or Danny. I will make sure of it." He crawled back up her body until his face hovered over hers. "We have this place. I cannot say that no one else will ever come...but you know we can defend it, if necessary. Especially once you learn more fully how to use your magic."

That was another thing she was getting used to—magic. It came and went, flaring up with her emotions, and learning to control it was a slow process. But with Merrick patiently guiding her, she knew it would, in time, become second nature.

Adalynn settled her hands on his arms and slowly slid them up to his shoulders. She smiled brightly; her joy returned to the forefront of her mind. "We're having a *baby*."

"I've had Danny setting up a nursery in the next room.

He's been moving down some of the furniture from the attic while you've been busy over the last few days."

"Even *he* knew?"

Merrick laughed. "Not until I said something to him. Don't worry, Adalynn—I don't give up secrets *quite* that easily. At least not usually."

"You could have let me in on it."

"I was waiting for you to tell me."

"Guess that won't be something I can surprise you with in the future."

Merrick smirked. "Does that mean you wish to have more?"

Adalynn blushed, stroking his arm. "Maybe."

He chuckled and lowered his face, brushing his lips over hers. The song within her flared, and her lips tingled.

"We have forever, Adalynn."

She smiled, looping her arms around his neck and raising her knees to cradle his body between her thighs. Teal tendrils of magic crackled across his skin, and similar energy rose from hers in reaction, creating a thrilling electric buzz on her flesh. He thrust his cock into her, pushing deep. Adalynn's breath hitched, and she tilted her head back to lock her eyes with his.

Merrick cradled her jaw in his hand, trailing his thumb over her lower lip. "Without you, I never would have learned to live again." He drew his hips away and slid back into her slowly, triggering another flare of scintillating magic and pleasure in both of them. "You've given me a family. A reason to be. Without you, I'd have stumbled through eternity without knowing love."

He pushed into her harder, and Adalynn clutched at him as their mana song—their shared song—swelled with each of his thrusts, building rapidly. They climaxed together swiftly, fiercely, with harsh breaths and strained cries that only added to their song.

Merrick gathered her closer and pressed his forehead against hers as they panted. "I would gladly give up the thousand years I spent alone to taste your lips a single time." He kissed her again. "You've given me everything. You, Adalynn, *are* my everything, and you're all the magic I'll ever need."

Author's Note

Thank you so much for reading *The Warlock's Kiss*! We hope you enjoyed reading it as much as we did writing it. For us, it was a trip down memory lane.

We've talked before about how Rob and I met, but for those who don't know, we met through a text-based fantasy roleplaying game. Roleplaying was something we really enjoyed doing, and because we lived so far away from each other when we first met, it was our primary way to spend time together. Even after we started living together in person, we continued to roleplay together. It allowed us to do what we both loved to do—write. We built worlds, characters, and stories, and *this* world, these characters—Merrick, Adalynn, and Danny—were created back in 2013.

Their story stood out in my mind, even after all these years, and we had logs saved of that roleplay. Though the original roleplay was much shorter than the story it became, the bones of it were all there, along with these wonderful characters—who were already fleshed out and alive. After we finished *Shielded Heart*, we wanted to write something short, something to cleanse our palates; we wanted a change of scenery. So, I brought this story up to Rob. And, well...we all know how it goes when we try to write something short. It doesn't happen. Not that it's a bad thing, haha! We planned this book to be around fifty thousand words, and wound up at over eighty-three thousand. We enjoyed delving into these characters and creating the deep, emotional connections they have with one another. Building new worlds is also something we really love to do.

Which brings us to this question at some of you might have: Will we write more books in this world?

The answer: Maybe. The Warlock's Kiss is a standalone, but we have other stories and characters that we had written before Merrick and Adalynn's story that take place when the Sundering began. It's just a matter of whether there's enough interest on your part. Of course, we can't say when we might get to them, as we have so many projects planned and lined up already, but you never know when we might squeeze something in.

So, if you loved *The Warlock's Kiss*, please leave a review on Amazon. We know you hear this from authors a lot, but reviews help author visibility on Amazon *and* can show authors how much you enjoyed a book and if you want a series to continue. You can also spread the book love by recommending it in one of your favorite book groups. Word of mouth is the best thing you can do for an author, and you have no idea how much we love and appreciate it each time we see our name mentioned. Like, seriously. I get all warm and gooey inside that you remembered us and that our book stood out enough for you to recommend it to someone else. Thank you so, so much!

Again, thank you all so much for being such amazing, supportive, wonderful readers. We can't express how much we appreciate you all. Every message, every post, every email, every review. Thank you again for reading our stories.

Also by Tiffany Roberts

THE INFINITE CITY

Entwined Fates

Silent Lucidity

Shielded Heart

Vengeful Heart

Untamed Hunger

Savage Desire

Tethered Souls

THE KRAKEN

Treasure of the Abyss

Jewel of the Sea

Hunter of the Tide

Heart of the Deep

Rising from the Depths

Fallen from the Stars

Lover from the Waves

THE SPIDER'S MATE TRILOGY

Ensnared

Enthralled

Bound

About the Author

Tiffany Roberts is the pseudonym for Tiffany and Robert Freund, a husband and wife writing duo. Tiffany was born and bred in Idaho, and Robert was a native of New York City before moving across the country to be with her. The two have always shared a passion for reading and writing, and it was their dream to combine their mighty powers to create the sorts of books they want to read. They write character driven sci-fi and fantasy romance, creating happily-ever-afters for the alien and unknown.

Sign up for our Newsletter!
Check out our social media sites and more!